THE AGE OF DARKNESS

WRAK WAVARA: THE AGE OF DARKNESS
BOOK ONE

LEIGH ROBERTS

DRAGON WINGS PRESS

CONTENTS

Dedication

To those of you who have joined the journey anew, and for those continuing on the journey with me from Series One, to answering the question—

What If...

CHAPTER 1

The sunset bathed the rolling verdant countryside around Kthama with a warm golden light. Moc'Tor breathed in the humid air that drifted up from the Great River below. His heavy full-body silver-white coat was tinged a pale orange by the setting rays, and he stood at nearly fourteen feet tall, with broad shoulders atop a thick muscular core. There was little that could stand in his way.

Moc'Tor gazed out across the rocky mountains and rolling hillsides from his favorite look-out place that was perched high at the peak of one of the paths leading to the entrance of their cavern home. Warmer days were coming, and with the Mothoc's heavy fur coats, the hot weather would be a burden to them all.

The Mothoc who counted Kthama their home considered themselves deeply blessed by the Great

Spirit to live in such an expansive underground cave system situated amid a land overflowing with riches. Moc'Tor's community had lived at Kthama forever. The story handed down was that many ages ago, the Mothoc had been formed whole by the hand of the Great Spirit from the dust of their world, Etera, to serve as the protectors of all creation.

As leader at Kthama, Moc'Tor's responsibilities were great. Added to that was his role as Etera's Guardian, and at times the mantle he wore weighed on him heavily. He had been Leader for some time now. The role was passed early to him by his father, Sorak'Tor, who was still alive. Sorak'Tor had seen great things in Moc'Tor and wanted him to have, for as long as possible, the additional benefit of a seasoned Leader's guidance.

It was years, though, since Sorak'Tor had been healthy. The Mothoc lived long lives, but they did not live forever. Moc'Tor watched his father's slow decline with great sadness. All would feel the loss of Sorak'Tor deeply. Moc'Tor put the thoughts of his father's deterioration out of his mind as he heard footsteps behind him. He turned from the view to see his First Choice, E'ranale, approaching.

"It is time," she said.

Moc'Tor sighed. "There are difficult times ahead; I can feel it. The Order of Functions is requiring more of my strength than ever before. Pray that I have the wisdom to guide our people successfully through the storm that is coming."

E'ranale regarded her mate. She could only imagine the pressure he felt as the Leader and Guardian. As with all the Mothoc, the flow of the Aezaitera also coursed through her veins. The Aezaitera was the very creative life force of the Great Spirit—the breath of life that continuously entered and exited Etera's realm.

But E'ranale was not a Guardian. Her physical body was not a vehicle called to bear the burden of supporting the Order of Functions, the creative blueprint of the Great Mind, which was constantly adjusting and reordering to maintain the perfect orchestration of life in their realm.

She placed her hand on Moc'Tor's shoulder. "I can see that something has been taking its toll on you. Come. Let us get this over with. We can rest together at the end of the day, and I will minister to you."

Moc'Tor and E'ranale made their way through the Great Entrance, passing the ever-present drips of moisture from the stalactites above, and headed for the Great Chamber.

Equally as vast as the Great Entrance, today the Great Chamber of Kthama was filled to capacity. Moc'Tor started to push a way through to the front to address his people, and a path opened as they realized it was their Leader. As he stood at the front, hundreds of pairs of deep-set eyes stared back at him, waiting for him to speak. The huge room was a sea of dark-haired bodies, crushed together shoulder-to-shoulder. He could barely tell where one began and the next ended. When one moved, the others pressed against them had to move in unison. Ordinarily, it would not have been this crowded, but both the males and the females had been assembled together for this announcement.

With the thick bark-covered Leader's Staff grasped firmly, Moc'Tor stepped up onto the raised platform he always used when addressing the crowd. "I am not sure everyone is here, but no matter. If anyone is absent, you can tell them later about today's announcement. If you look around, you will see that our community has grown considerably since my father handed the rule over to me. Unfortunately, it will not be long before we reach Kthama's limits. It is time we face the fact that we must look for another home. Scouts are out now as I speak. My hope is that they will find a place not too far from here where we can all share Kthama's bounty. Our food stores are full, but we have a long winter ahead, and we are in a race against time to expand our living space."

Moc'Tor stepped closer to the crowd but remained on the raised platform. "Does anyone have any questions?"

Toniss spoke up from the front row, "Are we leaving Kthama, Adik'Tar?"

"I doubt we will find another place that is big enough for us to leave Kthama together. We are hoping to find another dwelling nearby so that we can keep our community together even though some of us will relocate."

"How will it be decided who leaves here?" continued Toniss. "We have relationships, family."

"I do not yet know. But I will do my best to be fair."

The gathered Mothoc exchanged glances. Above their dark eyes, Moc'Tor could see furrowed brows.

"But we have always lived here; this is our home, Guardian," Toniss said.

"I know it is not easy to accept," Moc'Tor addressed the young female. "It will be hard for those who must leave. But we will still be one people."

Dochrohan, First Guard, approached to stand with Moc'Tor. His heavy dark hair covering contrasted sharply with Moc'Tor's silver-white Guardian's coat.

"Our stories tell us that we have always lived here," Moc'Tor went on. "But we can no longer hold onto what was. We do know this area is rich with unexplored hillsides. We have never needed to look for another cave system, but I am confident we will find something suitable for expansion.

"I will not order you to stop mating, but until we find more space, I am hard-put to justify the wisdom in continuing to reproduce. We do not know how long it will take to find another livable space. When we do, it will no doubt have to be modified. In the meantime, every offling decreases the living space for us all. I will let you know as soon as I have something to report."

Moc'Tor finished his speech with a few words of encouragement and stepped down. The crowd parted just enough for him to pass through. Even as one of the tallest of the Mothoc, Moc'Tor felt smothered as he pressed his way through all the bodies.

After much discussion, the crowd dispersed, glad to be freed from the cramped assembly.

E'ranale, First Guard Dochrohan, and Oragur, the Healer, weaved through the crowd, following the Leader outside, where they stood to speak.

"Quite a bit of talk afterward," Moc'Tor said. "It is obvious no one wants to leave Kthama. Who can blame them? We are blessed with our extensive tunnel system, the Mother Stream that sweeps through our lower level bringing fresh water and air, the large number of smaller caves for separate living spaces."

"This is their home," E'ranale said. "This is all they have known. As far back as memory goes, their parents and their parents' parents walked and lived within these same walls."

Moc'Tor paused, lost in thought, before continuing. "When did the last scouts go out?"

It was Dochrohan who spoke. "Two days ago. It is a long process. But I am confident we will find something. Like Kthama, any other entrances might be covered over and difficult to find."

"That is a good point, Dochrohan," said Moc'Tor. "But I doubt there will be another location with as rich a vortex as that beneath us here. Now, I have decided to visit the other colonies up the Mother Stream to see if they are also nearing capacity. I should be leaving in a few days."

"The crowd has probably dispersed; do you want to go back inside?" he asked E'ranale as Dochrohan and Oragur left.

"Not yet. I prefer it out here; the fresh air is a gift." She paused. "Toniss is seeded again."

Moc'Tor sighed. "I cannot bring myself to order them not to mate."

"It would be a hard adjustment. The males have always mated whenever they want to. I am not sure what the females would say, but many of them are tired of being constantly seeded, I can tell you that much." E'ranale took a deep breath. "My mate, there is no good time to tell you this, but I am also seeded."

Moc'Tor knew he should be happy, but this was not good news. Especially after telling his people they were near capacity and that more offling only added to the problem. But he did not want to hurt his mate's feelings.

He forced a smile.

"I am sorry," she said.

"It is not your fault, E'ranale. Only the Great Spirit decides when the male's seed will take root and produce an offling. And if anyone is at fault, it is me for not being able to stay off you," he said.

E'ranale was his First Choice. His two other mates lived with her in the smaller cave system next to Kthama. Only during assemblies like today's did the males and females mix freely. At least, now that E'ranale was seeded, he could mate with her at will. Later on, when the time came that E'ranale was too uncomfortable, he could pick one of his other females to mate if need be. *But I need to abstain from the others, considering our problem.* Moc'Tor knew it would not be difficult for him; it was only E'ranale whom he truly desired.

He ran his hand over the back of his head and smoothed the top of his hair, a habit he had picked up from his father. There was no mistaking Moc'Tor, with his silver coloring. His special status made him particularly attractive to the females, who frequently offered themselves to him. However, for some time now, Moc'Tor had limited his mating to three. E'ranale was his First Choice, and as time passed, he had stopped mating with his Second and Third Choice unless they presented themselves to him. He was content with E'ranale, and they shared far more than a relationship of physical release. She was more than his mate; she was his friend, his confidant, and in many ways, his chief counsel. He would choose his successor from her offling, although, in the lifespan of a Guardian, Moc'Tor was still very young.

While they were still talking, Drit came out to set

the wood for the evening fire. The Mothoc did not allow fire within the cave system of Kthama. Smoke accumulated at the top of the caves was difficult to clear since there was little circulation other than whatever breeze came up from the Mother Stream. But one of Moc'Tor's favorite ways to relax was sitting around a fire at night, enjoying the canopy of stars that blanketed the dark sky, even in warmer weather. It was perfectly safe, for the Mothoc had few natural predators, and hardly any had ever known fear.

Before long, Drit had a roaring fire going, sparked to life using his flint and striking stones. He always carried them in a pouch slung over his shoulder. Drit was the Fixer, the chief toolmaker, and brother to Oragur the Healer.

The last star to appear found them and a few others still sitting around the fire talking. "What if we cannot find another dwelling, Moc'Tor?" asked Oragur.

"If we cannot, then we will have to limit mating. It will be an unpopular directive and one I am not sure they will follow. The males are used to mating whenever they wish. Perhaps by the time I get back from visiting the other communities, our scouts will have returned with good news. Even if we split the community into different living areas, we still need to address the uncontrolled seeding of the females, or in a few generations from now, we will be right back where we are."

"If they report they have found a place before you return, what is your wish?"

"Move forward. Take a party and examine the place more closely. See what modifications would have to be made and report to me when I return. There is no use wasting time while I am away," replied Moc'Tor.

E'ranale rose to leave. "I am returning to my quarters."

"Stay with me tonight," said Moc'Tor. "There is now no harm in doing so."

E'ranale nodded. "As you wish. Wake me when you come in; I am going to rest."

"Why do you not mate with Ushca or Ny'on?" asked Oragur once E'ranale had left.

"This is the problem, Oragur. If I turn to Ushca and Ny'on, they will get seeded again. We are in this situation because we have no mastery over our desires. Our females are constantly having offling. Perhaps after I return from the other communities, I will have some new ideas about how to deal with it. At least some of them must be facing the same challenge."

The Mothoc stayed within their own communities for the most part. There was no conflict between them as the land was rich with resources and no need for competition. As a race, they were peaceful. Though the Mothoc were bound to protect and care for their neighbors, the Others, the two groups had virtually no contact. The Mothoc's seldom let themselves be known to the Others, and they shared no common language. The Others knew nothing of the extent to which the Mothoc watched over them, on both natural and spiritual levels.

A visit to the other Mothoc communities, especially by the Guardian, would stir much talk and concern. As a result, Moc'Tor rarely undertook it.

He tossed some acorns into the flames, watching the embers scatter as they landed. "I will see you at daybreak, then," he said to Oragur. He rose and retired to his quarters where E'ranale was already sleeping.

She woke when he slipped in next to her on the thick mass of grass and leaves.

"Do you wish to mate, Moc'Tor?" she asked, rubbing her eyes and rolling over toward him.

"No, not tonight. I want to talk to you. Get your ideas as the speaker for the females."

E'ranale propped herself up on one elbow.

"There are too many of us. And I do not know how to stop it," Moc'Tor said. "There is no guarantee we will find another cave system to meet our needs. At the rate we are going, we will be impossibly overcrowded in one more generation. Is there any talk among the females about this?"

"The females know it is getting crowded. They worry, too, about what will happen. But the males do not let up on them. The moment one of them becomes seeded, they mate with another. It feels like all we do is produce offling, one after the other."

"I am open to ideas," he answered, pulling her in close to him.

"I am afraid the males will not support any change. But I believe the females would."

"What if, for the time being, a male can only ever mate with one specific female?"

E'ranale remained silent, considering the thought. "That would certainly cut down on the seedings."

"Yes, although it would not be a very popular decision. But if it were only for a short time until we find another living space—"

"You know the males better than I do, but I think it will take a compelling argument or a strong hand to convince some of them. The females will support it, but it seems we have no say."

"What do you mean?"

"Well, if a male wants to mate, we have no choice but to comply. That is the way it has always been."

Moc'Tor sat in silence for a moment. *I never looked at it from their viewpoint. It did not occur to me they might want to refuse.*

"The females do not want to mate?"

"It is not that we do not want to mate, but we get tired of being seeded all the time. And we do not necessarily want to mate with just any male. We have preferences, too, just as you do. I am grateful to be able to accept only you."

Moc'Tor released his arm from around her, stood up, and paced back and forth. "What if it were the female who got to choose?"

"Got to choose what? To mate?"

"Not only whether to mate, but with whom to mate. What if it were the female's choice who to mate with—or not?"

E'ranale blinked a few times. "Oh, Moc'Tor, that would be such a relief. But I doubt you can sell that idea to the males. And what if more than one male favored the same female?"

"It would be the female's choice; that would be the end of it because we cannot continue as we are. I will think about this some more." He lay down again.

"Are you sure you do not wish to mate?" she smiled.

Moc'Tor let his eyes wander over his First Choice; her warm scent was inviting. He felt his response to her offer. "E'ranale. If it were up to you, would you choose me?"

"I would always choose you, Moc'Tor. And only you." She smiled again and pulled him closer.

Afterward, E'ranale kept thinking about Moc'Tor's idea and could not get to sleep. Having a say in who they mated with would be a great relief to the females. Some of them had feelings for particular males, and it was the same way for many of the males. If those who wished to limit their mating to only one other were given the choice, many hard feelings would be alleviated. But she would say nothing to the females yet for fear of getting their hopes up.

Because the females and offling lived in a smaller cave system adjacent to the males' larger one, their total numbers were deceiving. However, the assembly that day with all the males, females, and offling had shown just how overgrown their population was. In her head, E'ranale went through the females one by one, trying to figure out just how many would prefer to be paired to one specific male. She decided it was about three-quarters of the population. However, she could see conflict erupting when more than one male favored the same female, even though it would be the female's choice.

Morning came and found Moc'Tor thinking over his idea. Change came hard to the Mothoc, but if they were to survive, change they must.

E'ranale rolled over and found him sitting next to her. "Good morning. Have you been awake long?"

"Yes. I have been thinking about what we discussed. As I announced, I am going to travel along the Mother Stream to the Deep Valley and the Far

High Hills and talk to their Leaders. I will take the Healer with me."

Moc'Tor and Oragur followed the Mother Stream to the next population, a small establishment of only a handful of Mothoc. Past that was the Deep Valley, a day or so's travel further along the Mother Stream. Although visits to other communities were rare, many years past, the Mothoc had worked on the passageway along the route, carving out places to stop and rest, even to sleep. They had also created markings on the walls along the path to indicate to the traveler how far it was to the next community. Along the route, there were exit points to the surface, though they were few and far between. With a constant supply of fresh water, it was not difficult to travel, though being cut off from the topside for considerable stretches sometimes made it hard to tell day from night.

Moc'Tor and Oragur surfaced and checked the area for the tree breaks, the markers used by their people to signal the way to the small community named Khire. They quickly located them and traveled in the direction indicated. Before too long, they sensed the presence of the other Mothoc.

"I am Moc'Tor, Leader of the People of the High Rocks," he called out. "And this is Oragur the Healer, also from the High Rocks. We would like to speak with whoever you acknowledge as Adik'Tar."

As if by magic, three shapes stepped from the shadows. At seeing Moc'Tor, they exchanged glances before greeting him and Oragur.

"We will take you to him, Guardian," said the tallest, his face revealing his concern that a Guardian would be paying them a visit.

After traveling through the brush and up a slight incline, they came to a concealed opening—a small entrance compared to that of Kthama. A fire was being tended just inside, adding a warm glow to the otherwise gloomy interior. Before long, a shorter, stocky male approached, hobbling somewhat.

"I am Cha'Kahn. I am the highest rank here. Welcome to Khire. Visitors are an infrequent occurrence, and a visit by a Guardian even less frequent. What is your business?"

"I am Moc'Tor, and this is Oragur. We live downstream at the High Rocks. I am traveling to other tribes to seek counsel."

"Come, sit by the fire," said Cha'Kahn.

The two joined him around the dancing flames, which were welcome after the time spent in the dank tunnels along the Mother Stream. In the back reaches of the cave, both Moc'Tor and Oragur could see a number of females tending to figures stretched out on sleeping mats. Another female approached with a gourd and gave each one something to drink, one after another.

"Are you hungry?" asked Cha'Kahn.

"Thank you, but we are fine. Our problem is difficult to solve, Adik'Tar. We are outgrowing our mother caves. Are you facing the same problem?"

"We were, but we solved the problem by putting limits on mating."

"That has been my thought. But how did you get them to agree?"

As Cha'Kahn spoke, Moc'Tor's gaze kept shifting to the activity at the back of the cave. "It was difficult at first. Those who were unhappy left to find other communities. Since then, we have not had this problem, but I made the decree before it got out of hand."

"I am afraid we are past that point already," Moc'Tor sighed.

"I have heard of your community. Yours is the largest known."

Moc'Tor sat for a moment. While he was thinking, another figure was brought in and laid on the mats. Some females bent over solicitously, apparently trying to soothe the obvious discomfort.

"Would you be willing to meet with the other Adik'Tars?" asked Moc'Tor. "We could help each other with such problems if we band together."

"I would not object to that. The mantle of leadership borne alone is sometimes heavy."

Not able to ignore it any longer, and since Cha'Kahn was not going to volunteer the information, Moc'Tor had to ask. "You seem to have quite a few who are ill."

"Yes, but it is just a low fever and a bit of pain. We do not know what is causing it."

Moc'Tor tried to quell his unease over the number who were sick, but he felt a need to leave as soon as possible. After a bit more talk, he thanked Cha'Kahn, and he and Oragur continued on their way to the Deep Valley.

"Did you notice the number being cared for back there?" asked Moc'Tor as they walked.

"I found it a little disturbing, yes. They likely ate something the essence of which had long before returned to the Great Spirit, but I did not want to pry."

As Moc'Tor and Oragur arrived at the Deep Valley, the Guardian noted that the surroundings were even lusher than those at Kthama. His father had once told him this was the second-largest underground cave system, next only to that of the High Rocks. Those who lived there enjoyed a life of relative ease and plenty. As they approached, watchers greeted him and Oragur just as those at Cha'Kahn's settlement had done. Before long, they were engaged in a similar conversation with Hatos'Mok.

"I have no answers for you, Guardian," said the Leader of the community of the Deep Valley. "I believe you will find that all our people struggle with the risk of overpopulation. We have practically no natural enemies. Other than an occasional accident, most of us live out our natural lifespans until it is time to return to the Great Spirit."

Moc'Tor sighed. "I suspect I will find the same response at the Far High Hills."

"I know the Leader there; his name is Tres'Sar. Yes, you will find similar overcrowded conditions."

Moc'Tor noticed a parade of young females walking slowly through the area close to where he, Oragur, and Hatos'Mok were talking.

"It appears you can have your choice of females, Guardian," Hatos'Mok remarked, his eyes on the attractive maidens who were not even trying to hide their fascination with the Guardian.

"I have three to mate; they are all I need for my satisfaction. And I do not wish to add to the surplus population. But from what I can see, I will say that your maidens are particularly attractive."

Hatos'Mok nodded. "There are also three in my pod, though I find I have my favorite."

"I am considering bringing the leadership together to see if we can find solutions," Moc'Tor said. "If you are open to that, I will send a messenger when we are ready to convene."

Hatos'Mok agreed and offered Moc'Tor and Oragur lodging for the night.

The next morning the travelers left for the Far High Hills and met with Tres'Sar, garnering his support for the idea of coming together to solve their problems.

The sentries had returned by the time Moc'Tor and Oragur made it back to Kthama.

"Moc'Tor," said the head sentry, Ras'Or, "We have located a set of caves not all that far away from here. It is not as large as Kthama, but it is well-concealed and looks serviceable. We almost missed it because the opening was so well-hidden by bittersweet vines. There is a stream not far away, and there is plenty of cover."

"Do you believe it will suit our needs?"

"It will not be as comfortable as Kthama, but we can improve it—although it will take some time."

"How many do you think could live there comfortably?"

"Perhaps a fourth of our population."

"Are you sure there are no others?" asked Moc'Tor.

"None that we can find, and we have been diligent in our search."

Moc'Tor considered what Ras'Or had just said. *Not entirely big enough, but it will buy us some time.* Now he would have to decide who must leave Kthama. "Please take me there; I must inspect it myself."

That evening, after telling E'ranale he was leaving again and would not be back for several days, Moc'Tor gathered his hunting spear, collected Oragur and Drit, and set out with Ras'Or.

Darkness being no hindrance to them, they traveled with few rests and arrived just before first light on the next day. Ras'Or was right; the new cave system was virtually undiscoverable.

Moc'Tor set aside his hunting spear and pushed aside the covering that blocked most of the entrance. Later they could decide what to leave in place and what to cultivate further. Though they had few natural enemies, concealment provided some level of comfort.

The opening expanded into an entrance similar to that at Kthama, though on a smaller scale. From the main cave, tunnels extended in multiple directions. Moc'Tor chose the narrowest and set out along it with Drit and Oragur in tow.

The air was cool but not as humid as at Kthama. Moc'Tor knew from the dryness that there was no central stream running through the caves, though off in the distance on the way there, they had spotted the river mentioned by Ras'Or. The Mother Stream made life at Kthama convenient. Not only did it bring water, oxygen, and nutrients into their home, but it carried an easy supply of protein in the fish that swam through. It was a shame that the Mother

Stream did not also run beneath this underground cave system.

Moc'Tor followed the narrow tunnel with its familiar smooth rock walls. At its end, the passageway opened into several other caves. He turned to Drit, "Go back and take the next tunnel over. Oragur, you take the farthest. Walk about the same distance as we have here, then meet me back in the central area with a report. Look for signs of water, other exits, current or former inhabitants—anything good or bad. I will see you again shortly."

The two males did as ordered. Before long, they were all reassembled in the front cavern.

"The next tunnel was essentially the same as the first," Drit reported. "It wound around with several smaller caves along the way. There would be room for many single or shared quarters. I do not see an easy way to separate the females from the males, though."

"We would not want to send only males or only females here," mused Moc'Tor. "It has to be a mix like at Kthama. Oragur, what did you find?"

"Though Drit's tunnel does not sound suitable for both males and females, the route I took forked into two tunnels a short way back. I did not have time to explore both, but there may be a way to separate them by using that split."

Moc'Tor nodded. "Very well. Any signs of inhabitants?"

Both males shook their heads. It was no problem

for the Mothoc to remove any creature already living there, but they would not wish to deprive any of the Great Spirit's creatures of a home.

"I want to see the river," Moc'Tor said, and with that, they left the caves and headed toward the water.

It was clearly part of the Great River that also wove past Kthama. Moc'Tor felt a sense of continuity, the two locations connected by the same rich source of life and provision. In addition, this place was not as high up as Kthama, so there were none of the rocky outcrops that made travel around Kthama treacherous. Mature trees provided a canopy of shade, and the breeze from the river brought with it the smell of the rich soil along the riverbanks.

The three males stood for a while, connecting with their seventh sense to feel if the place welcomed them. Though this was not as strong in them as it was in the females, they could still feel the whisper of the Great Spirit speaking to them. Each searched for a sense of foreboding or a warning of any sort.

Moments passed.

Moc'Tor exhaled. He opened his eyes at the same time the others did. The three nodded to each other, intuitively knowing it was settled. This would be their next home; the Great Spirit had once again provided.

"There is no rich magnetic vortex here as there is below Kthama," conceded Moc'Tor. "But it will do. Let us stay the night; we can easily spear some fish and make a small fire. It will be our ritual of gratitude for this gift from the One-Who-Is-Three."

Before long, Drit had a warm fire going. With their bellies full, the males looked up at the wash of stars overhead. In the morning, they started out on their return to Kthama.

E'ranale was anxiously awaiting her mate's return. She smiled at the sight of Moc'Tor coming up the rocky path to home.

"I was just going out to gather some berries."

"I will walk with you," said Moc'Tor, handing his spear to Drit and signaling for the other males to go on without him.

He went ahead, brushing the branches out of the way for E'ranale, a courtesy more than anything as she was certainly capable of making her own path.

"What did you think of it, Moc'Tor?" she asked.

"It is a blessing to find something so relatively close. It is large enough and has quite a few branches for separate quarters. For gatherings, much like here, there is one large cave at the entrance, and the Great River passes close enough. Life will not be as easy there as it is here, with the Mother Stream passing through Kthama's lower level. But it will be serviceable. The hardest part will be deciding who stays and who leaves."

"Will the males and females be separated as they are here? Is there enough room?"

"There will not be separate entrances as far as I can tell. But within the recesses of the system, yes, they can be separate to a point."

That will be a big change, thought E'ranale. *Hopefully, by then, Moc'Tor's directive for males and females to mate selectively would have taken hold, if that is what he decides we should do.* She wondered if her mate had thought that through any further. In the next moment, she knew he had.

"E'ranale, do you know if Ushca and Ny'on favor any of the other males?"

E'ranale cocked her head, "You are asking if they have a preference for a mate other than you?"

"Yes, I am asking that."

E'ranale was not sure how to respond. She decided she should answer carefully, not wanting to hurt Moc'Tor's pride if that were possible. "I do know that Ushca favors someone."

"Who? Which male?"

E'ranale sighed and stepped into it. "Straf'Tor."

"My *brother*?"

"Yes." She sighed again.

Moc'Tor looked off into the distance. E'ranale surmised that he realized this might not be as easy as he had thought.

"Hmmph," he said, then continued. "Have they mated? As far as I know, Straf'Tor favors Toniss."

"I do not know if they have mated. I believe they

would think it disloyal to you, Moc'Tor, even though there is no prohibition against it."

E'ranale felt a twinge of jealousy that it bothered Moc'Tor if his Second Choice was interested in another male.

Moc'Tor ran his hand through his crown.

"What about Toniss?"

"Toniss mates with Straf'Tor because he chooses her. But she does not prefer him."

"This is getting complicated."

"It probably seems so to you, and I mean no disrespect. But you rightly do not spend as much time with the females as I do. I believe there would be less strife than you think. Given a chance, I believe that your brother and Ushca would choose to be together. I see them stealing glances at every opportunity."

"I am glad you know all this, but thinking about it makes my head hurt."

E'ranale stopped and turned to face Moc'Tor. She reached over with both hands and grabbed fistfuls of the thick hair behind his hips, pulling him to her.

"Then do not think about it."

Moc'Tor recognized her invitation and immediately fell to taking advantage of the opportunity. Obstructed by a fallen log was a small clearing to their left, and he broke from her long enough to heave it out of the way, opening up a secluded nook. Kicking aside the rocks and leaves, he laid her down on the soft soil and took her readily, then and there.

Knowing she was already seeded and he would not be adding further to the overpopulation allowed Moc'Tor fully to surrender himself to the relief she offered. For a moment at least, he was freed of the burdens of leadership, lost in the pleasure of claiming his First Choice.

CHAPTER 2

Time passed. Crews went out in series to the newly found cave system, each spending several days there to make it more habitable before coming back for additional supplies. Females whitewashed some of the interior to provide more light to the inner recesses, though everyone's night vision made much of it unnecessary. Moc'Tor named the new location. Kayerm.

He, Drit the Fixer, and First Guard Dochrohan were enjoying Moc'Tor's favorite leisure occupation —sitting in front of a pleasing fire on a starry night. Moc'Tor was still struggling with implementing his idea that the males should mate with only one female. As if that part were not hard enough, getting the males to accept the second part—letting the females choose them—seemed even more of an impossibility. He poked at the fire with a stick as Oragur joined them.

"Moc'Tor, I am getting alarmed," Oragur said. "More are getting sick. I am not sure what to think of it, and nothing I do is helping." He paused. "Rathic returned to the Great Spirit today."

Moc'Tor put down the stick. "Rathic is gone?"

"Yes."

"He was one of our Elders, but still— And my father?"

"So far, he has not come down with it."

Moc'Tor sighed. He needed to spend more time with his father; he knew it. Though Sorak'Tor had handed over the leadership ages ago to help mentor and guide him through being a new Leader, the Guardian was not ready to lose his father. "How many of us have it now?" he asked.

"Almost half. It is worse in the males than the females, and I fear it is a punishment from the Great Spirit."

"For what?"

"For what you told us some time ago. That we were being irresponsible with our mating."

"Why do you think that?"

"Because it is affecting the male's seed packs. Not all, but in many of them, the seed packs are painfully swollen. To try and limit the spreading, we have placed all the sick in one of the lower rooms, but it seems to have no effect. But it would not if it is retribution—"

Moc'Tor had lived long enough that he was not sure he believed in such punishments from the Great

Spirit. Still, even a loving father corrected his offling. "Keep me informed, Oragur."

He turned to his first guard. "Dochrohan, send a sentry up the Mother Stream to the other communities and see if they are also affected by this."

Over the next few weeks, Moc'Tor watched helplessly as a fourth of the males returned to the Great Spirit, and it was not restricted to those in their senior and twilight years. A dark pall hung over Kthama. Eventually, the sickness tapered off, but anguish remained.

Moc'Tor lay with E'ranale in the privacy of the Leader's Quarters, his worry drawing him to her. "I need to address the community. What is left of us, that is."

"There is nothing anyone could do, Moc'Tor."

"Oragur says it is a punishment from the Great Spirit."

"But you do not believe that."

"I do not know what I believe anymore. I have lived a long time, E'ranale, and in the end I have more questions than answers. Who is to say?"

"I can see why Oragur would believe it; he is the Healer for one thing, and it did come after you had admonished the community for overbreeding. Except, the sentries said it is impacting all the communities up the Mother Stream."

E'ranale was starting to show, her waist thickening and her breasts enlarging. It was noticeable even under her thick hair. Moc'Tor rested his hand on her expanding belly.

"Since we have been talking about it, I believe more and more that we males need to control ourselves. Even despite our losses." Moc'Tor sighed. "I must address the community. It is time."

The next morning, he called an assembly. In contrast to when he had last spoken with them, the Great Chamber was not packed with bodies side-by-side. It was a sobering demonstration of their depleted numbers.

Moc'Tor moved to the front and looked out into a crowd of dark, somber faces. The females were clearly in mourning with lowered eyes and slumped shoulders. Angry scowls and clenched jaws prevailed among the males able to attend.

"I remember that the last time I stood before you, my message was one of concern for our overcrowding and our lack of self-control in our mating. As I look out now and see our depleted numbers, I am deeply saddened and somewhat ashamed.

"Oragur believes that this sickness is a punishment from the Great Spirit for being disrespectful of the bounty that was given us. For eons, our people have been blessed to live here in a land rich with supply. But that does not give us the right to squander what we have been given by overbreeding. So perhaps Oragur is right."

Someone shouted from the crowd, "You believe this is a punishment?"

"I believe it is possible."

"If we are being punished, what are we to do now?" called out another voice.

"If Oragur is right, then we need to change our ways while there is still time. By reducing our numbers, perhaps the Great Spirit is giving us a second chance. But if we do not change, then we invite further correction."

"But what about finding Kayerm? Is that not a blessing?"

"Yes. It truly was—and is. I do not have all the answers; perhaps Kayerm is not a blessing for this time but for a time yet to come. At any rate, there is now no need to split what is left of us. We have already ceased work there and closed off the entrance."

Moc'Tor stood silently and let them speak among themselves. He spotted Oragur in the crowd and motioned for the Healer to join him at the front.

"Oragur, are we being punished?" called out someone else.

Oragur made it clear that he had no doubts. "We

are being corrected. We have been wasteful and let our numbers increase past that which even this great abundance could bear. Now we have suffered the consequences of our folly. Why else would the Great Spirit inflict a sickness that so targeted the source of our own demise? You have seen for yourselves the effects on the males who became sick and did not fully recover. Whether we listen or not will decree what happens to us next. Earlier, this room was packed to capacity; now there is but a portion of us left."

Moc'Tor did not completely agree with Oragur, but he saw the opening he needed and took full advantage of it. "Whether it is because we have been punished, or that the sickness is a result of our own foolishness, we have to change our ways. It will not be easy, but neither was what we have recently been through."

His Leader's Staff firmly in hand, Moc'Tor took a deep breath before continuing. "It is time for change. We males have had our way since the Great Spirit formed us from the dust of these walls. We now see where that has gotten us. We can no longer breed at will like the animals of the forest. We must be more than that because our future depends on it. From now on, the females will be the ones to choose whose seed to accept."

A gasp rolled through the crowd. The females stared at each other in amazement.

"Furthermore, the females will choose one male

with whom to mate for the rest of both their lives. That is it. It will be the female's choice of who and how often. The males have had control for too long. Now it is time to let our females have their way."

"Are you sick yourself, Moc'Tor? You want us to wait for them to decide to mate? And let them choose who with?" asked a male named Norcab.

Moc'Tor had known there would be resistance and anticipated that it would start with Norcab. The Guardian stood taller, took a confident step forward, and stared down at the angry male. "Do you have another solution? You see where we are. If Oragur is right, our numbers have been reduced because of our inability to control ourselves. As I said, mating at will is beneath us; we must be better than that. I will give the females five nights to select their mates. Once this has happened, I expect you to honor their selection. If a female does not wish to pick a mate, that is also acceptable. Females are not to be taken without their consent. Not any more. *Never again.*"

"I have never forced myself on any of them. Neither have any of the other males!" Norcab challenged the Leader.

"Have you not? Perhaps not physically forced, but have you ever considered whether the female you selected wanted to accept you into herself? Let alone to be seeded by you? They have given in because it was expected of them. Since we failed at treating them as equals, they are now elevated above us.

Anyone who does not agree with the new order is welcome to leave—now."

Moc'Tor's answer was a bedlam of voices. The females looked worried. The Guardian glanced at E'ranale and beckoned for her to join him. She frowned and remained where she was.

He motioned again, and this time she complied. Tentatively making her way through the crowd, E'ranale joined Moc'Tor on the platform. Then she suddenly realized that he wanted her to take the lead in following his order.

"People of Kthama."

The room silenced immediately at the unfamiliar voice—a female voice—speaking from the place of leadership where only males had ever stood.

"You have known me as Moc'Tor's First Choice. Now it is my choice as to whom I want to mate."

Utter. Abject. Silence.

For a moment, Moc'Tor actually felt afraid she was not going to choose him.

"I choose Moc'Tor," E'ranale whispered. Then, more loudly, she said, "I have always chosen Moc'Tor." She placed her hand in his, then turned back to the crowd. "I have exercised my right to choose. Females, I urge you to consider well and choose wisely for yourselves. We are fortunate to have a Leader who seeks wisdom and understanding. Through adversity, great change has come; Moc'Tor has given us a position of equality, even reverence.

My prayer is that we live up to the mantle that has been placed upon our shoulders."

All eyes followed E'ranale as she led Moc'Tor from the stage. He squeezed her hand as they left and murmured just loud enough that only she could hear. "Perfect."

The couple moved to the back of the room and watched the outcome of their display. Oragur stayed near the front and answered questions as some of the audience pressed forward.

"I need to be with the females tonight, Moc'Tor."

"I understand. Though now that you have freely chosen me, I regret that we cannot spend our first night together."

"I will make it up to you, I promise."

"Go and be with them. I agree; they need your leadership now, E'ranale. I have done all I can."

She took her leave of Moc'Tor and went into the crowd. After gathering the females, she led them to the meeting cavern in their own cave system, where she could hear their concerns without the males being present.

E'ranale had already prepared the females for what she believed was coming, so the idea of choosing who they wished to mate with was not a total surprise. The development was a boon for them, but still, the idea was not met without resistance.

Moc'Tor's former Second Choice, Ushca, spoke first. "The males are not going to accept this."

"They have little choice, Ushca. Moc'Tor has handed us the power to receive who we wish, and it is ours to accept or to give up. None of us has been pleased with the way things were."

"But I do not know how to choose," Ushca said.

"I think you do." E'ranale spoke gently. "What is really holding you back?"

"What if I choose someone who does not want me?"

"Doubtful. I have seen how he looks at you," said E'ranale.

Ushca lowered her eyes, thinking of her long-burning desire for Moc'Tor's brother, Straf'Tor.

"Moc'Tor and I discussed this at length," E'ranale continued. "This is the way it must be. If left to the males, we will only continue to have too many offling; you know this is true. When one female is seeded, the male goes on to the next even if she does not wish to be mated."

"We are not disagreeing with you, E'ranale. We just have no idea how to choose," said Toniss.

"You do not know how to choose, or you do not know who to choose? There is a difference."

The females exchanged glances and shifted uncomfortably.

"That is a good question," said Toniss after a moment. "Given the choice—"

The other females waited for her answer. They

knew Ushca favored Straf'Tor, but that he frequently chose Toniss. Ushca and Straf'Tor stayed away from each other, but only because Ushca was Moc'Tor's Second Choice.

"—I would not choose Straf'Tor."

Ushca frowned, "You would *not* choose Straf'Tor?"

"No. I am not sure why he even chooses me. Our mating is ritual and uninspired because he seems to burn for you, Ushca. Sometimes, I feel he is thinking of you when he is mounting me."

Ushca felt as if a fire had been lit within her at the thought that Straf'Tor might desire her as she did him.

"Well, this seems to be working out," E'ranale said. "Is it going to work out perfectly for each of us? No. But it is far from perfect the way it is now. We have been given power, and we have to try it. If you do not wish to choose now, do not. Wait until you know."

E'ranale let the females chatter among themselves for a few moments. Another question surfaced.

"If I know who I want, how do I know if he wants me?"

E'ranale now realized how truly out of balance the situation between the genders had become. And when things tilted too far, the Great Spirit made a correction. She leaned toward Oragur's interpretation that this was indeed a punishment from the

Great Spirit in an attempt to set things right. But it was sad that the females knew little about how to entice a male because the choice had always been made for them.

E'ranale answered, "Now that the males know they cannot mate any of us whenever they want, they are also going to be more selective. It is very simple. It is not so much choosing as offering. If you offer yourself to him and he does not move forward, then you have your answer."

"That makes it easier, E'ranale. Thank you."

"You do not have to be blatant about it. Brush up against him. Look at him, stare at him if you need to. Smile. Go slow. Believe me, he will be looking for the invitation. Just make sure he is the one you want before you make a move, as the odds are that unless he has a connection with another female, whoever you pick will accept you. Realize it is also hard for them."

The tension was easing, and E'ranale was exhausted. "Think about it for a while. There is no need to rush; we have five nights, and the males need time to adjust just as we do. Now I need to sleep. Tomorrow we enter a new age of control over whose seed we allow to be planted within us. A new age of choice."

Back in Kthama proper, Moc'Tor was dealing with the males, who were not taking the news as well as the females.

"Our numbers have been reduced, Moc'Tor. Why is this now even necessary?" asked one of the larger males.

"Trasik, if Oragur is right, it was a serious correction from the Great Spirit. If we do not heed this one, who knows how much worse the next correction might be?" said Moc'Tor. "I am not willing to take the risk."

"This is *krellshar*!"

"What exactly is bothering you about it, Trasik?" asked the Guardian.

"I no longer have the choice."

Moc'Tor scoffed. "I know your tastes, Trasik. You mated indiscriminately with anyone and everyone. You have never been selective to begin with, so what does it matter who chooses you? I doubt it is your loss of choice that you are complaining about. I suspect it is the control."

"Exactly. Now you have given them all the power," Trasik responded.

"They should have had it anyway. It does not mean you cannot approach them. But if you do, and one female accepts you, then you must limit yourself to her. It is very simple. One is the same to you as the other; I do not see your problem."

"We do not all feel that way, Moc'Tor," another voice spoke up.

Moc'Tor did not catch who had spoken, but he replied firmly. "I know this to be true. Some of you have been more selective in who you mated. If you admit it, many of you have your preferences."

It was time for Straf'Tor to come forward. "Moc'-Tor, E'ranale has chosen you. Are you to be content with mating only her?"

"I have been content for a long time, Straf. I seldom mated Ushca or Ny'on."

"What about you, Straf? Will you choose Toniss?" asked Trak, an alpha male of proportions equal to those of the huge Straf'Tor.

"I no longer get to choose; have you not been listening to my brother's words?" growled Straf'Tor in reply.

"You have mounted her in the past!"

"As have you! Not that who I have mounted is any of your business."

"I am making it my business. *Do you want Toniss?*"

When Straf'Tor did not answer, Trak stepped forward and snarled, "It is a simple question, Straf. Even a *PetaQ* such as you should be able to understand it. *Answer me.*"

Tension flared as the two giants squared off. Moc'Tor had expected this, though not from his brother.

Straf'Tor pushed Trak in the chest, knocking him off-center. Trak lunged in return and succeeded in knocking his opponent to the ground. Dust flew as each struggled to gain a stronghold over the other, rolling into rock slab tables and benches as they fought. Trak pinned Straf'Tor by his shoulders, but Straf'Tor wrapped his huge muscled legs around Trak's midsection and flipped him over.

Now lying on his back, Trak snarled and snapped at Straf'Tor, trying to land teeth in flesh, but he was straddled with both shoulders pressed to the ground. Pieces of rock from broken benches dug painfully into his back. Straf'Tor chose his moment and lunged down, canines revealed. If he now pressed his advantage, he would tear open the main artery and Trak would quickly bleed to death. But it was enough that Straf'Tor had won the fight; he did not need to kill his adversary. Instead, he pressed his teeth into the meat of Trak's shoulder, and blood trickled from the gash.

Straf'Tor had drawn first blood, and accepting his defeat, Trak surrendered. Straf'Tor resisted his impulse to tear out Trak's throat anyway, instead giving him a final shove into the ground before releasing him and standing up. Trak rose, and glaring at Straf'Tor, he circled away, a hand pressed against the wound on his shoulder. Straf'Tor kept his eyes locked on Trak while flipping over a table with one hand and shattering it to pieces, his final demonstration of dominance.

Moc'Tor and the others watched as the battle between the two robust males flared and ran its course. The Leader had allowed the fight, knowing that both males needed to discharge the sexual frustration triggered by his announcement and that aggression against each other was a natural outlet. He now stepped forward into the rubble of the battlefield and circled, eyeing the males one at a time.

"Go about your ways. I have made my decision, and any one of you who cannot comply must be gone by first light. We have more challenges ahead, and I will not tolerate your disobedience. You have had your way with whichever females you wanted. Accept that those days are gone forever; the females now have the right to choose. If you wish to approach one instead of waiting for her, do so. But you must be prepared to accept refusal. Anyone taking a female without her consent will be banished, or worse."

"You are weak, Moc'Tor. You have let the females take power!" called out Norcab as Moc'Tor turned to leave.

"Who is calling me weak, who himself shouts out from within the crowd like a coward?" Norcab had often challenged Moc'Tor's authority, and the Leader knew this was just one more way for him to do so.

"Who are you calling a coward?"

Moc'Tor stepped into the throng and pressed his chest hard into Norcab's, locking eyes as he did so. "I am not just calling you a coward. I am stating a fact."

Norcab roared, grabbing Moc'Tor by the shoulders and twisting as he swept a foot forward, trying to knock Moc'Tor's feet out from under him.

Moc'Tor was the alpha for a reason. He stepped back from the maneuver and Norcab had to bring his other leg back and plant it quickly or lose balance. As Norcab recovered his equilibrium, Moc'Tor brought up one knee squarely between his opponent's legs, and on contact, Norcab doubled over in agony.

While Norcab was still writhing in pain on the ground, Moc'Tor leaned over, and with one hand, threw him against the rock wall. Norcab slid down in a massive dark heap, still curled over and clutching his throbbing seed pack.

Moc'Tor looked down at the incapacitated male in front of him. He then turned and looked back at the others. "Anyone else?"

Met with nothing but silence, Moc'Tor left, knowing that those outbreaks were not the end of it. There would be more attacks and skirmishes, but as long as the males' aggression was discharged only against each other, he would allow it. Change came hard for the Mothoc.

For the next two days, the males and females remained pretty much separate, neither sure of what to do. On the third day, they started to mingle again.

Sitting on their own in the Great Chamber,

E'ranale asked Moc'Tor how it was going with the males after his announcement.

"As to be expected. Two skirmishes. One between Straf' and Trak. The other between Norcab and me."

"Norcab dared challenge a Guardian? What was that about?"

"The usual. Norcab is always looking for a chance to challenge me. I kneed him pretty hard and slammed him against the wall. He will be licking his wounds for a while. At some point, I will have to kill him, or he will kill me. It will not go away."

E'ranale knew her mate was right. Norcab had always been an angry beast. The day would come when Moc'Tor would have to end him, or his influence might spread to others. "Do not wait too long, Moc'Tor. Our people need a strong Leader to get them through these difficult times. You are both the Leader and a Guardian, and it is not good for them to see your decisions challenged. Even if Norcab is not coming at you directly, he might be working against you in the background, stirring up an organized backlash."

"You are right. For too long, I have allowed it to go on unchecked. The next time Norcab challenges me, I will end him as publicly as possible."

They both sat silent for a while.

Moc'Tor broke their reflection. "The females?" he asked.

"Relieved, I think, though unsure of their role

now. They will adjust. I suspect we will not have to wait long for your brother and Ushca to pair up."

Moc'Tor smiled. At least there would be some entertainment out of all this.

Ushca stood at the meal counter, looking over the food that had been assembled. The hair on her back pricked up, and she knew that Straf'Tor had entered the Great Chamber. She took a deep breath. It was the first time she would be seeing him since Moc'-Tor's announcement, and her heart pounded in her chest. She sensed his approach and feared she might pass out.

Straf'Tor stood behind Ushca, and she could feel the heat coming off his body. She did not dare look around and stood frozen like a wary deer. A quiet whimper escaped her lips, and she closed her eyes and swore under her breath.

Straf'Tor took a step closer; he was now directly behind Ushca and almost up against her back. Waves of desire swelled within her. Grateful that he had taken the lead, she realized that, nonetheless, she had to make it clear that she chose him.

Ushca stepped back enough to press up against Straf'Tor, and at the same time, she reached around and took his hand, wrapping his arm around her waist. She felt him respond to her and knew the deal was sealed. He pulled her harder against him, leaned down, and pressed his face to her neck.

"I choose you, Straf'Tor," she whispered into his ear.

His hot breath brushed over her. "Finally," was all he said.

Straf'Tor and Ushca were lost in their own world. Most of the inhabitants of Kthama had been aware for some time that the two desired each other. Seeing it come together before their eyes was an unexpected pleasure.

E'ranale and Moc'Tor also sat watching as, finally, the long-denied yearning between Straf'Tor and Ushca came to a head. When the couple suddenly realized they were still in the common area with all eyes upon them, Ushca took Straf'Tor's hand and led him out of the room.

Also watching was Toniss. Freed from Straf'Tor, she made a beeline for the other side of the room, where Trak had been standing quietly, staring a hole into her.

E'ranale and Moc'Tor looked at each other.

"I did not see that coming," said Moc'Tor. "But I should have known after Trak attacked Straf when Toniss's name came up. Wait; you told me Toniss is seeded. Will that not complicate things with her and Trak?"

"You are assuming the offling she carries was seeded by Straf," E'ranale answered with a chuckle.

"Trak?" asked Moc'Tor. "That explains everything."

Now everyone was watching Toniss and Trak circle each other like creatures in heat. The sexual tension filled the room.

"Well, this ought to get things going for the others!" exclaimed E'ranale.

"No doubt," Moc'Tor laughed. "And I am glad for them." With fire in his own eyes, he pretended to leer at E'ranale.

Over the next few weeks, many of the females chose males to mate with. There were a few skirmishes, but the pairing up went surprisingly well, proving what E'ranale had predicted; most of them did have preferences. For whatever reason, some of the females did not choose—in some cases because the contagion had left significantly fewer males than females.

Most of the sickness had left, and the husks of all who had died had been returned to the Great Spirit by ritual fire. However, despite the seeming calm, Moc'Tor was not relaxed. For one thing, Norcab, in particular, had been absent from the common areas.

First Guard Dochrohan found the Guardian walking outside Kthama. "Moc'Tor!" he called out.

The Leader stopped and waited.

"There is something you need to know. Norcab has been meeting in secret with several of the younger males."

"I am aware of it," he said, resuming his walk with Dochrohan beside him.

"Are you also aware of the topic of the meetings?"

"I would imagine my removal from leadership, with or without my demise."

"Yes, though I am not sure which they have decided upon."

"I will deal with it at the appropriate time, Dochrohan, though I do appreciate the information."

"There are quite a few of them, Moc'Tor— although I am not questioning your strength or fighting ability."

"Did you ever have to fight a Sarius snake, Dochrohan?"

"No, I cannot say that I have. But I know they are treacherous and can grow up to three arm-lengths and as thick as a grown male's thigh."

"Yes. And if you let yourself be distracted by its size, you will fail. There is only one guaranteed way to dispatch it."

"And what is that?"

"Cut off the head. Without the head, no matter how big it is, the rest of the snake is no longer a threat." Moc'Tor stopped walking and turned to face the first guard. "However," he added, "I am not so blind that I do not know I may need help in this matter. I will appreciate any other information you discover. Males like Norcab are not males of honor."

"The other males and I will stand with you. Nysas has joined the group and will keep me informed of their plans."

"I am the only target, correct?"

"As far as I know." Dochrohan stared at Moc'Tor for a moment. "You are not suggesting—"

"That in his hatred of me Norcab might hurt E'ranale and our offling? I would not put it past him or any other male stupid enough to challenge a Guardian."

"Who would go so low as to hurt a female, let alone one with offling? I am tempted to fight you for the chance to kill him myself," said the first guard.

"Place your strongest male to watch discreetly over E'ranale and our offling—with instructions to kill Norcab on sight if he or anyone else in his group goes near them. However, unless he makes such a move and is dealt with beforehand, he is *mine*."

Norcab and his males were waiting for Moc'Tor in the mouth of a tunnel that opened onto the Great Chamber. Norcab had enlisted a group of about twenty to his cause of unseating the Leader. They were mostly younger males blinded by their drives, and with nothing to lose, had been enticed by

Norcab. He had promised to strip the females of the power Moc'Tor had given them and grant the males the right to take at will any they wished to, even if the females refused to cooperate.

Moc'Tor's seventh sense had already alerted him to their presence. That and the heavy breathing that came from the passage.

As Moc'Tor neared the opening, Norcab stepped out of the shadows, blocking his path.

"You are in my way, Norcab."

"That is ironic. Because you are in *my* way, Moc'Tor."

"You are a fool. And I have no time for fools." Moc'Tor pushed Norcab out of his way but swung around and grabbed him by the back of the neck, catching him off guard. The Guardian easily swung him hard onto the rock floor, and Norcab's grab for Moc'Tor's ankles was met with a kick to the face. Blood spurted everywhere as Norcab's nose split with a resounding crack.

Enraged by the pain, he pulled himself onto all fours and lunged at Moc'Tor. Both bodies crashed to the floor, and the two giants rolled, each trying to gain the advantage. Norcab ended up on top with his hands around Moc'Tor's throat, but Moc'Tor brought up both his knees and pushed against his opponent's chest, catapulting Norcab several yards away. While Norcab was trying to get to his feet, Moc'Tor launched onto him and wrapped an arm around the rebel's neck, pulling hard to cut off his breath. Norcab clawed at Moc'Tor's arm, trying to get air.

Realizing that Norcab was losing, his band emerged from the shadows. Moc'Tor ignored them; his battle was first and foremost with Norcab, and without their Leader, they would most likely not be brave enough to pick up the fight.

By now, other Mothoc had entered the Great Chamber to watch the brutal battle taking place between the two behemoths. One of them ran to find Dochrohan, who had already heard and was on his way.

Moc'Tor knew that Norcab had only seconds left before passing out; it would be easy enough to crush his opponent's windpipe right then and there, but the Leader needed more than simply to kill him. He had to publicly destroy Norcab and any legacy of his defiance.

Seeing that the room was filling even further, Moc'Tor did not have to stall any longer. He released Norcab and moved away from him. "Get up. Get up and die like a warrior instead of the coward you are!"

Norcab gasped for breath in between coughing and spitting out the blood from his broken nose. He wiped his face and forced himself to his feet.

"*Va!* It is you who will die, Moc'Tor."

The Leader shook his head. "A coward and a fool both. Today is my lucky day."

At that moment, Dochrohan entered the room with his guards and made quick work of getting

Norcab's band under control, ensuring that this would be a fair fight.

Arms out, the combatants circled each other and Moc'Tor moved closer to the rock wall behind him, trusting that his opponent would fall for the appearance of opportunity it presented. Norcab moved unsteadily, his gaze locked on Moc'Tor.

Suddenly, the Guardian dropped his guard and looked to the side as if distracted by something. Norcab lunged at him, and Moc'Tor timed it perfectly, sidestepping to let the hulking giant's momentum carry him head-first into the hard wall. Crumpled in a heap, Norcab clutched his head and moaned.

By now, the Great Chamber was filled with spectators.

Moc'Tor was spattered with fresh blood that formed a stark contrast to his thick silver hair. "Give it up, Norcab. Admit you are beaten. You are done."

"If you are so sure you have won, Moc'Tor, then kill me and get it over with."

"You are no match for me, Norcab," taunted Moc'Tor. "I will not kill an unworthy opponent, even one who rightfully deserves it."

Norcab raised his head and growled. His eyes were already swelling shut, and his hair was caked with the blood from his broken nose. "I will not stop until I have killed you and restored order to our people."

"You would not restore order. You would return

our people to the path of destruction from which I delivered us all. And as for killing me, you are a greater imbecile than I realized. Cut your losses and get on with your life. There is nothing here for you but defeat, today and any other day on which you foolishly decide to challenge the Guardian."

Everyone was frozen in place. Norcab caught movement as E'ranale pressed her way through the crowd to stand in front of the other bystanders. Her hand flew to her face as she saw Moc'Tor and Norcab squared off in battle.

Norcab locked his gaze on E'ranale. Moc'Tor's blood ran cold.

"If I cannot kill you, Moc'Tor, I can at least make you wish I had." Norcab launched himself at E'ranale, who was standing exposed and defenseless only a few strides away.

The chamber seemed to split in two with the sound of Moc'Tor's rage as he flew after Norcab, felling him just inches from grasping E'ranale. As Moc'Tor brought Norcab to the floor, the first guard stepped in front of E'ranale, spear at the ready.

Driven by blind rage, Moc'Tor dragged Norcab to his feet, and holding him with both hands while bringing up one knee, slammed it into Norcab's head. Then he forced Norcab further down, and in one swift twist, snapped his neck before allowing the limp body to fall to the floor. The Guardian looked down at his own body, now drenched with his opponent's blood. Still enraged, panting, he stepped over

Norcab's crumpled frame and faced the remainder of the rebel group.

"Anyone else?" he roared. "Anyone else want to threaten me—or my family? If you do, step up now. Do you think you are male enough to challenge me? Then speak up!"

Every member of Norcab's group looked terrified. Dochrohan's guards still had them lined up and chastened by spears poised for action.

Moc'Tor passed down the row, looking each in the eye. Most could not meet his gaze; they were no match for the Guardian, not at any level. "*Va!* I thought not." Moc'Tor spat at their feet. "Take a good look at your champion. From now on, each of you is forbidden to be in the same room as E'ranale. Dochrohan, if any one of them is, you or your guards are to kill him on sight."

"We have done nothing, Moc'Tor!"

Moc'Tor turned and walked over to stand directly in front of the speaker. He was saddened to see it was Warnak, one whom he had thought had some promise.

"Nothing? Conspiring against your Leader is nothing? You have not done *nothing*. But I will grant you one point, Warnak; you *are* nothing because anyone who stands with a coward who would attack a female is nothing. And I will not spend one moment having my family looking over their shoulders at *nothing*."

In the swiftest of motions, Moc'Tor seized the

spear from the guard who stood behind Warnak, raised it overhead, and drove it straight down into Warnak's center, piercing the chest cavity. Killed instantly, Warnak remained upright, suspended by the spear. Moc'Tor rose, repositioned his grip higher on the shaft, and forced the spear down until it exited between Warnak's legs. He then stepped back and let the impaled body fall as he had Norcab's. A river of red gushed from the still twitching form.

For a moment, Moc'Tor stood watching before stepping over the carnage. "Remove this garbage," he ordered Dochrohan.

Then he turned back to face the rest of the rebellious band. "Because of Warnak's foolishness, the severity of your punishment has just been increased. Dochrohan, have your guards give them a few moments to collect their Keeping Stones, then escort them out of Kthama."

Turning to the rebels, Moc'Tor growled, "I do not know what awaits you out there, but you can see what waits for you here should you be stupid enough to return." He glanced first at Norcab's lifeless husk and then at Warnak's. "Dochrohan, you and your guards listen carefully. If any of them returns, kill him on sight and hang his body near the entrance to rot, a reminder for the rest of you who think they can defy me or threaten my family."

Choking down tears, E'ranale turned away from the gore. She knew Warnak's mother well, and her heart broke for the female who would soon learn that her oldest offling had paid the ultimate price for his poor choice in alliances. She knew that Moc'Tor had done what must be done, but it sickened her that it had come to this. She wanted to run from the room but steeled herself to wait for Moc'Tor as anything less would be seen as a lack of support for his actions.

Her mate came over to her, pressed his hand against the small of her back, and guided her from the room.

"Be strong," he said as they continued on to their quarters. "You are staying with me tonight. And every night for the foreseeable future."

Once alone, E'ranale broke down. Moc'Tor wanted to pull her to him, but he was still covered in blood.

"Lie down and relax. I will be back once I have cleaned up."

Moc'Tor stepped into the private area before realizing exactly how bloody he was. Though reluctant to leave her, he went to clean himself up in the males' bathing area.

"No good choices," he muttered as he dipped into the water, hating it and knowing it would take hours for him to dry. When he was finished, he squeezed as much of the water as possible from his coat.

He returned damp but clean to find E'ranale curled up on her side, fast asleep. For once, he regretted his prohibition against fire inside Kthama. He longed to sit outside to dry next to one of Drit's raging, evening fires but could not leave E'ranale alone. He stretched out alongside her, hoping she would somehow feel his presence.

Sometime in the middle of the night, E'ranale sat up with a start, twisting wildly about as if fighting someone. Moc'Tor sat up immediately and gently grabbed her flailing arms.

"E'ranale, wake up. Wake up; I am right here. It is only a dream."

E'ranale looked at Moc'Tor hazily, then flung her arms around his damp neck and sobbed. He held her tight against him as her tears released some of the horrors she had witnessed earlier.

"I know E'ranale, it was terrible, but you know there was no other way."

E'ranale's tears leaked more wetness into Moc'-Tor's heavy silver coat. She squeezed her eyes closed and clung to him tighter, trying to shut out the images of the crumpled and mangled bodies lying on the rock floor. "I have never seen such blood and gore. And I cannot stop thinking of Warnak's mother. Every time she passes down the corridor— We will never get the stain out, Moc'Tor."

"E'ranale, I do not want the stain out. It must stay as a reminder to others who may think to challenge my authority."

"What will happen to them?"

"Those I banished? They will live a life of

struggle and hardship unless they find another community to take them in. But that is doubtful. Few Leaders would take on young males in the prime of their drives who have been ejected from their own people. Banishment is one of the worst punishments we can impose. If they are wise, they will try to return."

"But I thought you said that if they return, they are to be killed on sight?"

"Yes. Exactly. A quick death would be better than the slow, agonizing death awaiting them in banishment."

CHAPTER 3

Time had passed. Moc'Tor's son, Dak'Tor, threw his first spear, impaling the target perfectly. The Guardian retrieved the weapon and handed it back to the offling. "Again."

"I am tired, Father."

"It does not matter. Set your physical body aside. A warrior who nurses his weaknesses will never build his strengths. Now, again."

E'ranale and Oragur approached the two. Without turning, Moc'Tor guessed the content of the message they were bringing.

"Another deadborn?"

It was Oragur who spoke. "Yes. Unfortunately."

"There are now more born dead than alive, and some of those who live seem to be sick or unstable. Starting with Trestle," sighed the Leader.

"Trestle is nearly full-grown, and his mind is still that of an offling," agreed E'ranale.

Moc'Tor closed his eyes and gave thanks for the health of his own offling and said a prayer for E'ranale's belly, once again swollen. So many others were not as fortunate.

"The females are saying the male's seed is ruined, poisoned. They are heartbroken and angry," said Oragur.

Moc'Tor stopped and took the spear from his son's hand. Placing his other hand on Dak'Tor's head, he said, "Alright, that is enough for today. Go and find your sisters and cousins."

He watched the offling scamper off. "Something has to change. We have to change."

"What are you thinking, Moc'Tor?" asked E'ranale.

As he spoke, Moc'Tor put his hand on her belly, and she placed her hands over his, resting them there. "It is time for the Leaders and what is left of the other communities to come together. We cannot solve this problem in isolation. Perhaps, if we combine our efforts, we can come up with a solution. We cannot stand by and let our people pass from Etera."

Moc'Tor sent messengers up and down the Mother Stream and into the far reaches of the outer regions. The words were simple, "Leaders and Healers, come to Kthama at the next full moon. We must join together, or all will be lost."

As the time passed, he readied Kthama for what he hoped would be a large assembly. Somehow, the excitement of something different breathed new life into his community. He knew they needed hope. If he could give them nothing else, he could at least give them that.

As the full moon broke through the clouds over Kthama, the turnout for the first Leader's meeting was a resounding success; the cave system was once again pressed to overflowing.

Enjoying a brief moment of solitude, Moc'Tor stood with his face to the moonlight and asked the Great Spirit for guidance and wisdom. The next morning between the first meal and the midday meal, he would address the other Leaders and their Healers.

As he had a hundred times before, Moc'Tor headed for the front of the room, head held high, with the Leader's Staff in his hand. This time, however, many different eyes followed his massive silver-coated frame as he passed by. To his right stood Oragur and Drit, to his left, E'ranale, his First Choice. He signaled for them to be seated and turned to address the large group of Leaders and Healers.

"Thank you for coming to Kthama. This is a momentous occasion, and we honor your presence with us—the first time we, as Leaders, have come together in unity. I hope you will find value in our assembly and that we will continue these meetings past our current crisis.

"I know that many of you will still be tired after a long journey here, and for that reason, some of our females will be bringing refreshments so you may relax somewhat before we move to a private meeting room to conduct our business."

A while later, in the large, secluded room, Moc'Tor got down to the issues before them.

"Ever since the sickness reduced our numbers, we have struggled with repopulation. Despite all our efforts, we seem to have come to an impasse. When our females do become seeded, many of the offling die or are born impaired. I know it is the same for your people. Each of you is in a position of influence. Each of you has a community that looks to you for guidance and protection. As for me, I feel that for a long time, I have failed in both regards. The mantle of leadership can become heavy at times. Perhaps, together as one people, we can solve our problems."

Solok'Tar from the Great Pines stood to speak.

"As Leader, I have willingly borne alone the burden of my people. But I believe Moc'Tor is right. It is time now that we band together and bring our collective wisdom to bear on this problem. If we do not, we will eventually all perish. Let us not forget our duty to Etera."

Next rose Hatos'Mok of the Deep Valley.

"We have done as you did, Moc'Tor. We gave our females the right to choose with whom to mate. At first, there was much dissent among the males. Uprisings. But that is behind us, and it was the right decision. But still, we have no favor with the Great Spirit. And the females' heartache at holding their deadborn is turning to anger. They demand solutions. They demand their right to produce life, and they look to me for answers. Yet I have none to give. I, too, welcome this new community of leadership."

Oragur stood to speak, "Not all the male seed is sour. Some males in each community are fathering live, healthy offling."

Moc'Tor took back the floor. "Oragur is right; some of our offling are still being born healthy, so all is not lost, but we need to maximize the benefit. Perhaps it is time for another change. When our numbers were overflowing, we had enough healthy young adults for matings within our own communities. Now, perhaps it is time to consider an exchange."

Those present started talking among themselves.

"An exchange? What kind of exchange?" The

anonymous question came from the middle of the crowd.

"An exchange of females. Or of males. Instead of mating within our own communities, as they come of age, our young adults could be paired with suitable mates from another community."

"And make them leave their homes to live with strangers?" It was a different voice this time.

"You make it sound like exile," the Guardian continued. "They would be welcomed to their new community, would they not? The promise of healthy new offling? New bloodlines? It should be a cause for celebration. In time it could become voluntary—but not until we have fully re-established our numbers."

"It would be unpopular, Moc'Tor!"

He laughed. "I have come up with unpopular decisions before, Krasus'Nol. It is one of my gifts. Yes, it will be unpopular, but only for the first generation or so. The next generations raised in this way will expect it, accept it as part of our culture. And further, it will knit us closer together. We have been isolated from each other for far too long. In each of our communities, the numbers are low; we have half-siblings and cousins mating with each other. Perhaps that is also part of our losing favor with the Great Spirit. Perhaps that is part of the reason why those of our offling who survive are born unhealthy."

Another voice arose, "We cannot change this quickly, Moc'Tor. What you ask is impossible."

"If what I ask is impossible, then we are all

doomed. Within a few generations, the Mothoc will no longer walk the land. What will happen when we are not here to worship Etera and protect her? Who will serve as keepers of the forest? What eyes will look out at the beauty of this world and give thanks and honor her bounty? Who will look after and protect the Others as we have always done? Our homes will stand, and the Mother Stream will flow, but without the Mothoc. And without us, the flow of the creative breath of the Great Spirit, which sustains our world, the flow of the Aezaitera, will weaken. Without the Mothoc and the Guardian, the future of Etera is at risk."

Moc'Tor walked closer to the group. "Dealing with change has always been our greatest challenge. We have to be backed against a wall with one last breath remaining before we will even consider it. But we cannot wait for that now. If we wait until change is comfortable, change will never come. If we wait until we *want* to change, the opportunity will have passed. It will be too late. If we must wait until change is forced upon us to open our minds to it, well, that time is here.

"So, instead of resisting change, I am asking you to embrace it. I am challenging you to embrace it. If I may be so bold, I am telling you that as a Leader, it is your responsibility to your people to *require* it. Order it. Shove it down their throats if you have to. Bear their wrath. Do whatever it takes but be the Leader. Be strong enough to do whatever is necessary to ensure that our people do not disappear from Etera. Without us, Etera's lifeblood will weaken and dry up, and eventually, all life upon her will pass into history."

As his speech ended, a commotion in the back of the room diverted everyone's attention. Two large Mothoc guards entered the room dragging a young male and followed closely by an older female. The guards looked around, realizing they had disturbed the meeting but unsure what else they could have done.

Moc'Tor strode toward them. "What is it? What is the problem?" He recognized Trestle suspended between the guards—the mentally impaired male he had been speaking about not long ago.

"It is Trestle, Moc'Tor. We found him near the Others' territory. He has been missing for days, and after finding no sign of him on our own land, our search finally widened to the land that borders their territory."

Moc'Tor looked at Trestle, who seemed terrified.

"Moc'Tor, he was with one of the Others."

Moc'Tor turned his eyes from Trestle to the guards.

"And?" The Guardian's eyes were steely cold.

"A maiden, Moc'Tor. He was about to take her without her consent. Or at least try to."

Moc'Tor closed his eyes as Trestle's mother rushed over and grabbed her son's arm. She quickly let go when the Leader opened his eyes and looked down at her. "Please, Moc'Tor," she begged. "We have been searching for him. He does not know any better. None of our females will have him. He does not understand; he has seen others of our people similarly occupied. He did not mean any harm."

Moc'Tor hated that this was the mother of Warnak, the defiant young male he had impaled years ago over Norcab's revolt. *Now, once again, more heartache for this poor female who has done nothing to deserve any of it.* "Where is the maiden?"

"We pulled him off her. She had passed out, no doubt from fear."

"Are you sure he did not—"

"No, Guardian, we caught him in time. If he had, no doubt it would have killed her. She could never have accepted the size of him. He would have torn her open beyond survival if she had not first died of fright."

"Clean him up, feed him, and confine him. I will deal with this later."

The accused's mother looked up at him pleadingly before following the guards as they led Trestle away.

"Leaders and Healers," Moc'Tor resumed. "Let us take a short break as it is almost time for the evening meal that our females have laid out for you in the Great Chamber. Discuss these problems among yourselves and bring back your thoughts when we meet here afterward."

Outside the meeting room, E'ranale approached Moc'Tor. "Trestle. What happened?"

"He almost violated one of the Others."

"Violated?"

"Without her consent."

"Moc'Tor, it would have killed her!"

"He *almost* mated her. They stopped him in time. We do not know that he harmed her other than nearly scaring her to death."

Oragur joined them. "This is a serious transgression, Moc'Tor. Perhaps it would be best to make her disappear."

Moc'Tor turned, grabbed Oragur by the throat, and pushed him back, pinning him to the wall. "Do not tell me how serious this is, *Healer*. I am well aware of the trouble Trestle has caused us all because of his mental impairment, but do not ever suggest doing anything of the sort to an innocent to cover up our sin. We are the Mothoc. The breath of Etera! Though they do not know it, we look after the Others. And above even that, you are a Healer; it is your job to foster life, not to take it. *What is wrong with you? Va!*"

He released Oragur, who rubbed his throat and glanced at E'ranale. She also looked as if she was about to snap.

"Enough! Enough." Moc'Tor threw up his arms. "Enough for now. I will be in my quarters."

"Are you not going after him?" Oragur asked E'ranale.

"Go after him? I am not going after him. But if you would like to, be my guest."

Oragur rubbed his neck some more. "No. I think it is better that he has some time to himself."

∗

After a while, E'ranale did go to find Moc'Tor. He was lying on the arrangement of leaves and mosses covered by a hide that, together, made up their sleeping mat. It was unusual to find him stretched out there in the middle of the day.

"Moc'Tor?" she asked as she entered.

"You may join me if you wish. It is safe; I will not bite your head off as I did with Oragur. I have no more answers, E'ranale. The females are about to revolt. I am tired of the fires that constantly burn for our dead offling, and I can only imagine how the mothers feel. Now we have Trestle, who almost violated one of the Others' maidens. And a room full of Leaders and Healers expecting me to have a solution. Why did I think it was a good idea to bring everyone together?"

"Because it *was* a good idea. Not just a good idea; it was a great idea. The Leaders need a way to come together and share their counsel with each other, and because most of the Leaders and their Healers— if not all—are here at the same time, decisions can immediately be agreed upon. And your idea of exchanging the youth was inspired."

"Why are my inspired ideas always so unpopular?"

"It is as you said; you have a gift."

Moc'Tor gave her a sideways look and pulled her over to him. "Make me forget about it all for a while, E'ranale. Or are you too close to delivering?"

"I am, but some of the visiting females have taught me a few tricks for times such as this."

"Tricks?"

E'ranale chuckled.

"You will see. Just lie back and close your eyes. And no matter what happens, keep them closed. Then afterward, I have something related that I need to share with you, also learned from those females who are visiting us."

Moc'Tor stretched out and let out a huge sigh, waiting for her to straddle him. But within seconds of closing his eyes, they flew wide open. "E'ranale! What the—" He partially sat up and looked down at her.

"Sssh, relax. Trust me, Moc'Tor, you will find this enjoyable. And I promise I will not bite."

Moc'Tor did as she asked and received one of the biggest and most pleasurable surprises of his life.

The Guardian did not realize he had fallen asleep until he woke up. E'ranale lay beside him, still asleep. He sat up for a moment and then allowed himself to flop back down, enjoying the relief from stress that his mate had so generously provided him.

Unfortunately, he was robbed of the moment by someone arriving at the entrance to their quarters.

"Who is there?"

"Drit, Leader. They are re-assembling; I thought you would want to know."

"Thank you. I will be right there."

Moc'Tor reached over and roused his mate. She should be in attendance when the meeting reconvened.

She blinked and finally looked up at him.

"We need to go. We both fell asleep."

"Alright, I am coming."

"E'ranale."

"Yes?"

"Before we go, I do not know what to say. What you did to me—I thought I had experienced everything."

E'ranale smiled, pleased she had satisfied him.

"You are happy because I just proved your point, Guardian, that an exchange of ideas is a good thing!"

He laughed, and her eyes lit up at seeing the stress leave his face, even for a moment.

"Later, we will talk more about what you did."

E'ranale chuckled and rose to leave with her mate.

Moc'Tor could feel the agitation in the room as he entered. Groups of Leaders and Healers were standing grouped together in discussion. Others had taken a seat and were talking to their neighbors. Moc'Tor checked his senses again. *No, not agitation. Excitement. Perhaps even a tinge of hope.*

His confidence renewed, he called for their attention.

"Let us return and focus. Now that we have had a break, does anyone have anything to add?"

Solok'Tar stood to speak. "I cannot speak for the others, but I support your idea, Moc'Tor. However, I think we need a smaller circle to work out the details."

Moc'Tor looked at the faces staring back at him. Many of them showed approval, but many were blank. He could not tell how much overall support his idea had. "Take a position so we can see where we are. Everyone who supports the idea of exchanging mating-age young, please stand up."

The vast majority of those in the room stood. Moc'Tor suppressed a smile of relief.

"I agree with Solok'Tar of the Great Pines," Cha'Kahn said. "We need a smaller group to determine how to put this into motion. Who among us has a mind for detail? If we do this, we must keep records. We will have to find a way to mark down our decisions."

"You mean like the marks on the Keeping Stones?" queried Moc'Tor. Each individual was given a stone at birth, upon which was recorded the significant events of their life.

"Similar, but more detailed. So we know who has mated with whom from which family."

There was a nodding of heads, and several looked as if they would volunteer.

"It is a good idea. Anyone interested in working on it, meet me after we have finished this discussion. Now, are there any other questions or observations?"

"How do we quiet the females?"

Moc'Tor recognized Tarris'Kahn, son of Cha'Kahn, from the tiny community of Khire immediately up the Mother Stream. "They are demanding their right to reproduce. They are saying that the males caused the ire of the Great Spirit. That we were punished with the sickness that took so many of us and fouled our seed. But they do not believe they should be denied offling because of our sins."

"What exactly are they asking for?"

"An abomination, Guardian. They are asking for permission to commit an abomination."

"Great. That is great news, Tarris'Kahn," Moc'Tor replied.

"*Va*, Moc'Tor! You did not hear me! I said they are asking for us to participate in an *abomination against the Great Spirit*."

"I heard you perfectly, Tarris'Kahn. But what you are calling an abomination may be the solution we are looking for. Regardless of the merits of their idea, this may be just what we need. We must learn to think in new ways. Try new things, be open to what we would never accept before, or that would never occur to us if our backs were not against the wall. Perhaps even ideas that we consider an abomination, because at the root of them may be an inspired idea that will bring us to the perfect solution. Now, just what is this abomination the females are proposing?"

"They want to mate with the Others."

Moc'Tor blinked. He rubbed his chin and then crossed his arms over his chest. He looked at E'ranale, who raised her eyebrows and nodded at him.

"Excuse me," he said, holding up one finger as he stepped over to speak with his mate. "You knew about this and did not tell me?"

"I was going to."

"Then why did you not?"

"You fell asleep."

Moc'Tor cleared his throat. "Oh. Alright. Well, we will talk about it later then."

He returned slowly to the front of the room. It was not unheard of; some races had been known to interbreed. But he doubted the Others would go along with it. And what would it mean to Mothoc culture? What would the offling look like? *It would have to be a male Other with a female Mothoc. Impossible.* But Moc'Tor had just chastised Tarris'Kahn for not having an open mind; he could not shut the idea off without considering it.

"How serious are they about this, Tarris'Kahn?"

"Dead serious."

"You cannot truly be considering this idea, Moc'-Tor!" shouted someone.

"And why not? Do you have a better one? I know your objection. The Others are our wards. It is our responsibility to watch over them, provide for them just as we do for Etera. Our people drive deer to their hunters. We keep the waterways open. We gather flint and leave it where they can find it. We move the weather, flare the vortex to increase the harvest when we expect a harsh winter. They are unaware of our protection and care.

"Maybe what the females ask is an affront to all the males here. But remember whose fault it is that we are in this situation? We have had our way with the females for eons, never considering their wishes nor the burden of keeping them in a continual state of being seeded. And then it was us, not them, whom the Great Spirit punished with the disease that destroyed the vitality of our seed packs. Perhaps it was a message; perhaps it was the Great Spirit driving us in this direction anyway. We do not know. So to abandon any ideas out of ignorance or because they threaten our personal sensibilities is going to doom us. Is that what you prefer?"

Moc'Tor walked across the platform. "Now, who wants to meet with the females on this idea?"

"Surely they do not mean for one of the Other males to mount them? Is that not what Trestle tried and was condemned for?"

"Of course not. I do not know what they have in mind, but I do know that the Healers have ways of which we are not aware. Perhaps they already have a workable concept. Now, who will consider this idea on its merits?"

Tres'Sar's Healer, one of the few females in the group, rose to her feet. "May I speak, Moc'Tor?"

"Yes. Please state your name."

"I am Lor Onida, from Amara—the Far High Hills. I am of the Onida Healer bloodline."

Moc'Tor nodded for her to continue, taking in her small frame.

"As a Healer, I can assure you that there are ways of accomplishing this with the male Others. And as a female, I can assure you that we are, as Tarris'Kahn said, deadly serious about this solution. You males ruled over us for as long as time remembers. You showed little concern for our needs or our preferences, mating us at will and assuming that one of you was the same to us as another. All the while having your own preferences about who you mounted, yet never considering we might also have preferences.

"And then you moved on to the next, never caring how shackled we might be with too many offling to care for, or how tired and worn out our bodies might be from the strain of constantly sustaining the seed you indiscriminately planted within us.

"We were created to bring life into this world. It is the right given to us, woven into the very fiber of our beings. But you can no longer give us what we need. And now that you can no longer perform your part of the process, you expect us to accept it and be punished along with you? We will not tolerate that. We are bringers of life. We serve the Great Mother; we have our own role, and we demand the right to satisfy our obligation to her as life-bringers, channels of the Aezaitera."

"But what if the Other males will not cooperate? Surely you do not expect them to—"

"Moc'Tor, so what if they will not cooperate? We need their seed, not their cooperation. Were we not taken by you males against our will for generation after generation? Bearing your offling whether we wanted to or not? But now the idea of taking what we need from a *male*—whether Mothoc or Other—without his consent is an affront? *Please.*"

Moc'Tor stood in silence, amazed at the power of this small female, Lor Onida, of the Far High Hills. She had chewed up and spat out every objection they could come up with.

"No harm will come to them," she continued. "Unbeknownst to the Others, we have protected them, provided for them silently through the ages. Now we need something in return. But there is no way to ask them, no possible way of making our intentions known. Even trying to explain would terrify them."

Moc'Tor felt the energy in the room shift as cracks in long-established beliefs opened under Lor

Onida's assault. The longer he listened, the more Moc'Tor believed that her words were inspired by the Great Spirit.

The room had fallen almost silent, and Moc'Tor was about to adjourn when one last voice spoke up.

"How do you know this is the will of the Great Spirit?"

Lor Onida turned to look at the speaker. "How do you know it is not?" Her dark eyes flashed. "If we do not do this, the Mothoc will disappear from Etera entirely—as the Guardian has said himself. And then what?"

Silence.

Moc'Tor stepped forward, and all eyes shifted back to him. "It is late. I can see the weariness on your faces. We will reconvene after first light. Those of you who are willing to work with us, please stay for a moment so we can determine who we are. The others of you, I bid you good rest and thank you for your willingness to be here. Having our ideas challenged, even threatened, is uncomfortable. But if we do not change, if we do not open our thinking onto a new path, even one that goes against what we have believed so far, then our future—and I assure you it will be brief—is carved in stone. Thank you."

And Moc'Tor stepped away from the platform to await those who would join him.

At first, the pockets of those open to change were small and few. But Moc'Tor met tirelessly with each group. One wanted to focus on the process of pairing up members from the communities. They met into the early hours, discussing ways of marking and recording the pairings. Drit joined this group, and his keen mind was a rare combination of embracing both innovation and structure. Not to Moc'Tor's surprise, Oragur joined Lor Onida's group, as did many of the other Healers. Straf'Tor and his mate, Ushca, also joined. And E'ranale. Small steps, Moc'Tor kept reminding himself. *Small steps will still carry us forward.*

Moc'Tor let the groups continue to work together over the following day. As the day ended, they would all reconvene to hear the thoughts and ideas of the working groups.

As he walked among them, he realized that they might not think it so now, but they were the Leaders of a new age. This handful of visionaries would be the ones to guide their people through the difficult unknowns into a future of uncertainty. But at least there *would* be a future.

At the end of the day, the Leaders of the workgroups came to speak with Moc'Tor.

Straf'Tor spoke first. "We believe we can make this work, but it will require a great deal of record keeping.

We will need a large area on which to mark the pairings. Only the wall of the Great Chamber is big enough, but it is part of our general community. We need something private, not open to everyone's eyes."

Moc'Tor nodded.

"But there is more. Even at best, with the numbers we have, we will only be able to vary our bloodlines across a few generations. Then we will be back where we are now."

"Do you have a solution?"

"We have a suggestion," Straf'Tor said.

"Speak, brother. You may not bear the title of Leader, but I recognize you as 'Tor, and I trust your wisdom."

"The two groups must work together. We must incorporate this idea of pairings with that of crossbreeding with the Others. Only if we have a complete plan will this work. We see no way around bringing the Others' seed into ours."

Moc'Tor turned to the Leader of the second group, the Healer Lor Onida.

"We agree with that," she responded. "We will work together. But we have suggestions of our own."

"Go ahead."

"The first requirement is that how we accomplish this must be confined to the Healers. There is no need for everyone to know. This is partly to control the process but also to reduce backlash. As Healers, we have a more detached view of what has to take place. We cannot trust the general population to understand."

"Who are you proposing should know?"

"Only those of us working together and moving forward; only Healers."

"I must know, Lor Onida," put in Moc'Tor. "As must some of the other Leaders. It is not just macabre curiosity about how you will accomplish it. I cannot be expected to blindly sanction this, no matter how much I trust you."

"Perhaps a small circle of Leaders, then," she reluctantly conceded. "But it must remain a closed group, Moc'Tor. Our efforts cannot stand or fall on the ground of public opinion."

"Very well, then. I support the two groups working together. Decide among yourselves what you wish to share with them. But I expect to know all your plans down to the last detail and to be kept informed as you move forward."

Both Leaders nodded and returned to join their groups.

"E'ranale, Straf'Tor, Ushca, Oragur, Drit, Dochrohan—come and find me here just before twilight. And bring Lor Onida with you."

Moc'Tor sat with his small hand-picked group, those he trusted most among his community. The only stranger was Lor Onida, the strong-willed spokesperson for the females.

"I asked you to come here to discuss the need for your work to continue undisturbed, away from the eyes of the general population. And to make a proposal as to how this can be accomplished. Ours is the largest underground community in the region. Kthama stretches great lengths back into the mountain and reaches down several levels. But there is also the adjacent cavern. It is where the females reside. It shares the Mother Stream as this system does. We have always kept the genders separate, but perhaps now is the time for that to change as well. With dissent brewing between the males and females, it would serve two purposes to merge them."

"Bring the females here to live among the males?" asked E'ranale.

"Yes. There is more than enough room. It would serve two purposes. First of all, it will force us to become one community instead of being separated gender groups. Secondly, it will free up the females' dwelling for the purposes of recording. There is a separate entrance, so you will be able to control access."

"There is only one entrance?" Lor Onida asked.

"Yes. Though both share the Mother Stream, the other side enters underground and is not accessible."

Everyone but Lor Onida was nodding approval. She frowned. "This means we will have to operate from Kthama."

"We have the largest population. It makes sense," said Oragur. "And locally, there is a large village of the Others. As we go down this path, we will need to expand to the other populations, but here there is the basis for a strong start."

Lor Onida sighed and added her consent.

"Let us keep this group together for counsel," Moc'Tor suggested. "Lor Onida, are you willing to stay here, at Kthama, for a while?"

"How can I ask others to leave their community to join another if I am not willing to do so myself? I concede that it is the wisest choice."

"You are welcome to stay in my quarters," offered Oragur.

Lor Onida shot him a look that would have killed a lesser male.

"I am sorry," he hastened to say. "I meant that if you wish, I will vacate the Healer's Quarters for your use. They are spacious and have all you would need. They are also a good place for a small group to meet, if you wanted. There is more room than I require."

With the fire leaving her eyes, Lor Onida backtracked. "That is generous of you, Oragur. I will consider it. I imagine staying in Kthama Minor would be lonely."

"Kthama Minor?" asked Moc'Tor.

Lor Onida turned to the Guardian. "I apologize. I am too headstrong; Tarris'Kahn is always reminding me. If this is the main system, then to me, this is Kthama Prime. And then it seems that the caves we will be using should be called Kthama Minor. Unless the females already named it?"

"No, it is just how it has always been," answered E'ranale. "We simply thought of it as home."

"So be it, then," approved Moc'Tor. "Once the council has disbanded, I will inform my people of the change. Dochrohan, I will need help from you and your guards to move the females across."

"They are not going to like this," said E'ranale.

"You must make them understand," Moc'Tor responded. "They are asking much of us males. Whether we are to blame for it or not, it is difficult to swallow. It is fitting that they give something in return."

"You are wise, Moc'Tor. I am blessed to be your mate."

"Do not speak too soon, female. After all this has passed, tell me if you still feel that way."

By late afternoon of the next day, Moc'Tor was in his quarters preparing to reconvene the group. He knew that while the members of the newly merged work-groups were putting their ideas and plans together, those not involved had been speaking among themselves.

"How are you feeling?" asked E'ranale.

"How am I feeling? It does not matter. All that

matters is that we keep moving forward, regardless of how difficult it is to do so."

"You are expecting trouble this afternoon?"

"Expecting it? I welcome it. All their objections must be aired here where they can be addressed, not carried back with them and nursed in dark corners to brew and fester, creating more conflict and dissent. If it appears I am dismissing or underestimating their concerns, then I must change my message." He paused. "And how are you doing?"

"I am pleased with the progress the group is making. Like you, I am prepared for a backlash from those who have not joined in."

"There are many reasons for them to have held back," Moc'Tor pointed out. "Only one of these may be disagreement with our approach. Some have more critical minds and need to be convinced of the feasibility before they will support an idea as radical as this one."

"If we can pull it off, I believe it will work. Though we will have to see how much influence the Others' seed has over the new offspring."

"Speaking of which, how exactly do you plan on making this work? Or is it too early to ask the details? And how do you know it will work."

"Oh, you already know some of the details." E'ranale gave him a conspiratorial glance.

"I do?"

"Well, yes. If you were paying attention, I think I

demonstrated the basic concept for you a couple of nights ago."

"What—?"

"What the females taught me. As I remember, you did not seem to mind what I practiced." She was toying with him now but could see his confusion was turning to anger.

"*Practiced?* No E'ranale. I forbid you to participate. The fact that you would even consider it—"

"I am not going to participate, Moc'Tor. I have no need or desire to do so. I want only you and our offling. I did what I did just so you would have a frame of reference. And to please you."

"But they are repulsive. Pale, small, with no covering. And what you did is so—"

"Personal? Oh, yes, it is. And as far as repulsive goes? Norcab was repulsive. As others were and are. And yes, it is unbearably personal. But do you think it any less personal to accept a male's shaft into your most intimate center, a male whose touch makes your skin crawl? Panting and straining while he slams himself into you as you grit your teeth, wishing to be anywhere else? It has taken years to learn how to put up with it, to block it out."

"The Others will not cooperate."

"They will not be awake to know. They cannot be. It would frighten them to death. As we have it planned, they will awake feeling very satisfied, with a story they can tell no one," E'ranale explained.

"How do you know they will not awake during—

Va!" Moc'Tor swore at not having the words to talk about this.

"You did not, the other night."

Moc'Tor narrowed his eyes at his mate. "E'ranale. You had better not have been toying with me, female. I may be your mate, but I am still the Adik'Tar!"

E'ranale chuckled. "Relax, Moc'Tor. I am only teasing. I did not experiment on you in that way. But some of the females have experimented on their mates. It is just a matter of administering enough tincture to knock them out long enough to collect what we need. With the Others, it will be different. At the chosen time, we will send them into a dream state. Once they are more or less asleep, let us say we will come to them in the Dream World. Except that they will see us as a maiden of the Others. It will be as real as if it were happening while they were awake, and the results will be as if they were having the real experience."

"But some Others may hear or see you. How will you handle that?"

"Simple. We do not just send those we want into the dream state; we send them all."

Moc'Tor sighed heavily. *Those they want.* It had not occurred to him that they might be selective, even with the Others. "One last question, and then I am done with this disturbing topic for now. After you have what you need, how will you keep them from talking about their dreams afterward?"

"This extraction process is not exactly established practice among the Others. Or us. You, yourself, were taken aback. They will have a very pleasurable and unusual dream about the attentions of an exotic maiden, and they will be too ashamed to discuss it. They are not supposed to spill their seed without procreation; it goes against all their prohibitions."

"And if you are wondering what we do once we have what we need—" E'ranale got up and came back with a little bowl of water and a small piece of clean moss, which she held up, then wadded and placed in the palm of her hand. She took a sip of water and then spat it out, soaking the little green wad and holding it up between her fingers. Then she smiled.

Moc'Tor held up his hand and walked away. "Remind me never to get on your bad side, E'ranale. You females are far too clever for me; I would never stand a chance against your inventiveness."

The Guardian left the room but stopped in the corridor just outside their quarters. He leaned his head against the wall. Was he a monster? Was this how he would be remembered—as the Leader who had brought unrest and division to his people? The Leader who had sanctioned an attack on their wards, the Others—an assault so shameful in nature that it could never be spoken about outside of closed walls? *We pride ourselves on our harmonious relationship with all the Great Spirit's creatures. What would the Others think if they knew what we plan to do without their consent?* And how could he condemn Trestle while approving a violation just as great though more shameful? What Trestle had nearly done was out of ignorance. What they were intending would be with full awareness of their wrongdoing.

E'ranale came up behind him. "Moc'Tor."

He was still braced against the cold stone wall, his head now cradled in his arms, and he did not look at her.

"Forgive me. I had no right to make light of it," she said. "I know that what we are about to do is a serious transgression. But in a way, they will have given their consent if they accept the maiden in the dream," she offered.

"That is true, as far as it goes, but they will not have given their consent to have their essences used to seed our females." Moc'Tor's voice was muffled against the wall.

"They are gentle and kind. They would help us if we asked."

"Yes, but we cannot ask. We have no shared language, and we virtually never make contact with them." He paused before continuing. "If I cannot convince the leadership waiting back in the meeting room that this is the right course, the only course, then how am I to convince the males of the general population?"

"You have said, so many times, Moc'Tor, that you are the Leader. You do not need to convince the general population. Nor do you need their permission. They do not have to know the details, and it is best that way.

"As for the leadership, they need to join with you and put their personal reservations aside. If we are to avoid extinction, we have two paths only, and we will have to go down both of them simultaneously in order to survive," she added.

Moc'Tor finally turned and met her gaze. "It is time. Walk with me."

As before, guards stood near the entrance to the meeting room, ensuring that passers-by could not be within earshot of the proceedings. As it was, curiosity, concern, and tension were at an all-time high.

Moc'Tor began speaking without waiting for the conversation to die down, and immediately the room fell silent.

"We are here tonight to finalize our plans for moving forward. The groups who volunteered to work out the initial details of the two possible approaches have joined to create one collective effort. I ask the original two Leaders to join me now." He signaled for Lor Onida and his brother, Straf'Tor, to join him.

"Before we give you our report, are there any lingering objections that we need to air?" asked Straf'Tor.

E'ranale looked at him as he stood next to his

brother, her mate. Straf'Tor had a dark coat, but they were almost identical in build and structure. A sadness swept over her, realizing that she might be looking at the last of their kind—the last pure strain of Mothoc.

Tarris'Kahn rose to speak. "We have talked about your proposals, Moc'Tor. We are ready to hear what the workgroups have to report before we make any comments of our own."

Moc'Tor nodded to his brother to continue.

"As Moc'Tor has explained," Straf'Tor began, "we have combined the efforts of both groups. Those of us working out how to plan pairings between young adults as they mature—well, we quickly discovered that while this is an excellent option, our limited numbers might bring us back to this exact point in several generations. After the sickness, we simply do not have the numbers to spread our seed widely enough. So there is no choice for us; we must bring in new seed or perish altogether. That may not be the news you want to hear, but it is the truth."

Lor Onida added, "We will not go into the details, but our plan for crossbreeding with the Others has been well-thought-out. If we do it as planned, the damage to our relationship with the Others will be minimal or nonexistent."

The Leaders looked at each other.

"If you do not mind our asking—" An unidentified male spoke up.

"I do mind. I understand your natural curiosity,

but what we will be doing is best kept between those directly involved. I know we have not earned your trust in this matter, which makes it harder for you to accept."

"The Others will know eventually," added the same male.

"Perhaps. But we only rarely have direct contact with them. Generations ahead, they may figure it out when the effects of their seed line are showing in us. But by then, the crossbreeding will be firmly established and completed."

"It is the end of us."

Lor Onida ignored him and continued. "Those in your communities who are producing healthy offspring will continue as they have been. Any female who has had a deadborn will be offered the chance to participate in our plan. Once we have it working, we will move to other communities and share our knowledge so they can do the same. If we are smart, if we are swift, if we are wise, within a few generations we will be far enough down the path that leads away from extinction."

Moc'Tor surveyed the room. He could read their reactions even if his male seventh sense hadn't been able to gauge their state of receptiveness. About half were convinced. Another quarter or so were still not committed either way, and the last quarter was mostly against it but for reasons having to do with the males' further loss of control. *The Others are our wards. We have always protected them, looked after them without their knowledge.* If there were any other way—

Moc'Tor took the floor once more. "You have heard from both workgroup Leaders. They will continue to work on their plan. As they said, once it is perfected, they will come to your communities and work with you and your people, if that is what you wish. I do not expect you to embrace this idea enthusiastically. But without your support, we will fail. It will require our collective effort to bring it about.

"This is not a tale to be told to offling at night to entertain them," he continued. "This is our reality. We change, or we die off. Forever. The choice and the power are in your hands. Once you leave here, it will be up to you which path you lead your own people down. But the truth is we cannot afford to lose the support of any of you. Our numbers are so low that we now need every one of our people if we are to survive. But I also cannot force you to participate."

The Leader walked down into the audience, intentionally heading toward the pocket where he had observed the most resistance. "You are all-powerful Leaders. Many of you said at the start that your people look to you for answers, but you know that the answers are not always easy. Sometimes we can soften them, but this is not one of those times. This will be difficult. You will meet resistance from members of your communities, just as I have met resistance from many of you.

"Before behavior can change, the thinking

behind it must change. When you go back, remember your own process, your own struggle with this. And consider the alternatives. You can go back and help them understand that this is a solution, a path forward, and then work with us. Not an easy solution, no. Not one to be proud of. *But there is one.*

"Or you can go back and tell them there is a solution, but that you do not support it. You owe it to your communities at least to let them know there is a way forward. And to give them time to adjust. If you do less than that, you are not a Leader; you are but a tyrant who uses lies as a shield to protect himself from conflict. They deserve to know the truth, and they deserve to hear it from you."

The room was quiet; Moc'Tor's words hung in the air. E'ranale felt the spirit move in her, and she knew she must speak to the group. She caught Oragur's eye and stepped forward, cueing him to stand beside her as a Healer and also as a male.

"I do not understand what it is like to be male," she began. "I do not pretend to bear your burdens or face your struggles. I do know that you have been taxed considerably over the past decades. And to hear what we are planning only adds to the weight you carry. The idea of our females, your females, using another's seed is no doubt repugnant to you.

"However, it is not too long ago that you openly shared us, not caring how many of you mated us or whose seed ripened in whose belly. This is not so different. But if you still struggle with what lies ahead, try to remember, *this is not our choice.* This is not something we choose willingly.

"We would never ordinarily seek out the males of the Others. *You* are our males. *You* are the ones we desire and long for. *You* are the ones in our hearts and the ones with whom we share our beds, our bodies, and our lives. We do not wish in any way to replace you. We can never replace you; we only wish for our people to survive, and therefore we must fill our purpose to produce offling for ourselves and for you. Offling for us all to raise as sons and daughters of our people. Nothing more. You will always be those around whom we build our lives. The rest will pass into history and be forgotten, just as the waters of the Great River flow downstream and disappear from view. If we do not take this path, the Mothoc and our responsibilities and gifts to Etera will cease. Consider those consequences. Which is the path you can most easily live with?"

E'ranale exhaled and released her tension. In her heart, she felt they had done all they could. Whatever happened next, it was out of their hands.

Through the upcoming years, the Mothoc females gave birth to more and more cross-bred offling. Knowing that the process worked, the two Healers, Lor Onida and her mate, Oragur, traveled to the other Mothoc communities with local populations of

Others and taught the process they had devised. As far as they were aware, the Others did not know what the Mothoc were doing. To begin with, the Mothoc had seldom interacted with the Others, and in time, if the Others became aware of the Mothoc's altered appearance, they might never make a connection between that and the past.

The first two generations of cross-breeding had produced offling still very much like the Mothoc. As the second generation was again crossed with the Others' seed, the Others' influence started to come to the forefront. As the years passed, each subsequent generation was bred as soon as possible. Eventually, there were two distinct new seed lines living at Kthama; those who resembled the Mothoc more— the Sassen—and those who had more of the Others' influence—who would become known as the Akassa.

As their population became stable, the sense of urgency faded, and unrest stirred among the two factions across all the communities—almost in unison.

Moc'Tor and his brother stood by their father's bedside. Sorak'Tor lay very still, his breathing growing more and more shallow. Moc'Tor bent over and drew the hide covers higher under his father's chin. The Healers, Oragur and Lor Onida, were standing with them for these final moments.

Sorak'Tor stirred and opened his eyes. He looked up at his two sons as they stared down at him.

"My sons." He reached out a hand. "I know my time to leave Etera is close. I am sorry to go during such great upheaval. Trust yourselves. Trust each other," he whispered. "I will wait for you on the other side."

Moc'Tor took his father's hand and squeezed it just as Sorak'Tor turned his head and let go of his last breath.

Kthama was in mourning over the loss of the male who had once been their Leader. As word spread, Leaders from the other communities sent consolation messages, while others came in person to pay their respects to Moc'Tor and his brother.

I cannot believe he is gone, thought Moc'Tor. Now he and Straf'Tor must carry on without their father. *If our faith is true, he is now reunited with my mother, and in time, when I also return to the Great Spirit, I will see them both again.*

For a while, there was quiet as they were all reminded of the preciousness of all life and that not even the Mothoc were immortal.

CHAPTER 4

Centuries later, the Great Chamber and corridors of Kthama were once again full of life. Moc'Tor still ruled with E'ranale by his side, but his subsequent generations of offling and those of his brother, Straf'Tor, had taken very different paths. Moc'Tor continued to pursue the introduction of the Others' bloodline, whereas Straf'Tor was steadfast that they dare not dilute the original Mothoc blood any further. The differences in ideology were creating dissent.

"Oragur and Lor Onida believe the differences will now be self-sustaining," said E'ranale to her mate.

"Meaning?"

"Meaning that those who wish to breed with others of their kind inside the community will produce offling true to their parents. We no longer need to introduce the Others' seed into our females for the changes to be handed down."

Moc'Tor breathed a sigh of relief. "How is this one doing?" he asked E'ranale, placing his hand on her swollen belly.

"She is quieter than the others. There is a sense of peace about her."

"Her? How can you know it is a female?"

"I do not know. But I strongly feel that she is."

"Have you thought of a name?"

"Yes. If you approve, I would like to name her Pan. Way-shower."

Moc'Tor thought a moment before answering. "Way-shower. For some reason, it strikes me as the perfect name. But then she comes from the perfect mate. I could not love you more, E'ranale. How you have stood beside me through all this."

She placed her hand alongside his face and stroked his cheek with her thumb. After a moment of silence, she asked, "Moc'Tor, do you really think the Others do not know we have been taking their seed?"

"I cannot say, E'ranale. On the one hand, it seems they must know something is going on. Maybe they do not want to admit any knowledge for fear of causing a direct confrontation. It is perhaps, as the females said, that the dreams are pleasant, but as a forbidden aberration in their pleasure practices, the males are reluctant to share them. It is possible there is no group disclosure. After all, we have taken what we needed as peacefully as possible, doing them no harm. They know we could easily overpower them if we wished, although it is perhaps an unspoken understanding. But then again, there is nothing about the dream that gives us away as the source."

"Since you gave the females the right to refuse a male, how easily we have set aside one of our most sacred tenets; Never Without Consent," sighed E'ranale. "I do not believe we are quite at the end of this path yet, but we do need to remember everything we have learned so far—that which is truly important."

"I am not following."

"Laws, Moc'Tor. I think the High Council needs to establish laws that we can all agree on. Laws that will direct and guide us in the future."

"That is a good idea, and I agree with you. I will present it to Straf'Tor and the other council members. If we can come to a consensus, such laws could unite all our communities."

The High Council had grown out of the original band of Leaders, back when Moc'Tor first proposed cross-breeding with the Others. He had become the official Overseer, and the group met regularly to get updates on the progress that Lor Onida and Oragur were making with the other communities. Kthama

Minor served as the central location of Lor Onida and Oragur's work.

Lor Onida and Oragur had since paired and were living at Kthama Minor. Deeper inside the system, the inner walls of the largest chamber were covered with markings. These represented the original pure Mothoc males and females, along with the chart of their pairings and offling—either offling with mates of their own communities or with those born of the Others' seed. When the Others' seed had been introduced, the Mothoc decided to trace the genetic line through the females until that line started breeding true and the Other's seed was no longer required. This, however temporary, bothered a fair number of the males, who resented that more and more power continued to be granted to the females.

Moc'Tor was deep in thought when the Healer interrupted him. "I bring you joyful news, Adik'Tar," said Oragur. "E'ranale has delivered your offling. It is a female."

"Is E'ranale alright. Is the offling healthy?" he asked, turning to face Oragur.

"Yes, both are fine, and yes, she is healthy. And —" He hesitated. "She is a Guardian."

Moc'Tor raised his eyebrows. "Are you sure?"

"There is no doubt about it."

Moc'Tor thought of his other offling by E'ranale,

Dak'Tor, his son, and his daughters Vel and Inrion, none of whom was a Guardian, though Dak'Tor sported a large amount of silver hair. "A double blessing," Moc'Tor replied, "though a surprise." According to legend, seldom had there been more than one Guardian walking Etera at the same time. Moc'Tor wondered if it meant that the Great Spirit planned to cut short his time on Etera.

"I know what you are thinking," said Oragur. "Whether it portends an early demise for you, Adik'-Tar, or is indicative of times of great need coming, I do not have the insight."

Moc'Tor shook his head and chuckled. "Never one to mince words, were you Oragur. No matter, the same thought had just occurred to me. I always found it a bit tiresome that Guardians are practically eternal. At some point, it just feels natural to move on."

He sighed. "No matter. Since there is no way of knowing, only time will tell. May I see them yet?"

"Yes."

So the two giants made their way back down the rocky path into the Great Entrance of Kthama.

Lor Onida, Oragur's mate, stepped aside when they entered, providing a view of E'ranale sitting up comfortably holding her offling. Her eyes twinkled when she saw Moc'Tor.

"We have a third daughter," she said softly, looking down at the tiny creature cradled in her arms.

Moc'Tor went to her side and crouched down so he could see the little face. He reached out and caressed it gently, at which the offling gurgled contentedly. Then she opened her eyes, and father and daughter exchanged their first look.

All the Mothoc possessed the seventh sense. The sixth was the ability to connect with the magnetic currents of Etera and pull from them not only information about their geographic position on Etera but also draw in the Aezaitera—the creative life force from the Great Spirit that was continually entering and exiting their realm. The seventh sense was their ability to know outside of the first six senses. At the moment in which Moc'Tor looked into his daughter's eyes, he knew that events both great and challenging awaited her on her life's path.

"What is it?" E'ranale asked, her eyes scanning his face. "What did you just see?"

"Only that this one— This one will be an even greater blessing to Etera than any who came before her, Saraste'," he answered.

"How is that possible, Moc'Tor—"

"Hush," he cut her off, taking her hand in his. "I feel your fear. But we are living in extraordinary times. Her birth does not necessarily signify my early transition. We should both have learned by now that what has been before is not necessarily the shade of what will be. We both know the turmoil enmeshing our people. Perhaps her coming is only the Great Spirit sending us additional help. This is a moment of great joy; a second Guardian will now help protect Etera."

E'ranale kissed the head of their new daughter. "Pan," she softly addressed the offling.

"A strong name. You have chosen well," said Moc'Tor. *Pan*, he thought, *meaning way-shower.*

Moc'Tor smoothed his mate's hair back from her forehead. "If there is nothing you need, I will leave you now and let you rest. I will be back by twilight unless you want me to return earlier."

"Pan and I will be fine. Oragur and Lor Onida are taking very good care of me, I promise. "And no doubt, soon Dak'Tor and his sisters will be here to see little Pan." E'ranale took his hand and kissed it.

Irisa, who had been sent by Lor Onida, poked her head through the doorway. Straf'Tor waved her all the way in.

"I come bearing news. E'ranale has delivered her offling. It is a female, and she bears the Guardian's markings."

Ushca and Straf'Tor looked at each other before he spoke. "Give them our blessings. I am sure they will let us know when E'ranale is ready for visitors."

Krin nodded and retreated, leaving them to their sudden concern.

"Come, Ushca," said Straf'Tor, "lie with me and let us forget all our troubles for now." He led her to the sleeping mat and took comfort in their lovemating.

Word spread quickly that a second Guardian had entered Etera. Oragur's hands had been full with quelling everyone's fears, and he was currently addressing a large gathering.

"We cannot lose Moc'Tor," said Toniss, mother of Straf'Tor's first offling. "We are not ready. We are still in the midst of all this change. What does it mean, Oragur?"

"Like most mysteries, it can mean nothing, or it can mean everything. We simply do not know. I understand the concerns of all of you—that the appearance of a second Guardian has always portended the transition within centuries of the current one. But these are unprecedented times. We should all know by now that what has been in the past does not necessarily dictate what will happen in the future."

Oragur's words did little to quiet their fear. His mate, Lor Onida, stood by, also feeling helpless in the presence of so much emotion.

"Guardians are practically immortal. Moc'Tor

has not walked Etera anywhere near long enough for his time here to end," stated Toniss.

Lor Onida found the words to reply. "Look at Moc'Tor. He is as robust as ever. He stands tall. His stride is without falter. His mind is sharp, his wit even sharper, and he holds Kthama in the palm of his hand. His steps will guide ours for centuries to come. There is no waning in Moc'Tor's power. Fear is difficult to master, but you must use your reason to look at the facts of the situation instead of listening to the voice of panic that threatens your peace of mind.

"As always, Moc'Tor needs our support; do not let your belief in him waiver. He has gotten us this far, and he will take us the rest of the way through what lies ahead."

"The fact that a second Guardian has entered Etera should be received as a great blessing, not as a harbinger of doom." All heads turned to see Straf'-Tor, who had entered the assembly from the back of the room.

The large dark-coated male strode confidently to the front.

"Now, go about your lives. Try to focus on the positives of the situation and keep your thoughts from running away from you."

Though he was not the official Leader of Kthama, Moc'Tor's brother spoke with an authority that was recognized by all.

Straf'Tor, Oragur, and Lor Onida stood on the

speaking platform, watching as the crowd slowly dispersed. Where once the assembly would have consisted of giant dark hair-covered bodies nearly identical to each other, they now saw a variety of heights, builds, body coverings, facial structures. Straf'Tor watched with a heavy heart.

The division he had feared was not coming. The division was here.

Pan turned out to be a delightful child, full of wonder and joy. She looked at everything through eyes of appreciation and gratitude. She took care of every orphaned creature and had to be stopped from feeding the mice that found their way into Kthama. When she was not allowed to feed them, she negotiated that they must be caught and safely returned to the outside. Kthama was dotted with various contraptions designed to capture the little creatures without hurting them. Pan would also sit quietly for hours, watching the birds and studying their calls. She quickly found her way into the hearts of everyone at Kthama, regardless of the faction they favored. All offling were precious and cherished, but there was no way to dispute the special place Pan held in everyone's hearts.

Breaking the mold of many Mothoc fathers, Moc'Tor spent hours with Pan from when she was a tiny offling, just as he had with her older sisters and her brother, Dak'Tor. And while she would learn hunting and marksmanship, the turning of the seasons, the patterns of the stars, and everything else Dak'Tor and her sisters had learned, Pan's training would include even more. She must be taught her role and responsibilities as a Guardian of Etera.

The day finally came when it was time for Pan's indoctrination into the duties of a Guardian. It was time for Moc'Tor to start teaching her how to use the Aezaiterian current that moved through her body. And in time, he would teach her how to engage the Order of Functions.

"Is it not too soon? asked E'ranale. "She is still so young."

"It is an honor to be a Guardian," Moc'Tor replied, "but it is also a burden. She needs to learn now to accept the mantle. The longer I wait, the more difficulty she may have embracing it."

Father and daughter stood outside in the lush meadow above Kthama. The meadow was off-limits to anyone but Moc'Tor. Sentries monitored the two paths that led there, ensuring his privacy for however long he visited. A small stream meandered through the meadow, which was ringed with trees, flowers, and thick grasses. The spring blooms would soon burst open, announcing the return of new life to Etera.

Pan was mesmerized by the beauty of the place and its energy—the loving, calming energy that was like nothing she had experienced before.

"Today starts your training as a Guardian," said Moc'Tor, breaking her out of her reverie. "We will begin with connecting with the Aezaitera. The Aezaiterian flow is the very creative life force of the Great Spirit; it is the breath of life entering and exiting this realm. All Mothoc are connected to this current, and though it flows throughout Etera, there are places where it is particularly accessible. Are you listening to me or watching that deer and her fawns?" he asked.

"I am sorry, Father."

"Very well." Moc'Tor started again. "Underneath Kthama is a great vortex of this current. We do not know, but we surmise this is why Guardians are only born of the 'Tor seed line. We have a connection to this physical location. It is more than the great practical blessings Kthama offers—the expansive cave system, the Mother Stream, which brings fresh air, water, and richness through all the levels—our very souls are connected here."

Pan nodded.

"Alright. Enough talk; we will begin," he said. "Close your eyes and make sure your feet are firmly planted on the ground."

Pan did as her father had said.

"Now, reach into the core of Etera. Send your awareness down through your body, through your feet, and straight into the vortex beneath us. You will know when you connect directly with the Aezaitera. The moment you do, come back to your body immediately."

Pan stood silent, and then a small shudder went through her frame.

"Father—"

"Shhhh. I know. You will have to build up your ability, but bear all that you are currently able to."

"Ahhhhhhh—" a moan escaped her lips. "I cannot—"

"Break it off, Pan. Come back to your body."

Pan became deathly still. She stopped breathing, though she remained standing.

"Pan! Open your eyes!"

Her eyelids fluttered, and she staggered. Her father reached out to steady her and gave her a gentle shake. Finally, she opened her eyes but was staring blankly ahead. Moc'Tor crouched down so that she had to look at him.

"You did not listen to me. You must build up the ability to bear the Aezaitera's current."

"I did not want to let go." She looked at her father with wide eyes.

"Of course you did not. Connecting with the Aezaitera puts you directly within the creative current. That is life itself. It is pure joy and pure creative love. While we bear an overwhelming responsibility, a Guardian is blessed to be able to experience the power of the Great Spirit in a way no other creature on this side of the veil can."

"I want to reconnect."

Moc'Tor laughed. "You are so like your mother. Ready to take life head-on. We will practice again tomorrow. But you must never engage the Aezaitera alone. It will be a long time before you are strong enough to withstand it without getting lost. For now, you will always be standing up when we engage with it. That way should you lose yourself, the fall will most likely bring you back. In time, when you are able not to lose yourself in it, we will enter the Aezaitera lying down. But not until then, as the temptation to stay immersed is too strong."

Pan nodded her understanding.

"I am glad you are anxious to learn. But trust me, Pan, you have nearly an eternity here to fulfill your role as Guardian."

"What do you mean?" she frowned.

Moc'Tor sighed and looked up at the sky. *Quat. I had not meant that to come up yet.* "Go and find your mother. It is time for midday meal. I will explain later."

"No, father. I want to know now," she said, standing firm. "What do you mean an *eternity*?"

"All right. We may as well sit down; this is going to take a while." Moc'Tor led his daughter to a soft grassy spot.

"The Mothoc live very long lives on Etera. Many, many years longer than all the other creatures here."

Moc'Tor put an arm around Pan's shoulders. "You are a Mothoc, but you are also a Guardian. As a Guardian, you play a specific role on Etera. Life is always entering and transitioning out of Etera—what we call being born and later returning to the Great Spirit. This life force, the Aezaitera, is continuously moving in and out of our realm, just as we are continually breathing in and out. This movement, the coming and going of life in our realm, happens at different speeds based on the lifespan of each creature; but it is always in motion. So you may think of the life and death cycle on Etera as the life force—the breath of the Great Spirit entering and leaving our realm with the taking on and shedding off of physical form—the birth and death of every living creature here. Now, what happens to us if we quit breathing?"

"Well. It seems obvious we would die."

"Exactly. It is the same for Etera. If the flow of the life force in and out of this realm were to cease, Etera herself would die."

"You speak of Etera as if she is alive."

"Etera is alive, Pan. Although it appears we are all separate from each other—the creatures of the forest, the Mothoc, the birds in the sky, even the blades of grass—the truth is we are truly all one life. We see separation, but in fact, there is no separation. I see the look on your face but stay with me. We, as the Mothoc, are connected to this breath, this constantly flowing current. Each Mothoc serves as a channel to facilitate the movement of the Aezaitera in and out of Etera. That is why we live so long. We are rejuvenated by the flow of the life force in and out."

Moc'Tor bent his head down to look into his daughter's eyes. "Do you understand so far?"

"I think so."

"As a Guardian, you are not only part of the Great Spirit's breath of life, but you have the power to cleanse the Aezaitera as it returns to the Great Spirit."

"Cleanse it? Why would the breath of the Great Spirit need to be cleansed? The Great Spirit is perfection in all things," said Pan, perplexed.

"That is a good question. A great question. Yes, the Aezaitera, the breath and inflow of life coming from the Great Spirit and entering our realm, is perfect. But once it enters this realm, it is affected by what is happening on Etera. In time you will realize how challenging life can be. Distortions in our souls, like anger and fear, affect the Aezaitera and change it from its original pattern of perfection. Guardians have the ability to return the Aezaitera to its original state before it leaves this realm. And because of this, we are always in the positive flow and are continuously imbued and refreshed by the life force. We are virtually never sick, we heal incredibly fast, and our life spans are even longer than the other Mothoc."

Moc'Tor stopped talking and waited, knowing what was coming because he had experienced this same understanding of the burden endured by a Guardian.

"But Mama. Dak'Tor—and my sisters."

Moc'Tor drew his daughter closer. "Yes, Pan. At some point, you will have to finish your journey here without them."

He felt the sobs wrack her body as she understood that she would outlive everyone she loved—her mother, her brother, her sisters. Even the half-siblings her father had sired by other mates before E'ranale had become his only choice.

Everyone she knew except her father would at some point transition to the Great Spirit—long before she did.

"I do not want to be a Guardian," she said in muffled words as she buried her face in her father's thick white chest hair. Her arms were snaked around his neck, and she clung to him.

"I know, daughter. I know. But I hope that in time you will come to see what a great blessing it also is. I will not lie to you; there are drawbacks, painful, heartbreaking drawbacks, but there are also great joys. In time you will come to see the balance."

They sat there together for a long time, the father and the daughter, bearing the burden that had been placed upon them and them alone. The Guardian was revered, but few understood the great cost that came with being chosen.

CHAPTER 5

Dak'Tor approached his father. "May I speak with you?"

"Of course, son; sit with me."

Moc'Tor's only son by E'ranale had long ago matured into a fine male. Though not a Guardian, the top of his head was almost white, and the color continued over his shoulders and below, covering almost all of his back. It gave him a striking appearance. Moc'Tor was not sure what it meant, or if in time, Dak'Tor might develop some Guardian-like powers. If nothing else, he seemed to have a highly developed seventh sense.

"Father, you seem to sit down a great deal nowadays. Are you ill?"

"You know better, Dak'Tor. There is no cause for worry; I am the Guardian, and we do not fall ill. But tired—yes, I am tired; the strain on our people grows daily. But that is not what you came to talk about, is it?"

"I am concerned about the strain I see on *you*."

"We live in a tumultuous age. So many changes, many of them good, such as the idea of the Leaders coming together in a formal Council. In fact, very soon, we will be convening to agree on some common laws—conduct that we will all be expected to follow. This agreement will be critical as we move forward; I fear that a great division is coming as my brother and I cannot see eye-to-eye on the future of our people. Perhaps you should join us tomorrow. You are, after all, heir to my leadership."

Straf'Tor had stood up to address the Council. "A suggestion has been made to set down agreements, standards of behaviors—laws if you would—to guide our fellow communities and us as we move forward into this new age."

"Give us an example, Straf'Tor," a female from the crowd asked.

"I am not talking about restrictions that go against our general nature. I am talking about statements with which we can all readily agree. Such as *never commit violence against another except in self-defense.* Or that *the needs of the community come before those of the individual.*"

"Or—*never without consent*?" added a sarcastic male voice.

Straf'Tor had known that was coming. Much of the rising strife had to do with the very practice that had saved them from extinction. "Your point, Garl'-Tar, has been made often. Move on."

"My point needs to be made again, Straf'Tor. There are many of us who agree with it, and you are one of them. This has gone far enough. We have achieved our objective, and we must cease this abomination against the Others. We agreed to it in the beginning because it was the only way to avoid the complete dying-off of our people. But our population is re-established. There is no need to continue. Already, the next generation looks more like the Others than the Mothoc. Where will it end? When no part of the Mothoc is left at all?"

In the background, voices joined in to support Garl'Tar.

"And what of our culture?" he persisted. "The genetic lines used to be traced through the males but are now traced through the females. The balance of power was off in the beginning, it is true. We males treated the females as if they were ours to mate with as we wished. But that has all changed. We corrected our error only to go too far in the other direction. The females have too much power now!"

Even more voices, louder ones, joined that of Garl'Tar.

Straf'Tor did agree with Garl'Tar. The cross-breeding had gone almost dangerously far and certainly far enough—but that was not the point of the assembly, and he had to bring it back on track.

"That is not the subject of this meeting. We came here to agree on guidelines, standards of conduct. We all recognize there are strong feelings on both sides, but for now, can we not put them away so we can at least accomplish this goal?"

After the mumbling had quietened down, the group agreed that there should be at least three laws for the community at large; The Needs of the Community Come Before the Needs of the Individual, Honor the Females in all Matters, Show Forbearance for the Failings of Others.

The second statement had been hard-won, but Straf'Tor and Moc'Tor argued strongly for it. They did not want to forget the sins of the past, especially with the resentment now brewing against the females. In the face of this growing sentiment, there was a need for a statement lifting the females, not pushing them back down. Neither would budge, and the Council members all stayed into the late hours before Moc'Tor was finally able to dismiss them.

Straf'Tor had returned to his quarters where he could consult Ushca and enjoy some solitude with her. "There was dissension again in the Council meeting over how far to continue using the Others'

seed. There is a large group that feels we need to stop where we are. What do the females think about this?"

"I do not know what they think in other communities, but here, most of them wish to continue. The females are now used to their appearance, and with each generation, they see the benefit to the offling increasing. The younger generations are now more inventive, faster, and have finer muscle control. They are not as strong, but they are still far stronger than the Others. Like us, they will have few natural enemies."

"Has Lor Onida told you anything at all about the other communities?"

"Yes," she sighed. "There is something that fits directly with your concern, Straf'Tor. The People of the Far High Hills are rumored to have taken it further. Several of the females produced offling from Waschini seed."

Straf'Tor stopped cold and stared at his mate. "Waschini? Are those not the rumored pale, fragile versions of the Others who are said to have come across the icy waters in huge floating shelters? How is that possible? I thought they were a myth. *They do exist*?"

"That is how the story goes, yes. Some females came across what seems to have been several sentries on foot. They were far separated from any others. The females were attracted to their startling hair coloring, almost the color of the sun."

"I do not believe it. I am not convinced they are even real. I would have to see one. Did they bear offling?"

"From what I was told, yes. For some reason, they are even smaller than any of our other combinations produced. They have very little overall body covering. And what they do have is very light—almost the color of the winter wheat. They will have to take after the Others in wearing wrappings. But the mothers were already several generations modified."

"I need to confirm with Lor Onida how true this is. If it is accurate, then it is time. The line must be drawn, and it must be drawn hard. It is one thing to do what we have to do to survive; it is another to spit in the face of the Great Spirit by taking matters too far. After having come this far in recovery, if this is not stopped, it will bring destruction upon us all, and on Etera."

The next morning, Straf'Tor requested the presence of Lor Onida and Oragur. Before long they stood before him, and Straf'Tor had his answer. He was enraged. The females of the Far High Hills had indeed stolen seed from the Waschini and produced offling. The Waschini had not survived the encounter.

Straf'Tor stormed across the room, his arms

stretched wide. Lor Onida, Oragur, and Moc'Tor watched him in silence.

"Is this what we have become? Is this who we are now? Is it not bad enough that our females use their abilities to subdue the Others, sneak into their villages, and take what they want from them? Have we forgotten they are our wards whom we are supposed to be protecting? Oh yes—I know that no harm is done *if you do not consider performing such an intimate violation on another as harming them*. The fact that it is females doing this to males should make no difference. Oh—but now it has gone further. Now they have *killed* to get what they want."

Moc'Tor stepped forward. "Straf'Tor, that is not true. They did not kill the Waschini—at least not intentionally."

Straf'Tor continued, unfazed. "We have no fear of the Waschini. The stray washed-out ones that are said to come across the waters are no threat to us. But it is of no benefit that they become aware of our existence. It may be better that they were frightened to death—or whatever caused them to die. But that does not change the fact that this abomination has to stop. And you heard Lor Onida.

"There is even more to the story," continued Straf'Tor. "The females were far, far out of their territory. There is no explanation, no excuse for what they did. They should be punished, but as far as I know, their Leader, Tres'Sar," he pointed at Lor

Onida, "*your* Leader, looked the other way. Enough. *Enough*."

Moc'Tor reminded them that he had said words to that effect many years ago. He had said *enough* over another instance where an act had almost been committed without consent—the young maiden of the Others, whom Trestle, the impaired young male, had intended to violate. He was one of the first born with problems, the specter of things to come. Now, again, they were arguing about the same issue—imposing one's will on another. "To him, it was a drive, no different than eating when hungry or drinking from the stream when thirsty. Luckily, the maiden survived the trauma. So I gave his mother a choice—we could either kill her son or crush his seed pack, permanently removing his mating drive."

Moc'Tor still struggled to get the image out of his head of how Oragur had carried out the act, though after Trestle recovered, he was gentle and quiet and never caused any trouble again.

"We must come to an agreement, brother," said Straf'Tor. "We must stop this before it goes any further. Say you agree with me, and together we can put an end to this."

Moc'Tor slowly shook his head. "I wish I could, Straf, but I cannot. It seems we are at an impasse. You have a following that wants to stop where we are. My people want to continue because we see the benefit of the Others' seed line mixed with ours. We intend to move forward another generation to make sure we continue to breed true. Perhaps then we will stop."

"*Perhaps* then? So you admit you see no end to this?"

"I am not saying either; we will decide according to my people's wishes. This is not something I alone can dictate."

Straf'Tor glared. "Is it not? Decades ago, did you not give a speech stating exactly that? That it is our place as Leaders to do exactly that? And were you not just now talking about laws and standards of conduct? For the love of the Great Spirit, if this is not where we should be setting limits, then *what is*?"

"Straf'Tor, our father has been gone for some time now. It is just you and me; we must lead together."

"And yet you are the one making it impossible. How can we lead together when we are divided on this critical aspect?"

"It is late. Perhaps we should stop and calm down," said Moc'Tor.

"We can stop, brother. But nothing will change tomorrow. Or the next day. Or the day after. If you have made up your mind, if you will not stop this abomination, then there can be no peace between us. I can no longer stand here and condone what you are doing."

"What are you saying, Straf'Tor? Are you talking about war?"

Straf'Tor scoffed. "It would be a short war, Moc'-

Tor. Your followers are frail compared to mine. They are stronger than the Others, but there is no comparison with us in strength. You may think your offling are more inventive, but that matters little when our offling can, at will, snap any of yours like a twig. They disgust me!"

"If our community splits, Straf, we are the largest. It will divide all the other communities. Is that what you want?"

"I never wanted that. But if it has to be this way, then so be it. You are ignoring our obligation to the Great Spirit to provide for Etera. I am appalled that you, the Guardian, would do so. Even you, brother, will not live forever. Yes, there is your daughter, Pan, but she is not well-enough versed in the Order of Functions, and we can all see the strain this division is having on you."

"Do not lecture me on the importance of the Order of Functions. And do not bring my offling into this. When it is time for her to take her place as Guardian, she will be ready. You speak of the strain caused by division, yet it is you who support that division. And how can you support division when it goes against everything we believe?"

Straf'Tor started to walk away but paused for a moment, his back to his brother. Hardly turning his head, he said, "We will stay until the laws are agreed upon, and then we will leave Kthama. There are fewer of us than of you; it is only fair that we are the ones to leave. I am sorry it has come to this, but this is where we are. And once we leave, there can be no contact between our people ever again. If it has fallen to us to serve Etera alone, then so be it. But I will risk no more contamination of my people with your thinking."

Moc'Tor watched his brother walk away. His heart was heavy, and he was more tired than he remembered ever being. He walked the corridors aimlessly until he found himself outside Kthama.

The Guardian looked up at the canopy of stars. What had he done? But what other choice had the Great Spirit given him? There was no other choice; it was this or perish. But was it still what the Great Spirit truly wanted? Had Moc'Tor taken his community too far down that path? He could not believe they were wrong. *Our offling are far more advanced than we are. The future belongs to them. Why can Straf and the others not see that?*

Moc'Tor felt he had failed in some way; had he failed his people? They could not afford a rift, but neither could Moc'Tor prevent one. Straf'Tor was right. *Our offling's ingenuity is no match for their offling's size and strength.*

If Moc'Tor could not change their minds, then he must allow this division because in a battle between the two branches of offling, without a doubt, Straf'-Tor's following would be the victors. And as Straf'Tor had stated, what of the Mothoc blood? In the rush to find a solution, maybe Moc'Tor had not given that enough consideration. In a flash, the realization hit him. Straf'Tor was right; the Mothoc blood must not perish from Etera.

Moc'Tor bent over, resting his hands on his knees. *I, of everyone, should have kept this need at the forefront of my decisions.* How had he lost his way? Perhaps he was indeed no longer fit to lead.

He would give Straf'Tor time to calm down and then talk to him again.

I will try one more time. If he still wants to take his band of followers and leave, then I will concede. I could not stop them, anyway. But at least they had set out their laws first. Perhaps if they could achieve that much, they could maintain peace—some form of unity in spirit.

Moc'Tor returned to Kthama to seek relief and a few moments of peace in the arms of E'ranale but found her curled up on their mat, already asleep. However, he needed to talk to her.

"E'ranale, are you awake?" he asked. She stirred a bit but did not reply.

"E'ranale, are you awake?" This time he touched her shoulder.

She sleepily turned to him, thinking, *Well, I am now.* "What is it, Moc'Tor? Is everything alright?" She brushed the hair from her forehead.

"I am worried, E'ranale. I have been so focused on ensuring our survival that I forgot our first duty to Etera. Straf'Tor is right—we cannot breed so far with the Others that the Aezaitera is compromised. What-ever happens next, we must keep the two seed lines separate. For the protection of our offling and for the continuation of what is left of our Mothoc blood. I fear I have taken it too far already."

"What are you planning to do?" she asked.

The next morning Moc'Tor sought out his brother.

"We need to talk."

"What would be the point? We said everything last night."

"I have given much thought to your words. And I have come to realize you are right. We cannot allow the Mothoc blood to be diluted much further. But there is room on Etera for us all, and the division between us, which I have seen as a loss, I now see as necessary protection of the different paths we are taking. I am truly humbled at the wisdom in the Order of Functions—that which you have rightfully accused me of abandoning, but which directs us without our conscious awareness."

Moc'Tor paused a moment in reverie.

"I am calling the original Adik'Tars together," he continued, "those who are still alive from when we started down this path. I believe there is a bigger plan of which we were unaware—something more complex than a disagreement between two brothers. We are the largest population, and what we do will affect the other communities as well."

"I am glad you have come to your senses. What are you thinking?" asked Straf'Tor.

"I have a plan," said Moc'Tor, "but it will take both of us, and perhaps others, to make it happen. I have already sent sentries out with word to assemble, and I expect that within several days we will have enough Leaders to meet. I hope Lor Onida will be able to attend. I have lost track of how far along her seeding is. She is an integral part of what has happened and can answer any questions."

"I agree that we need her there. I believe she has some time yet before she delivers."

"I will find out how Lor Onida is doing. I can send for Oragur or that female who is often with her, Irisa. Let me know when the Leaders start to arrive. But first—"

Straf'Tor listened as his brother laid out what he proposed they do.

Within days, there were enough of the original Leaders, including Lor Onida, for them to go ahead with the meeting.

Moc'Tor looked out at the circle of familiar faces. Hatos'Mok of the Deep Valley; Tres'Sar from Lor Onida's community, the Far High Hills; Tarris'Kahn from the small group up the river— even Solok'Tar had made it from the Great Pines. Not everyone had come, but it was enough. Moc'-

Tor, E'ranale, Straf'Tor, Toniss, and Oragur brought the number to ten.

As Overseer, Moc'Tor spoke first. "Fellow Adik'-Tars, I will get straight to the point. The path laid out before us for our survival, the path we all agreed to take, has now become a source of division. For many generations, we have used the seed of the Others to provide offling. As we all know, the longer we continue this practice, the greater the physical changes. But not just size; there are changes in physical abilities too. Some of us see these as positive, and others see them as negative. That is part of our division.

"My brother and I are on opposite sides of the matter. Our father died some time back, and I find it particularly hard that the only solution we can see will end up dividing forever what is left of my family. No matter—it is clear that a great division is about to come. But before that takes place, it is my hope that we can agree on a set of laws to collectively follow as the basis of our culture, so though our physical differences will increase, our foundational ones will not.

"If we agree that we cannot agree and the division has to go ahead, let us at least have laws on which we can agree."

No one said a word. The silence told Moc'Tor everything he needed to know. He stepped down, and to start the discussion, joined the others at the table.

Accepting that the division might take place somehow helped them focus on what they needed to do. Before the day's end, they had agreed on the rest of the laws.

1. The needs of the community come before the need of any one individual
2. Honor females and do not subjugate them
3. Show humble forbearance for the failings of others
4. No hand may be raised against another except for protection or defense
5. In conflict, use the least amount of force necessary
6. Protect, heal, and shelter the sick, helpless, and those in need
7. Offling are our future and are sacred
8. Never take more than you need
9. All contact with Outsiders is forbidden
10. Never without consent

These were declared the Sacred Laws and would be made known to everyone. Lor Onida recorded the laws as clearly as she could in symbols on a piece of hide for later transfer to the great wall of Kthama Minor. Memories were short, and she was a believer in records, as was her mate, Oragur.

Despite the progress made, a pall hung over the

group when they disbanded for the evening. As hard as that day had been, the next day they would start the even more painful discussion of division and exodus from Kthama.

Back in their quarters, Moc'Tor sat with his family. E'ranale was there, as were their son Dak'Tor, their daughters Vel and Inrion, and their youngest daughter, Pan.

"Before long, Straf'Tor will be taking his followers and leaving Kthama. They will travel to Kayerm, the cave system we discovered generations ago when our numbers were so great that we believed we would have to split our community. Then the contagion came and reduced our population to frightening levels. How ironic that we now find ourselves back at a place of division."

Sensing the heaviness hanging over Moc'Tor, none of the others spoke.

"I have offered them whatever supplies they need," he continued. "Your roles tomorrow are to stay out of the way. No doubt tempers will flare. No doubt harsh words will be spoken. As I contemplate the events of the past generations, I can see the Great Spirit's hand bringing us to this point. Although I fought this division for a long time, I now believe it is the best way—perhaps even orchestrated by the Order of Functions. And that leaves me to trust what is yet to come, however painful."

"Do you think there will be a war between us?" asked Dak'Tor.

"That is the point of the division—to avoid such a war. Our people, our descendants who have been inter-seeded with the Others, are no match for Straf'Tor's people.

CHAPTER 6

Straf'Tor could not sleep. The upcoming events were weighing on his mind. He was glad that Moc'Tor had come to his senses about their roles on Etera. Ushca lay sleepless next to her mate, feeling how tense his body was.

"Talk to me," she said and rose onto one elbow to look at him.

"The day of division has come. You were there. I am prepared to take my followers and leave—I have been for some time. But once we leave, we will never return. Everyone and everything at Kthama will be lost to us forever. The other communities are also divided, so perhaps several dozen from those will join us."

Ushca grew silent, knowing that her offspring by Moc'Tor would not be going with her but either staying at Kthama or dispersing to the other communities that embraced Moc'Tor's philosophy. Already her daughters had chosen to be seeded by the Others and had produced the crosslings that Straf'Tor rejected.

"What will it be like at this new place, Kayerm?"

"It will not be as easy as life here. There is no Mother Stream running below, but the Great River is nearby. And there is plenty of room. Our numbers are not that great, so it is right that my brother and his group stay here. And I have some peace now that he and I agree this division is necessary."

Ushca listened quietly.

"My brother said something the last time we talked," continued Straf'Tor. "He came to me and agreed that he had taken it too far but that he also wondered if perhaps this was not part of a greater plan. He mentioned the Order of Functions and that perhaps this division was all along meant to be. I do not know what to believe."

"He is the Guardian. Despite our differences, we must have faith in his connection to the Great Spirit," Ushca whispered.

Straf'Tor regarded her. "I can do this as long as you are by my side."

"Always," she said and pressed her lips to his, and for a while, Straf'Tor forgot his troubles. But morning found him still awake, going over and over what was to come and hoping they would all play their roles well.

All the Mothoc Leaders, the Adik'Tars, were assembled. Once they had agreed on the details, they would address the entire population of the High Rocks.

As usual, Moc'Tor opened. "Let us make this as thorough as it needs to be, but as brief as possible. Straf'Tor, tell us your plans."

"Since we cannot agree on the collective future of our people, my family, my followers, and I will vacate Kthama. We will be leaving as soon as we can. The Leaders who are in support of continuing to interbreed with the Others, are you willing to release those within your communities who would join with us instead?" Straf'Tor looked around the group, unsure who was of the same mind as him.

"I support our current path, but any of my people who wish to join you certainly may do so," said Hatos'Mok of the Deep Valley.

"I think we all would agree to that, Straf'Tor," said Solok'Tar.

"I agree, too," said Tres'Sar of the Far High Hills.

"That surprises me, Tres'Sar," sneered Straf'Tor.

"Why would that surprise you, Straf'Tor? I do not wish to hold anyone against their will."

"Oh, but you will allow your females to suck the male seed from the unconscious bodies of the Waschini *without their consent*! That is an interesting set of standards you have there. Who knows what matter of abomination your females are producing up there now!"

Tres'Sar had finally had enough of Straf'Tor's insults and leaped across, knocking him against the wall. "Who do you think you are, Straf'Tor? Do you think you are above this? You agreed in the beginning that it was our only way. Would you rather we had all died out by now? Because that was our only choice!"

"I did agree!" shouted Straf'Tor, breaking away and spinning around to pull Tres'Sar's hands behind his back. "But we are past that point. We have done what we had to do, and there was no need to take it this far. We have shamed ourselves. You and my brother have shamed us by bringing us into this age of darkness. Look at your offling. They barely resemble us any longer. They practically shiver in the halls of Kthama. Their modesty is hardly covered. In some cases, their skin is not even as dark as the Others. And all are so pale compared to ours—like the creatures that scramble in the deepest levels of Kthama, deprived of light too long. Is this your legacy to our future? Each generation becoming weaker and frailer? And what of the Aezaitera? *Krellshar!*"

The others stayed back, letting the two enraged warriors burn off their anger. They were well matched; it was unlikely that one would do irreparable harm to the other before they drained each other's reserves.

Tres'Sar struggled and broke one hand free from Straf'Tor's grip, spinning around in turn and slamming his free fist directly into Straf'Tor's jaw.

Straf'Tor released Tres'Sar's other hand, which Tres'Sar then brought around, landing an uppercut to the bottom of Straf'Tor's chin, snapping his head back.

Both males were thrown apart in opposite directions and collapsed, bent over on the floor, catching their breath.

Straf'Tor rose, his hand nursing his chin as he locked a bone-chilling stare on Tres'Sar. Tres'Sar pulled himself to his feet and circled, looking for an advantage.

"You do not want to continue with this, *fine*," Tres'Sar said. "But do not tell us what we can or cannot do. You lead your people; I will lead mine, as will the other Leaders. But do not come crawling back to us when, five generations down the road, you are back to where we were before, with grieving mothers cradling deadborn offspring and imbeciles who do not know any better than raping their sisters."

"Enough!" shouted Moc'Tor stepping between the two males. "Enough! Nothing good is being accomplished. You are not listening, Tres'Sar. There are two paths open to us. No, we do not agree, but we can at least part on good terms instead of creating this bitterness and division between us."

"It is too late for that, Moc'Tor," said Tres'Sar. "Bring your message to my people, Straf'Tor. Anyone who wants to is welcome to leave with you. But once you have had your say and collected your following

—if any—they may never again return to the Far High Hills."

Though they were not part of the inner council meeting, by now, guards had entered the room and stood ready to intervene at Moc'Tor's command.

Moc'Tor addressed them, "Your services will not be needed; this is nothing more than a friendly dispute between family members."

The guards stood down but remained against the wall.

Having had his final say, Tres'Sar spat at Straf'-Tor's feet and stalked to the back of the room.

Moc'Tor turned to those remaining.

"Nothing more will be accomplished here. Tres'Sar is right. The best we can do is go our separate ways as soon as possible. Make your arrangements, Straf'Tor, and let me know when you will be leaving. I will address the people of Kthama this afternoon."

With that, almost all the others dispersed to their respective corners of Kthama.

Almost all.

The room fell silent—more silent than seemed naturally possible. Quiet and still under the weight of the heavy mantle carried on the shoulders of those who remained. They had decided. Enough. It had fallen to them to bring the end to Wrak-Wavara, the Age of Darkness, and to protect the future of Etera.

After a moment of reverence, Moc'Tor's voice

broke the quiet. "Now, we wait. Once the division is complete, we will put an end to Wrak-Wavara."

Straf'Tor's sentries had visited the other Mothoc communities and returned with those who agreed with Straf'Tor's ideas. It was time for the division to take place and the Great Chamber was a sea of activity. Heavy bodies, some with darker coats and some with lighter, moved among smaller ones of similar variation. Some were saying their goodbyes; others were only watching the activities. Moc'Tor stood to the side with First Guard Dochrohan, observing what was taking place.

"At the end of the day, Kthama will consist only of your followers. It will feel empty by comparison," said Dochrohan.

"We are fortunate they chose to leave. Their numbers are less, but an argument could have been made that by their physical size alone, they should retain Kthama. And we would have been hard-pressed to win that battle." Moc'Tor turned to face his first guard. "Thank you for secluding my family elsewhere."

"Of course. They are safe, Adik'Tar."

The Leader nodded as he watched his brother enter. Leaving Dochrohan, he walked over.

"We shall be out by midday," said Straf'Tor.

"That argument with Tres'Sar was a nice touch," said Moc'Tor. "It truly set the mood for the division."

"Well, it was not planned if that is what you are thinking."

"Oh no. I was not thinking that. It was far too convincing to have been staged. Now we must wait until the division is complete and hope that in time everything we have set in motion will come to fruition. I only regret that I will not be alive to see it."

"I do not know why you would say that. You are the Guardian. I will not live to see it, but no doubt you will. Through you, we all touch the future. And it is for the good. When the time comes for the Age of Shadows to fall, both our communities will need all the help they can get."

"Have you decided what you will be calling yourselves?" asked Moc'Tor. "You and your generation are Mothoc, but your offling are not."

"We will be known as the Sassen, and we are calling you the Akassa."

"As in, people of a smaller build?" Moc'Tor asked.

"No, as in people who are frail or feeble," Straf'Tor answered with a grin.

"*The frail ones*? Not very flattering. Especially compared to Sassen, the *righteous*?"

"Oh, we have other names as well if you would like to hear them—"

Moc'Tor chuckled, glad for the good-natured sparring between them. "No, thank you. Since we will never cross paths again, the Akassa it is. My intention is that you and your people should pass from our history."

As they were speaking, Wosot entered and hurriedly approached Straf'Tor. "Adik'Tar, there is a problem at Kayerm."

"Well, speak up," grumped Straf'Tor. "What is it?"

"The scouts went to check on Kayerm and have just returned. It is occupied."

"By what? Bear? Cougar?"

"By Mothoc."

"*Rok!* Who? Another community traveling through? That is unlikely. But it would be good news for our bloodlines. Do the scouts know who they are?"

"Yes. It is the band that was following Norcab."

Straf'Tor turned to Moc'Tor, "Those you exiled from Kthama after you killed Warnak. At the time, it did not occur to me that any scouts who could lead them there were in that group."

"I doubt you will receive a warm welcome. What will you do?" asked Moc'Tor.

"I will take a group to confront them. Wosot, did the scout say how many were there?"

"He only saw them from a distance, and they kept moving about. He saw perhaps eleven or so. They were outside talking, so there could have been more inside. He does not think they saw him."

"Very well. Arm twenty of our males with spears.

I cannot take my followers there without dealing with them first. Whichever way it goes."

"Whichever way it goes? Surely you are not going to let them take over Kayerm?"

"No."

"Then what are your choices?"

Straf'Tor turned back to face his brother. "Remember, brother, they disagreed with *you,* not me. You exiled them with no regard to whether they perished or not. In fact, I believe you preferred they did. But we are not in a position to lose any more Mothoc."

"I am afraid you will find rebels are rebels, Straf. Whether it was my decisions or my authority to which they objected, I fear you will soon learn for yourself," said Moc'Tor. "If you need more guards, I can send some of mine along."

"No, thank you. Our paths are diverging. The sooner and the cleaner it happens, the better."

Straf'Tor sent word through his followers that they would not, after all, be leaving that afternoon. The same group who had just finished saying their goodbyes, their bundles of belongings stacked by the entrance, now milled around, worrying and speculating about the reason for the delay.

Straf'Tor, Wosot, and twenty of Straf'Tor's largest males left for Kayerm. Wosot took them behind a small grass ridge to the place where the sentry had crouched and observed the other Mothoc. Now there was no one to be seen.

"I do not want to confront them inside the cave," said Straf'Tor. "We need to bring them out."

"I could go in and ask to speak with their Adik'-Tar," Wosot whispered. "With Norcab gone, I wonder who that is now."

"No," said Straf'Tor flatly. "We must bring them out into the open. By now, they know Kayerm's layout, and we could easily be ambushed. Although we may outnumber them, I would prefer a more relaxed meeting. I do not believe they are going to welcome us, but there is no point in riling them more."

"A distraction then."

Straf'Tor nodded, and Wosot signaled to several of the others to come with him. They moved out of sight until they were perched above Kayerm's entrance. From that position, they began throwing large boulders, landing them just outside the entrance. Each thud also sent up a dust cloud. Within a few moments, several of the rebel Mothoc had come out and stood staring at the huge rocks.

They turned abruptly when they heard Wosot call out from above. "What are you doing here, and who is your Adik'Tar? I wish to speak with him."

Straf'Tor watched the exchange carefully, sizing up the response and waiting to see what numbers would appear. If their Adik'Tar was wise, he would not send his entire group out at once.

"Wosot?" one of them called back, recognizing him.

"Yes. Ser'Hun?"

"Ridg'Sor is our Leader," said Ser'Hun. "What are we doing here? You should know. Because that *PetaQ* tyrant, Moc'Tor, threw us out of Kthama after he murdered Norcab and Warnak in front of us all. So what are *you* doing here?"

"Bring Ridg'Sor, and we will talk," Wosot answered.

Ser'Hun glanced around at his fellow Mothoc and shrugged his shoulders.

The rebel leader, Ridg'Sor, strode out of Kayerm, immediately defiant.

"What is it you want, Wosot? We left Kthama as Moc'Tor ordered. There is no need for more trouble."

"I do not come bringing trouble. We only want to talk."

"We? How many are *we*?"

Wosot thought for a moment. *Is Ridg'Sor sizing up our numbers? Perhaps he prefers to fight rather than talk.* "Follow me to the clearing down the first path to the Great River. We will talk there."

Ridg'Sor looked Wosot up and down. "Alright."

Ser'Hun stared at his Leader. "Surely you are not going down there?"

"No, *we* are going down there. There is no other choice; whatever they want, they will not go away because I refuse to talk to them. Best we get this over with and find out what it is about."

A few moments later, they were in the clearing, and Straf'Tor and his remaining males silently crept closer.

"Now tell me what this is about," Ridg'Sor demanded of Wosot, his voice edged with steel.

"No, *I* will tell you what this is about."

Ridg'Sor spun around as he heard Straf'Tor's voice behind him.

Straf'Tor coolly eyed Ridg'Sor before continuing, "We have come to a point of division within the population of Kthama. My followers and I are moving here, into Kayerm."

Ridg'Sor frowned hard. "How many of you are there?"

"Far more than there are of you," answered Straf'Tor. "Looking at the condition you are in, I am willing to bet that my people are healthier than yours, too, and far better prepared for battle. I suggest you think before you let the next words come out of your mouth."

Ser'Hun looked at Ridg'Sor and nodded almost imperceptibly.

Ridg'Sor clenched his teeth. "So, you are leaving us no choice."

"You have several choices, Ridg'Sor. You can take your band of followers and leave Kayerm to us. You can decide to fight us, though I can assure you that your group will be defeated—in which case those of you who survive will still be leaving Kayerm. Or you can make room and try to live amicably among us."

"Ridg'Sor," hissed Ser'Hun.

"*KahTah!*" Ridg'Sor snarled back, shutting him down.

The rebel leader rubbed his forehead. "Very well then. When will your group be coming, and how many are there?"

"A better approach is that you show me how many are in your band. The last I remember, you had only about twenty," said Straf'Tor, motioning for the rest of his crew to show themselves.

Seeing their numbers and knowing full well that Straf'Tor would not have brought his entire following, Ridg'Sor's upper lip curled, revealing his sharp canines. "Alright."

Straf'Tor and his group followed Ridg'Sor and Ser'Hun back to Kayerm. When they reached the entrance, Ser'Hun went in and called for the rest. They piled out, blinking against the light, their faces contorting as they saw what was waiting for them.

Straf'Tor counted eighteen without Ridg'Sor.

"What is going on, Ridg'Sor?" demanded a smaller ruddy-colored male.

"We have guests, Laborn. Or rather, we are taking in new members."

Straf'Tor's glance passed quickly over the group, logging the somewhat emaciated forms, darting eyes, and shifting stances.

He stepped forward. "I have no direct quarrel with you. But my followers and I are taking over Kayerm. If you accept this and we come to a truce, you will be permitted to stay. If not, then you will be removed, though I will not be as lenient as my brother was."

He took another step forward, and the group took a step back. *Good. They recognize my superiority. There is no need to fight—not today.*

"You no doubt took over the living areas closest to the entrance. I suggest you relocate further in. I will be back at twilight and how we proceed is entirely up to you."

Straf'Tor turned to leave. Once they were out of sight, he took Wosot aside. "Stay here. Do what you can to make sure we are not returning to an ambush. I do not want to expose the females to harm, and I may leave them at Kthama for a while longer until we can get more of a feel about the situation."

"From what we just saw, I do not believe they will accept our terms," said Wosot.

Moc'Tor was alerted that Straf'Tor had returned. "Is there a problem?" he asked, concerned.

"Nothing I cannot handle. I may need to leave the

Mothoc females and offling here for a few more nights, though."

"Of course."

"And all the Sassen."

Moc'Tor said nothing as he realized that Straf'Tor had larger problems than he was letting on.

Ridg'Sor stormed around Kayerm's entrance, pounding up dust clouds with each step.

Ser'Hun followed after him, raising his voice, trying to get a response. "There is nothing you can do. Perhaps this is a good thing."

Ridg'Sor stopped, and flinging his arms high and wide, whirled around to face Ser'Hun. "Straf'Tor is no better than his brother. They are both arrogant, and I am the Adik'Tar here!"

"Apparently not for long, and it seems you had better get used to your change in station. It is not worth dying over. At least we will have shelter, and perhaps they will bring females."

"*KahTah*! That is all you have ranted about since we came. *We have no females. We have no females.* You act as if that pitiful rod of yours will fall off if you do not stick it somewhere."

Ser'Hun glared at Ridg'Sor and came to a stop. "Well, *Adik'Tar*, do you have a better idea? Do you intend to fight him? Our numbers are, without question, smaller than his, and we have struggled with everything since we came. I could use a good meal provided by some females. *And* a good 'rokking too! Yes, I admit it."

"Well, you can forget about that. No doubt whoever he brings will already be paired, and if not, they will have no interest in such a pathetic scrawny male as you. Remember the days are gone when we get to decide who and when to mate."

"We are suffering here. It is better than having no shelter, but not by much. I, for one, am glad they are joining us."

Ridg'Sor slammed Ser'Hun against the nearest wall. "Joining us? They are not *joining us*. They will take over. We will be lucky to get the scraps from their leavings."

He abruptly released Ser'Hun and spat at his feet. "Go. Tell the others to move their quarters farther back and make room for our *guests*. Straf'Tor is smart; he has chosen the living areas closest to the exit, ensuring that he and his intruders are in no danger of being trapped by us."

Straf'Tor returned to Kayerm just before twilight, meeting up with Wosot before going any closer.

"I was able to get near enough to listen," Wosot explained. "So far, there is only grumbling and a fair amount of moving around. They are pitiful; I doubt they have much real fight left in them."

"That may change after they have had some relief from their current struggle," replied Straf'Tor. "The Mothoc were not designed to live in small numbers."

"They will see us as intruders for quite some time yet. Perhaps they will never accept us," said Wosot.

"I am tired of battle and division. We will share our stores with them as a show of goodwill and hope for all our sakes that Ridg'Sor influences them to accept the change."

"We are forgetting. Your brother exiled this group before the females started cross-breeding. They know nothing of cross-breeding with the Others." Wosot paused. "If they could not accept the rise in status of the females, how are they going to accept the Sassen?"

"It will no doubt come as a shock, but it cannot be helped. We must be prepared for a battle." Straf'Tor let out a huge sigh before turning to leave. "Let us get on with it, then. We will move in almost all our Mothoc males and give it a few days before fetching the Mothoc females and the offling. The last group to bring in will be the Sassen."

"That raises another issue."

"I know, Wosot. I also saw no females among them."

That evening, Moc'Tor stood in the silent emptiness of the Great Chamber. Straf'Tor's females and offling, and as his Sassen followers were still at Kthama but in their quarters.

Never before had he felt so alone. From wall to wall, there was nothing but empty space. He remembered a time when there were so many bodies pressed together that when one moved, all had to shift in unison.

"Is this your will?" he asked. "Was this your intention all along? In my core, there is peace, but in my heart, there is none. My community, my people are divided, and now half of us are cast out to find a new life, to create a new home. My brother and I, perhaps never to see each other again for centuries? Yes, we survived. We are still here. But our differences are now greater than our similarities. There is no longer anything to bind us. We are the Sassen and the Akassa, and as a result, comparatively few Mothoc still walk Etera. What will become of Etera when the Mothoc no longer walk this realm? Surely you have a plan, but it is beyond my understanding."

E'ranale had entered the Great Chamber, but on hearing Moc'Tor speaking into the void, she turned to go.

"Do not leave me," he said without moving.

She came up behind him and wrapped her arms around his waist, leaning into his back. "You feel cold. I have never felt you cold before." Her voice was filled with concern.

"It is nothing; I am merely tired. The Order of Functions is taking a great deal of my strength.

Perhaps it is time to take Pan to the next level of being a Guardian. I could use her help right now."

"When did you last take time to enter the vortex, the Aezaitera, and replenish yourself, my love?"

"Too long. Too long; you are right. I have spent so much time dealing with this and training Pan that I have not taken time for myself."

"You have led us well. No one could have seen this coming, just as, despite our seventh sense, when there is this much turmoil, none of us can feel what is coming. But it has always been our faith in the Great Spirit and the Order of Functions that things are unfolding as they should."

Moc'Tor did not correct his mate, though he wanted to. It was not true that no one could see what was coming. He *could*. And it was a path he did not want to walk.

Pan trudged up the path from Kthama to the great meadow where her father was waiting.

"Are you ready?"

"Yes, father. Are we going deeper into the vortex again?"

"No. Today you are to learn about the Order of Functions."

"I have heard you speak of it, but I have never understood it."

"Then sit and listen as we begin the next phase of Guardianship."

"Before I can continue," he started, "you must remember that Etera herself is alive. *Everything* is alive because everything that exists is created from the living force of the One-Who-Is-Three. Even objects like rocks have the life force in them; it is just moving so slowly compared to our own vibration that we do not think of them as having a life force. Everything in existence is made up of the creative life force, though not everything has awareness. And that is often what we are unknowingly referring to when we say something is *alive*. What we mean is that it has some level of awareness. And at higher levels, that becomes self-awareness."

Pan interrupted. "Does Mother know all this?"

"Yes. She has heard this speech many times. Now, hush."

Pan sat silent as told.

"What we call life and death is the life force, the Aezaitera, moving in and out of Etera like the inhalation and exhalation of a breath. I have already covered this. So life and death are the life force—the breath of the Great Spirit—entering and leaving this realm.

"The three aspects of the Great Spirit work together in this ongoing creative act. The Great Heart is the creative substance, Love, from which everything is formed. The Great Mind is the unfathomable intellect that effortlessly thinks everything into existence in infinite combinations, complexity, and order. Through the Great Will, the creative force of the Great Heart and the exquisite design of the Great Mind are continuously called into being.

"Without the entry and exit of this life force, the Aezaitera, Etera will stagnate and die—just as does the physical body if breathing ceases, though much more quickly. Etera would not fail all at once, but system by system over time."

Finally, we are getting somewhere, Pan thought impatiently.

"Daughter, I know you know most of this," Moc'Tor said, sensing her impatience and hearing Pan's not-quite inaudible sigh.

"Sorry, Father."

He continued. "The Order of Functions is the collective rules, patterns, and inherent wisdom in each cell and piece of Etera that knows its place and works together to create the complex creation that surrounds us—and beyond, even to the halls of the Great Spirit. No doubt you can remember cutting yourself and how quickly your body heals. That is the inherent wisdom built into each of the tiniest pieces of what makes us and everything in our realm. Pieces so tiny that we cannot even truly conceive of their size. It is this same intelligence that sends the ants into collective action the moment their hill is damaged. It is this same intelligence that lets the birds flock together in the sky, swooping back and forth in patterns without ever getting in the way of each other. So, this pattern of intelligence is every-where; it is inseparable from life itself because it is the intelligence willed and knitted into being by the creative force of the Great Spirit"

"The Three-Who-Are-One."

"Yes, and the One-Who-is-Three. We have many names, but they all point to the loving intelligence that created us and sustains us."

"Now, the Order of Functions. The Order of Functions is the pattern built into all of creation. But like the Aezaitera, it can be affected from within this realm. You have played games with other offling, stacking stones as high as you could without toppling them. As long as they are balanced and carefully placed, the tower stands. And like that example, all life on Etera depends on balance. Because imbalances occur, you must connect to the Great Spirit and use your life force to bring it back in line."

"How is that possible?"

"That is a very good question. And the answer is that I do not know. I only know it is given to us to do, and it is part of our function here. It is the role of the Guardian, in addition to cleansing the Aezaitera before it leaves our realm, to strengthen and realign the Order of Functions when needed."

"How do you know when it is needed?"

"It is a feeling. A deep-seated unsettling. A knowing that something is *off*. It is beyond the plea-sure of entering the Aezaiterian flow. It is a *need* to engage the Order of Functions. And the longer you wait, the greater the need grows until it actually turns to discomfort."

"Why do I not feel this discomfort?" she asked.

"Because I am strong enough to bear the full load. You have been shielded from it."

"Is that why you look so tired? Why is it wearing on you?" she asked, frowning.

"Now is a time of great change. Great challenges require me to return to the Order of Function more often, with fewer breaks in between."

"So, it is different from the feeling of being one with the Aezaitera?"

"Yes. It is different. And I will not lie to you, Pan, because to do so would be unfair. I must tell you that your first time will be terrifying."

"Terrifying?" Her eyes were wide. "But being connected to the Aezaitera has always been so pleasant. So intensely good that it is all I can do to leave it."

"I know. That is why you must be prepared; this will not be like that. But the good news is, it becomes less frightening each time you experience it. You must trust me, for when it begins, you must remember my words and cling to them. You will survive this. You will return to Etera. And that this is what you were born to do."

Pan was clearly shaken. "I am afraid."

"I know. That is why I am speaking so bluntly. If you do not know beforehand that it is going to be uncomfortable, and you do not understand, regardless, how critical it is, you would never willingly go through it a second time. And if the Guardians had not, Etera's systems, like the unbalanced tower of rocks, would have toppled very long ago."

Pan sat quietly before saying, "When do we have to do this?"

"If you are ready, we will do it now. Those standing guard are among my most loyal males and are aware of our need for privacy and protection. They will not allow anyone to approach this place when they know I am working."

Pan was silent for quite a while. Finally, she said, "I am ready now, Father."

Moc'Tor told her to lie flat on the ground. "Get comfortable. And just as when you were learning to enter the Aezaiterian flow, you must never attempt this alone until I say you are ready. You must also always immerse yourself in the Aezaiterian flow before and after engaging the Order of Functions. Do you understand?"

Pan nodded.

"Say it. I need you to proclaim it."

"I understand."

"I will be with you the entire time, though you may not realize it once you engage the Order of Functions. No matter what happens, focus on the truth that you will come out of it, and you will return unharmed. That is all I can say, Pan. Beyond that, there are no words to describe what you are about to undergo."

Pan tried to hide her trembling.

"Now. Close your eyes and reach down to the vortex below Kthama and enter the stream as you have before. Once you have done so, I will join you and lead you from there."

Pan closed her eyes and sent her awareness down through her body as her father had taught her, down to the rich vortex deep within Etera. The moment she made contact, indescribable pleasure overtook every spark of her consciousness. She was joy itself. There was nowhere else to go, nowhere else to be. It was everything her soul longed for, and her only desire was to be joined with it forever.

After a moment, she felt her Father's presence. It was difficult to describe; she was separate from him and yet not. And then suddenly the distance was closed, and he was leading her somewhere, somewhere deeper, and the bliss of the creative life current was receding. She steeled her will to surrender to her father's guidance. With a jolt of searing pain, Pan suddenly felt as if she were being torn apart—as if each cell in her body was being disassembled and spread to the edges of eternity. Terrible anguish and burning coursed through every part of her consciousness. Stretched beyond bearable, the distance between her thoughts became infinite. And in that space, there was nothingness. Every part of her felt disconnected, spread to the corners of the universe, and then split apart again into an unimaginable number of disconnected pieces. She was nowhere and everywhere at once.

Then, just when she could not stand it a moment longer, she started to reassemble. The infinite number of shards of what had been her were drawn back to themselves. Piece by piece, her consciousness re-formed. The pain started to fade, and she could feel the current of the Aezaiterian flow just out of reach. And her father's presence was back, this time leading her to the current, back into the lifeforce of the Three-Who-Are-One. Unbearable fragmentation was replaced with indescribable peace, belonging, and joy. And it was all the sweeter for the horror of what she had just been through.

Slowly, she felt herself re-enter their own realm and once more became aware of her breathing and the weight of her body lying on the soft grass. Fresh air filled her lungs, and she inhaled sharply. As soon as she was fully returned, she rolled over and curled into a fetal position, sobbing.

Moc'Tor immediately pulled her up and started rocking her. On Etera, he alone understood what she had just experienced. "I know, I know," he soothed her. "Listen to me; it will never be that bad again. Never. You have been through the worst. And now that you know what to expect, it will only get easier."

"How could that have been of the Great Spirit? That was worse than annihilation. I would rather not exist than go through that again," she sobbed. "Oh, Father."

Moc'Tor let Pan cry it out. Right now, his daughter needed comfort, not another speech on what an honor and gift it was to be a Guardian. He kissed the top of her head and committed to holding her for however long it took.

After some time, she raised her head and wiped her tears with her arm. They glistened on the silver-white hair. "I know you want me to be strong. I know you want me to tell you I can do that again. But I do not think I can."

"You can, Pan. You can, and you will. I promise you, it will never again be that bad. And each time, it will get easier. And it will also not seem to last as long."

Taking in what he had just said, Pan looked around. "It is twilight. How can that be?" she asked. "It felt as if only moments passed."

"Time behaves differently once we engage the Creator's realm."

Pan sat up properly. "How often do I have to endure this?"

"It depends. You will learn to 'feel' when it is time for you to enter the Order of Functions."

"The Order of Functions. It is so different from the life current. I will never understand how it can be so painful when the life current is so pleasurable, and they are both of the Great Spirit."

"You know how the lines of sinew we use can

become tangled?" said Moc'Tor. "And sometimes impossibly so?"

"Yes."

"And the only way to untangle them is to stretch them out as far as possible and then unknot and separate them from there."

Pan nodded.

"That is similar to what happens when we engage the Order of Functions. Through being fragmented, dissipated, and then re-assembled, we are put back together in alignment with the divine pattern."

Pan shook her head. "Having been through it, I can understand what you are saying. Had you told me this before today, I would have avoided it. But even now, I was afraid. Even though you told me you would be with me, I have never felt so alone and so frightened."

Moc'Tor nodded. "I promise it will get easier. It will never be enjoyable, but you will know that because of your sacrifice, you are bringing the proper order back into Etera."

"What would happen if there were no Guardian?" Pan asked.

"If there were no Guardian, then the Aezaitera would become poisoned by the build-up of negativity, and in time Etera's lifeforce would become sick, much as our bodies do if toxins are not eliminated. And without our engaging with and re-establishing the Order of Functions, the systems, which work together to make Etera the paradise she is, would falter. In time, different aspects would fall out of balance and degrade. Negative forces would grow in power. It might take eons, but at some point, without the Mothoc blood facilitating the flow of life entering and leaving Etera, without our cleansing of the Aezaitera and aligning with the Order of Functions, Etera would become a barren, toxic husk."

Moc'Tor could see from her stillness that Pan was taking in at the deepest level of her soul everything he was telling her.

Finally, she asked, "Can we get stuck in the Order of Functions and not be able to leave?"

"No. There is no risk of that because it takes our will to stay as it is so unpleasant. And you will learn that shorter, more frequent visits are easier to bear than putting it off and having to stay longer. But the longer we stay engaged, the greater the benefit to Etera."

Pan thought for a moment. "When we return to our bodies, is that what re-aligns the Order of Functions here on Etera?"

"No. Our souls are the link. Returning to our bodies does not re-establish divine order. Our engaging the Order of Functions does that," he answered.

Pan put her head in her hands. "I need some time to think about this."

"Of course," said Moc'Tor. "But first, we must

return to the Aezaiterian flow. Remember, you must always end with returning there."

After they were finished, he stood and pulled Pan to her feet. "Let us go find something to eat. I am always famished when I have completed this duty."

E'ranale was waiting for their return. "Where have you been? I was getting worried. And where is Pan?"

"Today was Pan's first introduction to the Order of Functions. She got through it, but she needs time now to heal from the experience."

"Should I go to her?"

"No. Let her come to you. Solitude is the best medicine for her right now. She has a lot on her shoulders, and she must find her own way to accept the burden that has been placed on her, one for which she did not ask."

"What will happen if Pan refuses to accept the mantle of the Guardian?"

"She will not. No Guardian ever has. She may struggle with it, but she will accept it. It would be as impossible for her to refuse as it would be for you to refuse to love and care for your offling. It is who you are. It is who she is." Moc'Tor went to the sleeping mat and stretched out. "I need to rest."

He was asleep within moments.

CHAPTER 7

Several days later, having moved in most of the Mothoc males and having sized up Ridg'Sor's group and decided who the troublemakers would be, Straf'Tor sent for the remaining Mothoc males and the Mothoc females and offling. He and Wosot stood watching as they nervously filed into Kayerm. The newcomers' attention was drawn to the six huge Mothoc rebels lining the entrance and whose gazes seemed to lick the females all over.

The paired females were immediately claimed by their mates, who had been waiting for them, and with the offling were taken to their new living quarters. To the unpaired, Straf'Tor said, "There are larger group quarters on the second level. Together, you will be safe there." He shot a warning glare in Ridg'Sor's direction, and Wosot's males helped the last females with their belongings and escorted them down the tunnels.

"I want you to keep Salus and Laborn away from the females," said Straf'Tor, his eyes fixed firmly on Ridg'Sor. "I will be watching them both, and so will the other males. As far as Ser'Hun is concerned, he seems harmless enough, though it is obvious he is the worse for wear from having been so long without a female.

"I also want you to put together a schedule of hunting parties. Since you know where they are, you will need to show Wosot the best places. Also, put together a list of any repairs that must be done. You have been here longer than we have, you must know."

Ridg'Sor nodded. At least Straf'Tor seemed to be entrusting him with assignments. *Perhaps I can appear to make peace with it—for the time being.* "What are your plans for retaking Kthama?" he asked.

"I have no plans to retake Kthama."

"Surely you do not mean to scrape out an existence here while they live in incomparable luxury? We are far stronger than they are; it would be a quick battle."

"I left willingly, for the sake of us all; Mothoc, Sassen, and Akassa."

"Sassen? Akassa? What are those?"

"A great deal happened after you left Kthama. More are there now than just the Mothoc. My brother and I agreed that the females should be seeded by the Others. It was either that or have the Mothoc blood perish altogether. The Akassa have more of the Others' blood in them. The Sassen do not have as much."

"What kind of abomination is that? How in the name of the Great Spirit was such a horror achieved? And you are bringing them *here*?"

"Just the Sassen, and you will treat them with respect, or I will deal with you as Moc'Tor did Norcab and Warnak. This is home to all of us now, and you had better get that straight," snarled Straf'-Tor. "Forget about Kthama. Put it from your mind. The sooner you make peace with the fact that we are never going back, the sooner we can move forward into making this place more comfortable."

He is insane, thought Ridg'Sor. *Just like his brother.* But Ridg'Sor knew he must be patient and bide his time to build up strength, and hopefully, numbers. He was certain that not everyone in Straf'Tor's camp could be in full support of what had been done.

The new arrivals quickly sized up Kayerm. It did not have the deeper levels of Kthama, and there was no life-giving Mother Stream running through its lower levels. The walk to the Great River was not far, though more taxing for the Sassen than the Mothoc. Straf'Tor would have preferred that Kayerm was farther away from Kthama, but they had neither the time nor the resources to scout out another location.

Straf'Tor left to fetch the Sassen males, females, and offling, and when he returned with them to Kayerm, the tension was palpable. To their credit, the Sassen ignored the stares and whispers of Ridg'Sor's group. All Straf'Tor's Mothoc would be keeping their eyes on Ridg'Sor's band to make sure the Sassen were not mistreated.

Later that day, Straf'Tor's mate, Ushca, approached him.

"Something is on your mind," he said.

"The unpaired females are nervous," she told Straf'Tor.

"I have seen how Ridg'Sor's males look at them, so I do not blame them for being afraid. But no matter how much his males want to mate, I doubt they will risk the penalty of forcing themselves on anyone. Unfortunately, in our group, there are more unpaired females than there are males. Some of our females will have to pick mates from Ridg'Sor's group or give up on having offling. Another concern is that the females will be going out to gather what they can for the coming months. But they will be accompanied by more than a few of our largest males, you can be assured."

"If you wish, I will help organize the gathering," said Ushca. "We will need more strong storage baskets; I do not believe we brought nearly enough. As for Ridg'Sor and his group, perhaps they will soften over time. They will soon find that if they wish to attract any of the females, they will have to change their ways. They cannot cling to the old customs; it is the female's right to choose now."

Then she rose. "I am turning in. Please do not be long. I need to feel your arms around me."

Ushca looked around their barren room. *A good chalk washing would help.* Perhaps after she and the other females had gathered berries and roots, and reeds for more baskets, they could pick some flowers to bring some life into Kayerm. And maybe some fluorite rocks because of their beauty at night. There were no light-bearing channels to charge them under, though. Everything did seem harder at Kayerm.

She gave the sleeping mat a good stir to fluff it back up. She would ask one of the males to carve out a channel in the floor for it to rest in. Perhaps more soft mosses and leaves to go under the sleeping mat would cushion it more. *We should have brought more hides with us; the floor and walls of Kayerm seem so cold compared to Kthama.* Her mind was racing. So much to do!

Eventually, Ushca curled up on the sleeping mat and closed her eyes. Life was much harder at Kayerm, and Straf was right; she must get used to it and stop thinking about Kthama. She was never going back. It was time to focus on what they could do to make Kayerm feel like home—for everyone's sakes, and more personally, for the sake of Straf'Tor's offling, who Ushca still prayed she would someday bear.

Time passed. Back at Kthama, Lor Onida once again sat perched on the birthing stone. Because he was a Healer, her mate, Oragur, was present, as was their oldest daughter, Krin, who was apprenticing to become a Healer. Time passed as everyone waited for news of the birth. Too much time. In the hallways outside, rumors spread up and down that things were not going well, and Lor Onida was in trouble.

E'ranale and Pan were waiting in the eating area, trying to give them privacy. There was enough commotion already, and though they were very concerned, they did not want to add to the congestion.

"Mother, I fear the worst."

"Is that a premonition, Pan, or just concern over one of our community?" asked E'ranale.

"It is both. I believe it is Lor Onida's time to return to the Great Spirit. Even though she is far too young."

Just as they were speaking, Lor Onida's oldest daughter, Krin, came running up to them.

"Something terrible has happened," she panted.

"We have lost my Mother. There was something wrong; we could not stop the bleeding."

E'ranale sprung up and put her arms around Krin, and held her while she sobbed.

After a few moments had passed and Krin stopped crying, Pan softly asked, "The offling?"

Krin turned her head from E'ranale's embrace to answer. "The offling seems to be well."

"Your father must also be disconsolate. Come, I know this is unbearably hard, but let us get back to them," and E'ranale turned and guided Krin away.

They found Oragur clutching his mate's still body to his own. In the corner stood Irisa, an older friend of Lor Onida's. The offling was in her arms, warmly wrapped up, as Oragur rocked all he had left of Lor Onida.

E'ranale wanted to approach but felt it would be an intrusion. "Please tell the Healer I stopped by. I will immediately arrange a wet nurse for the offling and send her to you. Can you care for her for now?"

"Temporarily, yes," said Irisa.

"Thank you. Krin, do you want to stay here or perhaps spend the day with me? It is not good for you to be alone right now."

"What will become of my—my mother's offling?" Krin asked. "I am almost old enough to raise her, but my father refuses. And my other sisters are even younger."

"Do not worry about that for the moment. You, your sisters, and your father have too much to deal with right now. Irisa will keep her for the moment, and we will find a wet nurse to help with her care. Now, come, let us go back to my quarters, and I will keep you company while you try to rest."

Once there, E'ranale sat next to Krin, waiting for the young female to fall asleep. *Great Spirit, what will happen now?* Not only had Lor Onida's offling lost their mother, and their father his mate, but Kthama had lost one of its Healers.

Two days passed, and Oragur kept to himself. He had not left their living quarters, refusing most of the food that was brought to him. He also refused to see his new daughter. When they were with him, he barely spoke to Krin, her older brothers, or her younger sisters.

Moc'Tor felt that enough time had passed and insisted on seeing Oragur. He entered the Healer's Quarters to find Oragur on his own, lying on a sleeping mat and facing the wall.

"Oragur, I do not pretend to understand the depth of your pain, and there is nothing I can say to console you. I can only imagine how I would feel if I lost E'ranale."

Oragur said nothing, not moving or in any way acknowledging the Guardian's presence.

"If there is anything you need, only ask. But at some point, you must accept your new daughter and move on. We will find someone to help you raise her until her sisters are old enough to be of more help."

Oragur turned over abruptly and sat up.

"I never want to see it. If it were up to me, it would be thrown into the Great River and returned to the Great Spirit."

"The offling is not to blame," said Moc'Tor. "You know better than that. It is your heartbreak speaking."

"Whatever is speaking, my feelings will not change. I never expected to be paired, and then Lor Onida came along. And then, one by one, we had our offling, and our joy multiplied. Every other birthing went well, so why did this one not? And now she is gone, and I cannot live life without her. That *thing* you wish me to accept is the reason she was taken from me."

"We cannot wait any longer. We need to lay Lor Onida's husk to rest."

"I will not attend; nothing is there for me. I know she is gone; I said my goodbyes while she was still warm in my arms."

"Very well. I will leave you to your sorrow. You know where to find me."

"Do not wait for that to happen. My other offling and I will be leaving soon. I will never find peace at Kthama—my Saraste' is everywhere I look. I will take my family, and we will move to the Deep Valley. Perhaps I can find peace with them where there is nothing there to remind me of Lor Onida. She has family at the Far High Hills, and I do not wish to see them. I want no new reminders of her, and I do not wish to see the offling that killed her."

Moc'Tor left the Healer to his suffering and went to find E'ranale.

"Oragur will not accept the child. He wants nothing to do with her," he told his mate.

"She is with Nisere now," said E'ranale, "who has just had her own offling and can nurse her. But we must make more permanent arrangements. Nisere cannot raise her, and we cannot keep passing her around. The news has brought great sadness to the community, and I am sure someone would be prepared to take her, even knowing that it may be temporary if Oragur comes out of this at some stage. Lor Onida's other offling are too young yet to be of help."

Moc'Tor let out a long, deep breath.

"Oragur told me he is taking his other daughters and their brother and moving to the Deep Valley, where there will be nothing to remind him of Lor Onida. Perhaps in time, he will change his mind. But I do not see it in the foreseeable future. His faith in the Great Spirit was deep, and now his despair is equally deep."

"Mama," interrupted Pan. "I would take her."

Both Moc'Tor and E'ranale turned to look at their daughter.

"You are not even paired, Pan. And you are a Guardian," Moc'Tor said, too quickly.

"I do not understand, father? You are a Guardian, and yet you have offling."

"Yes, but—" Moc'Tor stopped short of saying it was different because he was a male Guardian, and she was female.

E'ranale chuckled, reading Moc'Tor's mind.

"Your father is right, Pan. And not because you are the first-ever female Guardian, but because you have not even begun to take on your full role. You are still learning. This is not the time for you to embrace motherhood as well."

"On the contrary, Mother. Since I am not, as you said, fully encumbered by the responsibilities of a Guardian, it seems the perfect time. By the time I have to assume those responsibilities, this offling could well be full-grown."

E'ranale looked at her mate. She leaned in and whispered, "Your turn."

"I am not sure I have anything else to say," he replied.

"You know I can hear you both," smiled Pan.

"All right," said E'ranale. "You are grown enough to make your own decisions. But you must be prepared to relinquish the offling if, or when Oragur changes his mind."

"Or you could pair with him," said Moc'Tor, his eyes twinkling.

"Ohhhhhh! He is far too old for me. You are just getting even because you lost this debate."

"Maybe," he smiled. "I still suggest that we make

the offer to the community first, Pan. We do not want to use our positions unfairly, and she will need a wet nurse for some time."

"I understand. I will accept whatever decision is made."

That afternoon, Moc'Tor sent an announcement to the females in the community. Whether they were afraid of Oragur changing his mind, even though he had said he was leaving, or had heard rumors that Pan wanted the offling, no one came forward to claim her.

Before too long, Pan was holding Lor Onida's newest and last daughter. She looked down at the tiny bundle wrapped in the soft hide reserved for newborns and rejoiced in the feel of the tiny fingers wrapped around one of her own. She looked into the innocent eyes that gazed back at her with only trust and the longing to be loved.

"Did Oragur name her?" Pan asked.

"No," E'ranale said. "But Krin told me that their mother did before she died. Her name is Liru."

"*Liru*. I will make sure you know how much your mother loved you. And I will do my best to be as good a mother as she would have been." *You are such a joy. How am I ever to explain it to you? That it was through no fault of your own that your father wants nothing to do with you.* Liru's tiny, beautiful heart should not have to bear such a burden, ever.

Pan wiped away a tear and then went back to cuddling the tiny miracle she held in her arms.

Over the next few days, the Leader's Quarters were modified to create a nest for Liru. E'ranale stood admiring it when the other females had left after helping her set it up.

Moc'Tor came in and stood behind his mate, his hands resting on her shoulders. "This will do for now, but since Pan is older, perhaps she needs a place of her own?"

E'ranale turned to look at her mate. "A place of her own?"

"Before too long, Liru will be crawling. If Pan is going to raise this offling, she should establish some independence about it. She will still need Nisere's help as long as Liru needs to nurse, but she must move out. And we need some privacy back. After all, Vel, Inrion, and Dak'Tor all left long ago."

E'ranale squinted at her mate. "So that is it? You are tired of sneaking around when she is gone, trying to fit in our lovemating. Admit it!"

Moc'Tor smiled. "No, that is not it. But now that you mention it—" and Moc'Tor placed his hands on E'ranale's face and hungrily pressed his lips against hers.

At that moment, Pan entered and stopped suddenly, "Oh! Am I interrupting something?"

Moc'Tor released his mate, raised his eyebrows, and shook his head.

"Daughter," said E'ranale, "There is something we need to discuss."

Moc'Tor once again stood facing the Leaders from the other communities. "I have invited you here to continue our practice of meeting on and off, but also because I have some very sad news. Tres'Sar from the Far High Hills and Hatos'Mok of the Deep Valley already know what has happened, but others of you do not.

"Oragur, our Healer who paired with the Healer Lor Onida many years ago, has left Kthama. He has taken his son and three daughters with him to the Deep Valley. Lor Onida died giving birth to their latest offling, and he found it unbearable to remain here."

Moc'Tor waited for the murmuring to die down. The loss of anyone, let alone a Healer, was deeply felt.

"Lor Onida's last offling is being cared for by my daughter, Pan. Lest you entertain considerations of favoritism in this decision, I canvased our females, and no one claimed her. Before returning to the

Great Spirit, Lor Onida named the offling. Her name is Liru."

Moc'Tor paced around the front of the room a moment, head down, before continuing.

"With the loss of both Lor Onida and Oragur, at the moment, Kthama has no Healer. Lor Onida's eldest daughter, Krin, was apprenticing with her parents but had not progressed far enough to take over. And, of course, she has left with her father. With this in mind, I propose that we consider whether each community should have more than one Healer. I further propose that we should consider whether Healers should be allowed to be paired and have offling." Moc'Tor stopped again, waiting for the backlash.

Hatos'Mok from the Deep Valley was the first to speak. "At the moment, we have two Healers now that Oragur has left Kthama and joined my community. We are not as many as you, and I can attest that having more than one Healer is comforting. But those called to be Healers are not that common. And if we cut off their bloodline through forbidding them to have offling, how is that furthering our cause of avoiding a shortage?"

Tres'Sar stood. "To the first point, having more than one Healer would be a luxury. We do well to come up with one to replace the current one before he or she returns to the Great Spirit. As for not allowing them to pair, I understand what Tres'Sar is stating—however, not every Healer's offling becomes a Healer. We do not know whether there is a blood component or not—it is not consistent."

The discussion continued for some time. In the end, the council agreed to establish the position of an official Helper to each Healer. In this way, at least the practical aspects of the profession would be passed on should a community lose its Healer.

"This has been a productive meeting." And Moc'Tor summed up the conversation. "It is agreed that the Healers will each select a helper to work with them. The helper will learn the selection and gathering of the herbs and supplies and anything else about the healing trade, including the practices of basic care. Should another tragedy ensue and a Healer is lost, at least the knowledge will be preserved to pass on to the next Healer. It is a work-able compromise since, as several of you have stated, Healers are in short supply, to begin with."

Tres'Sar spoke again, "If Lor Onida were here, she would be reminding us that we need to record our decisions. Did she not write down the Sacred Laws that we and the Sassen agreed on before the division? Does anyone know where she put them? They need to be transferred to the Wall of Records at Kthama Minor."

"If anyone knows, it would be her mate, Oragur," said Hatos'Mok. "I will ask him when I return."

"While we are assembled, however, there is another matter of bloodlines we should address," said Tres'Sar. All heads turned to follow him as he walked to the front of the room and stood next to Moc'Tor.

"As we have learned, the loss of a Healer can be devastating. I put it to you that the loss of a Leader would be equally devastating. Up until now, it has not been a requirement that Leaders pair and produce offling. But if we are going to set rules about pairing and mating for Healers, we should consider them for the Leaders also."

Some in the group turned to one another, frowning and shaking their heads.

"Is that really necessary? Have we ever had a Leader who did not pair?" asked Hatos'Mok.

"No," answered Tres'Sar. "Not in my memory; however, we have never lost a Healer prematurely either. We are speaking of possibilities here."

Moc'Tor spoke next, "I agree with both points. And since there is little risk of a Leader not pairing and producing offling, I see no harm in a rule that states they must. We might also consider what our recourse is should an heir not be produced."

"That has an easy solution," said Solok'Tar from the Great Pines. "We simply find someone else in the bloodline."

The others nodded in agreement. "As long as we continue to implement the pairing guidelines and the selection of mates by the council, it would help return some of our culture to normal."

Moc'Tor thought a moment, wondering if things would ever be *normal* again. "The Leader should be allowed to choose his own mate without the council's participation. The role of the Leader's mate is crucial to his ability to function efficiently. And the Leader's mate is often his closest counsel."

He gave them a few moments to look around and see if they were in accord. This time the entire group nodded in agreement; Moc'Tor's logic was self-evident. "It is late, and I am sure you are tired. We have decided then, in the matter of the Healers, we are establishing a Helper position. We are also agreeing that Leaders should choose their own mates, and should the union produce no offling, another in the bloodline will be selected. I did not hear agreement on whether Healers can continue to pair and have offling. We will discuss that in future meetings when we have had more time to think it over individually. If there is nothing else, then let us go to the evening meal."

Moc'Tor walked into the Leader's Quarters just as Pan was leaving with Liru. He carefully hugged his daughter as she walked by.

"We were just deciding where her quarters would be. Not too far away, but far enough," E'ranale chuckled. "How did the council meeting go?"

"It was productive. What do you think about Healers not being allowed to pair and have offling?"

"This is because of Lor Onida's death?" asked E'ranale.

Moc'Tor nodded.

E'ranale sighed. "On one hand, I do not like it because it denies a Healer the greatest blessing there is—that of a loving mate and offling of their own. On the other hand, it would facilitate greater dedication to their calling. Without the influence of a mate, he or she would be more independent."

"That is a good point. I was just saying how important selecting the right mate is. You are my closest and wisest counsel. You lighten my burdens every day. I cannot imagine what it would be like to be paired with someone I could not trust or turn to."

E'ranale could see that Moc'Tor was tired. "It is late. Have you eaten?"

"No."

"Let me bring you something to eat, and we can sit together while you tell me about the rest of the discussion. It feels as if everything here is starting to settle down. I do wonder, though, how Straf'Tor is faring at Kayerm."

Straf'Tor sat next to the evening fire, which was just getting going. His son by a mating with Toniss, many years ago at Kthama, came to join him.

Straf'Tor motioned for him to sit.

"It is a fine evening," said Nox'Tor.

"Indeed it is. How is your mother?" He'd had little contact with Toniss in the time since she had chosen Trak as her mate, even though the couple had traveled to Kayerm with the rest of Straf'Tor's followers.

"Mother is fine, but she is having a hard time adjusting to life here," he said quietly.

Straf'Tor put a hand on his son's shoulder. "And how are you doing with it?"

"I would like to be paired."

Straf'Tor raised his eyebrows. "Do you have a female in mind?"

Nox'Tor blinked. "Is it not the female's right to choose?"

"Hmph," Straf'Tor replied. "Yes, there is that, but I am Leader now. Do you have your eye on someone?"

A huge smile crossed Nox'Tor's face. "Kyana."

"A fine choice. Does she return your interest?"

Nox'Tor nodded.

"Then tell her of your desire for her, and we will make it official. Let me know when you are ready, and I will call everyone together."

Nox'Tor practically jumped up and ran back into Kayerm in search of Kyana.

Straf'Tor let out a long slow breath. That took the pressure off. If Nox'Tor and Kyana produced offling, then he could stop worrying about whether or not he ever seeded Ushca. Nox'Tor was the logical choice to replace him, though Straf'Tor hoped it would not be sometime soon. He was not ready to be parted from his beloved Ushca, and times were still turbulent; he would never place on anyone else that burden of leading such a divided community. *Nothing I have tried has healed the rift between Ridg'-Sor's rebel group and my people—and there is also their resentment of the Sassen.* At least matters seemed to have settled down for the time being—and there were considerably fewer rebels compared to the rest of the population.

Chuckling, Ushca came to join her mate at the fire.

"Why are you laughing?" he asked.

"I do not know what is up, but Nox'Tor almost ran me over in his rush to get somewhere."

Straf'Tor laughed. "He just told me he wishes to pair with Kyana."

"He wishes to pair with her? I thought the females had the right to choose," she frowned.

"It is time for our culture to return to what it was. We have deviated too far from the old ways, so the females must give up their right to choose."

"What about the agreement reached back at Kthama? The trade of females between communities?"

"And who would we trade with? The Akassa? That was the point of the division—that what is left of the Mothoc blood would remain as pure as it can. We know of no other Mothoc communities. If they exist, they are far out of our reach."

Ushca conceded. "You are right, although there are not that many of us. But within time—"

"Yes, within time. But the challenges of today are sufficient to handle. I will pray that the future Leaders of Kayerm will come up with a solution. When I announce the pairing of Nox'Tor and Kyana, I will also announce my decision to eliminate the females' right to choose."

Ushca was silent for a moment. Then she said, "Straf, I do not wish to challenge your decision, but please reconsider. If you give the males the right to choose, where does that put our females in the hierarchy, considering that the rebel males are also living with us at Kayerm."

Straf'Tor turned to look at his mate. "You are right. I almost made a terrible mistake. Until our community is at peace, the females must retain the right to choose. But eventually, I hope to return the choice to the males."

Ushca let out a huge sigh.

Later that evening, Straf'Tor let his son know that he had changed his mind, and for the time being, the females would retain the right to choose. The next morning Straf'Tor called an assembly.

Straf'Tor waited for everyone to exit Kayerm. He walked up a nearby hillside so they could all see and hear him more clearly. It was just after first-light and cool with the welcome morning breezes of fall. As they assembled in front of them, he noticed the rebels collected off to themselves at the back. *Ushca saved me from making a huge mistake.*

He signed for Nox'Tor and Kyana to come forward. Everyone fell silent. "This morning, I am announcing that Kyana has chosen Nox'Tor as her mate." Then, placing a hand on Kyana's back and the other on Nox'Tor's, he drew them to face each other. All those assembled began the pairing chant, words spoken in unison. When it stopped, Straf'Tor turned to Kyana.

"Do you choose Nox'Tor over all others?" he asked.

Kyana placed her hand over Nox'Tor's heart and said, "I, Kyana, daughter of the House of 'Nul, choose you over all others."

Then Straf'Tor turned to his son and asked, "Do you accept Kyana as your own, over all others?"

Nox'Tor gently placed his hand on Kyana's head and said, "I Nox'Tor, son of the House of 'Tor, choose you over all others."

Nox'Tor and Kyana embraced before turning and smiling at the group. Many congratulated them as they moved out into the crowd.

Straf'Tor allowed his gaze to flick from his son to the rebels who were grouped together at the back, whispering among themselves.

With the ceremony over, Ushca joined her mate and followed his gaze. "Trouble brewing?" she asked.

"I do not think it ever stopped. Even after all this time, they are not merging in with any of the Mothoc, and certainly not with the Sassen. There are still decided lines of demarcation, and as long as Ridg'Sor keeps them riled up, there will never be peace."

Just then, Ridg'Sor looked up and caught Straf'-Tor's gaze. A wry smile crossed his lips before he went back to talking with Salus, Laborn, and the others in his troop.

Later, Ridg'Sor approached Straf'Tor, who was sitting at the evening fire. As the rebel drew closer, Wosot looked over at Straf'Tor, who motioned for him to stay back.

"Straf'Tor. I would speak with you."

"You already are," Straf'Tor replied. "What is your request?"

"How do you know I am going to ask for something? You assume much."

"I assume you are going to ask me for something because that is always why you seek me out. It has been the one constant since we came here. You wish for some further adjustment to the rules, I assume?"

Ridg'Sor kicked away one of the firepit stones. "And why should I not? You came here and took over. This was our home first, and now you give us no consideration at all."

"Kayerm was never *yours*. Kthama's scouts discovered it when we were overrun with our numbers because of the males' inability to control their mating practices. It was open to the Mothoc and now to the Sassen. We have been willing to live with you in peace, but you seem unable to accept your position."

"My position is Adik'Tar. You are the intruder."

Straf'Tor sighed. He picked up a stick and started poking the fire. "After all this time, still the same complaint; I am tired of this. Make your request or leave. Now."

"We need access to females."

"The females live among us as they have for centuries. They are no longer living in a separate cave system as they were at Kthama. I do not see your problem."

"They will not have anything to do with us."

"And you cannot imagine why. Very well, let me make it clear. You have as much of a chance to woo a female as any male, and always have had. It is the female's choice with whom to pair. If you and your males do not have enough sense to know how to be pleasing and helpful to win their hearts, then there is nothing I can do to assist you," Straf'Tor said.

"You have warned them off of us."

"I have done no such thing. They do not need me to warn them away from you. Anyone can see how angry you are. Females desire a pleasant mate. One who can provide, who has a reasonable personality.

Who will make her feel safe in the world and look after her offling. I see none of those qualities in any of your males. Oh—and clean yourselves once in a while. You stink something terrible."

"*Rok* you," shouted Ridg'Sor.

Straf'Tor stood to face Ridg'Sor. "Lose your anger. Accept my rule. Accept the Sassen. Make the best of the situation. The path you are choosing leads only to conflict and more division. There is nowhere else for you to live. The sentries scouted the entire area long ago to find this place, but if you are *krell-bent* on leaving, then go. I certainly will not stop you."

"*Qa!*" spat out Ridg'Sor and stormed away.

Wosot had sat silently watching, and he now stood up.

"He will never accept you as his Leader. Why do you not expel or kill him? Perhaps with him out of the way, the others will back down."

"There are so few Mothoc left. We need as many of us as we can gather. Even the loss of one would diminish our ability to diversify our bloodlines. You are right; he will never back down. But should it end up being a fight to the death, he will become a martyr to his followers and inflame their anger more. Come," Straf'Tor continued. "Sit back down with me. The evening is still young, and the stars are just starting to come out. Let us forget our troubles for a moment and give thanks to the Great Spirit for the blessings we do have."

Ridg'Sor had stormed into Kayerm and called out for his group. "Salus, Laborn, Ser'Hun, Kaisak, Gard, and all the rest of you. Meet me at first light down by the Great River."

The next morning, Ridg'Sor stood on the river bank waiting for his group to join him. The sound of the water rushing by, the damp smell of the leaves, the calls of the songbirds—all were lost on him; his mind was elsewhere. He turned as he heard footfalls.

"Gather round; I will be quick. I am done waiting, and I have a plan."

CHAPTER 8

Pan bounced Liru on her knee, causing the tiny offling to burble with delight. Then Pan set her down on the floor, and Liru scampered as fast as she could toward E'ranale, who grabbed her and kissed her little belly over and over, which made Liru giggle more.

"She is such a happy little thing. She brings me joy each day," said Pan. "Well, and challenges too. I have had to move everything up and away now that she is so mobile." Pan fell silent. "Mother, this makes me want my own offling. But how would I ever be paired?" she asked.

E'ranale smiled at hearing this from her daughter. *Finally.* The role of the Guardian was demanding, and having a mate would lighten the load.

"We will ask your father to speak with the Leaders' Council. They are in charge of pairings now. As a Guardian, you might not be bound by their selection, but they might have an idea of some suitable males for you to consider."

"I may not be bound by their selection?" Pan asked.

"The council has decided that Leaders are allowed to choose their own mates. And I think it is appropriate that the exception should also apply to a Guardian." E'ranale stood and put Liru on her hip. "Coming?"

They found Moc'Tor outside Kthama, over-looking the verdant fall landscape that stretched out to each horizon. He turned as he heard them approach, and reaching out, he gave his mate a kiss on the cheek.

"Your daughter has an announcement," she said as she kissed him in return.

"Oh?" Moc'Tor smiled, realizing by their actions that this was good news.

"Having Liru to raise, I know now that I wish to be paired."

Moc'Tor exchanged a quick glance with his mate, and seeing the smile on her face made his own heart soar. "This is a big decision, Pan. Congratulations. Do you have a male in mind?"

"Mother and I were just speaking of this. Am I not bound by the Leaders' Council's choice for me?" Pan asked.

"I do not believe that applies to you. How would you like to proceed?" he asked.

"Mother suggested that perhaps the council

Leaders might have some suggestions from their own communities—for my *consideration*." She let out a little chuckle.

"I will bring it up at the next meeting. I promise."

Pan threw her arms around her father's neck and whispered in his ear, "Thank you, Father. I love you so much." She took Liru from her mother and practically skipped away.

Once Pan was out of earshot, E'ranale said, "That is a relief, yes?"

"Yes. Not only will she have the help of a mate, but she may indeed produce offling."

"Surely not another Guardian?"

"There is no telling, E'ranale. The Great Spirit seems to be full of surprises lately. I am proof of that. We have centuries to live yet, as does Pan, and who knows what the future holds. In the meantime, let us cherish today."

Moc'Tor pressed a small red rock into E'ranale's hand.

"What is this for?"

"Just something I found. I thought you might like it."

"I do, thank you," said E'ranale. "It is a piece of red jasper, is it not?"

"Yes."

"Oragur taught me that this stone represents the heart of the Great Spirit and assures us that we are loved and cared for," E'ranale said with a smile, then her face crinkled up.

"What is wrong?" he asked.

"Nothing. Just a little pain. It is gone now."

"We have no Healer, and you are in pain? Tell me where."

"Moc'Tor, it was a slight twinge, probably a touch of indigestion, which is not unusual," she answered.

"*Since when*?" he asked.

"Since I am seeded again!" A huge smile crossed her face.

Moc'Tor took her up in his arms and hugged her. "That is wonderful," he exclaimed. "You had me worried there." He placed her back on her feet again.

"I am glad you are happy, my love. So am I," she said. "We will have a new offling by the warm weather!"

Months passed, and it was time for the Leaders' Council to meet again. Moc'Tor opened with an announcement that his mate E'ranale was with offling, then continued with his daughter Pan's request.

"On top of my joy at my mate's seeding, my daughter, Pan, has stated that she desires to be paired. She is raising Lor Onida's offling, who was rejected by her father, Oragur, when Lor Onida died. I believe that has helped Pan realize what a great blessing a family is. Although as a female she has the right to choose her mate; she did say, however, that she would be interested in beginning by meeting any choices recommended suitable by the council."

The Leaders exchanged glances and nodded. All saw the logic of allowing a Guardian to choose his or her own mate.

"I am happy for you," said Cha'Kahn. "But in this circumstance, I assume the male of her choosing would have to relocate to the High Rocks?"

Moc'Tor nodded. "Yes. She is still undergoing her training, but, regardless, the Guardian must remain here at the High Rocks," he said. "A Guardian's duties are tied to a vortex. Although there are others across Etera, there are none as strong that we know of."

The other Leaders nodded in understanding.

"I have several in mind. Would you object to her traveling to meet them?" asked Hatos'Mok from the Deep Valley.

Moc'Tor signaled for Dochrohan and asked him to fetch Pan.

After a while, she arrived, Liru on her hip.

The Leaders stood as Pan entered, and the act of respect was not lost on Moc'Tor.

"I am very sorry," she whispered to her father. "I could not find anyone to take Liru." Pan had never attended a Leaders' Council meeting, and she looked out at the group and the faces staring back at her, some older, some younger. *It must be peculiar to them to see two Guardians at one time,* she suddenly realized.

"I have put to the council your request about

suggestions for a possible mate. They have questions, and I could not presume to speak for you," he answered. "Are you willing to travel to meet prospective males?"

Pan nodded and stepped forward. "Greetings, Council members. Thank you for allowing me to speak with you today. Your question is fair, and I thank you for your help. From growing up witnessing the blessing that is my father's union with my mother, I see that not to pair is to miss much of the sweetness of life. But I also know that selecting the right mate is of the highest importance in achieving the kind of bond and mutual support that my parents enjoy. I am willing to travel to meet any suitable males you suggest. I do prefer to start with the Deep Valley and the Far High Hills."

"Thank you, Guardian," said Tres'Sar. "I will send word as soon as I have news."

"So will I," said Hatos'Mok from the Deep Valley.

"Thank you."

As Pan left the meeting, her mind was full. Was she really going to be paired? Have offling of her own? How would she know if he was the right one? How would she select him? A bad pairing could ruin someone's life—her mother had said it many times — just as a good one could make everything easier. If she could find someone to love who would love her just as it was between her parents— But how? And how much would her stature as a Guardian affect it?

Before long, word came that both the Far High Hills and the Deep Valley were ready for Pan's visit. She made arrangements for Liru and prepared to set out.

"This is your first trip away from home. Do you not wish for one of us to go with you?" asked E'ranale.

"I saw how they looked at me at the council meeting, Mother. For the first time, it sank in that I have an obligation to meet. It is time I stepped out on my own and started acting like a Guardian," said Pan. "But I am concerned."

E'ranale waited for her daughter to continue.

"What effect is it going to have that I am a Guardian? When I saw the reaction of the Leaders, it seemed they were almost in awe of me. I do not want my situation to entice someone to pair with me on that basis alone."

"You will know, Pan. Trust yourself. Trust your heart and your guidance. If a male is not what he seems or is concealing his true motives, you will know," said E'ranale. "And you do not have to decide on one trip. Perhaps if you narrow it down, it would be wise to have them come here to visit before you make a final choice."

"How did you know that Father was the one for you? Were you swayed by his being a Guardian?" she asked her mother.

"His being a Guardian actually made it harder. I

knew that, as a Guardian, he would outlive me by centuries. And that as a Guardian, he would have obligations requiring his focus to be on more than me and any family we might have. Add that to his being the Leader's heir, and it was a difficult decision. Except—" and her voice trailed off.

"Except what?" Pan asked.

"Except that despite all the reasons not to pair with him, I could not get him out of my mind. Just being in the same room with him made my heart race. I knew that, despite all the reasons not to accept the offer of being his First Choice, if I refused, I would regret it for the rest of my life."

The next morning, Pan set out along the pathway at Kthama's lowest level, through which the Mother Stream flowed. The exit for each community was well marked, and cozy nooks and alcoves were situated where she could stop for a while as needed. She passed the marker for the small community from which Tarris'Kahn hailed. Story had it that this was the origin of the contagion, which, centuries ago, had nearly wiped out all the Mothoc and had driven them to breed with the Others. As a result, its name had long been struck from mention. Even those who lived there merely referred to it as home.

Eventually, she reached the exit to the Deep Valley. She followed the path to the surface and looked for the tree breaks that would show her the rest of the way. As she neared the cave entrance, two sentries greeted her.

"Welcome, Guardian. We have been awaiting your arrival," the first one said. "Come this way."

The entrance was similar to the High Rocks and, in fact, looked so much like Kthama that she was immediately at ease. Within moments, Hatos'Mok had arrived.

"Welcome to Awenasa, Guardian," said Hatos'Mok. "Rohm here will show you around and help you settle into your quarters. At the evening meal, you will meet the males I have selected. If you wish to rest until then, I will send for you when it is time."

Pan nodded and followed the tall male whom Hatos'Mok had referred to as Rohm. He chatted with her as he led her through the eating area and then through the general layout. He seemed to be taking a long time to show her around, but he was interesting and kind, and despite how tired she was, Pan found she was enjoying his company. For her to get her bearings, he finally led her back to where they had started and then down a nearby tunnel to a fairly large living area. He stood at the doorway and motioned for her to enter.

She looked around and could see it had been prepared for her visit. Dried flowers hung suspended over the eating area. A ventilation shaft had been pierced through the roof to the surface to let in light and fresh air, just as was done at Kthama. When she had finished looking around, she turned to Rohm. "Thank you. It is very pleasant and comforting. Will you be coming to get me later"?

"I do not know, Guardian. I hope so," he said. "If there is anything you need, just let anyone know."

After he left, Pan thought how peculiar his response had been. She wondered what he meant by *I hope so.*

Pan poked around the room a bit, looking in each of the woven baskets lined up along the wall and those placed on the work surfaces. The baskets were both decorative and functional, some holding dried fruits and nuts. She could see they had made an extra effort to be welcoming. Her curiosity satisfied, Pan stretched out on the large sleeping mat. It smelled of lavender and mint.

Within what seemed like moments, she was awakened by someone clacking the announcement stone on the outside wall. She rubbed her eyes and rose to find Rohm standing in the passage.

"Are you ready?" he asked. "Or do you need a few moments?"

"Yes, please. I will be right with you," she said.

She smoothed down the top of her head and the rest of her ruffled silver-white hair. She was nervous. *I wonder if I am an attractive female? I know my silver coat is striking, but what about the rest of me?* She had never thought about it before.

Pan stepped out into the hallway and Rohm led

her to the eating area. All heads turned as she was escorted in and over to a table where Hatos'Mok and several others were waiting.

As she approached, the Leader stood, "Welcome, Guardian. I hope you were able to rest. Let me introduce you to the others. On my right is my First Choice, Deparia. Then her sister, Alewar. You will be seated on my right, and next to you will be Zyhot, then Raksar, and then Ondram." Then he turned to Rohm and said, "Also joining us tonight will be my son, Rohm'Mok."

Son? This Rohm is Hatos'Mok's son?

The meal was pleasant enough. Pan did her best to be polite by eating some of it but found that her nervous stomach left her with little appetite. She joined in the conversation, finding Hatos'Mok's mate to be delightful and charming. As far as the males were concerned, her attention was drawn to Rohm more than all the others presented to her. More than once, she caught him watching her, and he smiled warmly each time. But she did not know if he was a candidate or just joining his family for the evening meal. She still wondered about that remark, *I hope so.* Did that mean he was interested in being considered? *Oh, I wish Mother were here to ask her advice.*

When the meal ended, Hatos'Mok asked Zyhot to escort Pan back to her quarters. As Zyhot stood, Rohm'Mok interrupted. "I will take her, Father," and he extended his hand to Pan.

Pan stood to leave, "Thank you, everyone, for

your hospitality. And the living quarters are beautiful. I appreciate your efforts to make me feel welcome. Will I see you at morning meal?"

Deparia said, "Of course. We will send someone at first light." Pan nodded and left with Rohm.

He made conversation on the way. "So, how did you feel about the males you met tonight?" he asked as they walked.

"It is a huge decision. Clearly not one to be made in one evening," she answered.

"True. And you must take care that whoever you pick is not just enamored with your stature as Guardian."

Pan nodded.

"How long will you be staying?"

"Two to three days, I imagine. Then I am on my way to the Far High Hills," Pan answered. "I may stop in again on my return to Kthama."

"I hope you will. If you find yourself bored tomorrow, send for me. I know some great berry-harvesting places this time of year. I would love to show them to you."

Pan nodded, and Rohm'Mok left. She stood in the doorway, watching him walk down the tunnel. He did not turn back before he rounded the corner and she found she was disappointed.

Why would they have him escort me if he were not for consideration? But he was Hatos'Mok's son and possibly heir to his leadership. If he was the heir, he could not leave the Deep Valley. It was best that she put him out of her mind.

〰

The next morning, Pan was ready for the clacking of the announcement stone. When she went to the door, her face fell. "Oh. Good morning Deparia. Thank you for coming to get me. Where is your son Rohm'Mok, might I ask?"

"He is with his father, discussing whatever it is they discuss," she laughed.

"I see," Pan answered quietly.

"He did send a message, though. He said if you are interested in berry picking, to meet him down by the Great River after you have eaten. Apparently, you discussed this last night? I have to admit, he does know the best places," she smiled.

"Deparia. I feel I can talk freely with you. May I?" asked Pan.

"Of course, Guardian. What is it you wish to know?"

"Was Rohm'Mok assigned to escort me so I could get to know him better than the other—males?"

Deparia tilted her head. "No. He was assigned to escort you as a matter of respect for your station."

"I see." She looked away, her voice devoid of any lilt. "Thank you for clarifying,"

"Oh, I am so sorry, Guardian. I did not think how it might appear. Rohm'Mok is heir to the leadership at Awenasa, and whoever you select would be expected to live with you at the High Rocks; that was made clear. His place is here. I apologize that we have created confusion," she said softly.

"Thank you for your honesty. Please let Rohm'Mok know I will not be joining him this morning, though I appreciate his thoughtfulness." Pan put her head down and then collected herself. "I am ready if you are." She forced a smile.

They walked together in silence. On the way, Deparia stopped to speak with one of the sentries, who left immediately to deliver the message to Rohm'Mok.

Pan forced herself into conversation with the males who had joined them at the table. Her thoughts kept drifting to Rohm'Mok, and as many times as she brought them back to the moment, they returned to him again. She was being rude to Zyhot, Raksar, and Ondram. *I hope they cannot tell I am distracted.*

At the end of the meal, Hatos'Mok asked, "How would you like to spend the rest of your day?"

"I think, Adik'Tar, with your forgiveness, I will continue on my travel to the Far High Hills. But I will stop back on my return to Kthama if that meets with your approval."

Hatos'Mok nodded and gave a slight bow. "Of course, Guardian. We look forward to your return."

Pan nodded to Deparia, Zyhot, Raksar, and

Ondram. "Until later, then," she added and made her way to Awenasa's exit.

She found herself hurrying down the path, almost desperately looking for the entrance back down to the Mother Stream. When she was almost there, someone called out to her.

"Oh!" she exclaimed, turning to see Rohm'Mok running to catch up.

"Rohm'Mok. What are you doing here?" she asked.

"Mother told me you were leaving early. I am sorry to hear that. I came to ask if it was anything I did?" he said, skidding to a halt.

"No. No, of course not. You have been nothing but welcoming and kind." She felt color come into her cheeks, and she knew that with her light skin, it was noticeable.

"Will you stop on your return as you said?"

"Of course," Pan replied. "If you like."

"Pan—may I call you Pan?"

She looked up into his soft dark eyes and nodded.

"I am disappointed you are leaving so soon. I had hoped to spend some time with you. Forgive me for saying this, but I hope you do not select a mate at the Far High Hills," he said softly.

Pan shook her head. "I have to go." She stepped around him and disappeared.

Once out of sight, she ran the rest of the way to the

entrance to the Mother Stream. When her feet hit the rock floor of the tunnel, she stopped to lean against the cool wall. *Why did he say that?* He had acted as if he was interested in her. But he could not leave the Deep Valley; his own mother had confirmed it. Perhaps he was like other arrogant males who thought they could convince a female to their way of thinking. Perhaps he thought that if he was charming enough, she would leave Kthama to join him. If that was the case, then it would be better if she did not stop at the Deep Valley again. Her confusion was enough without adding more to it.

Pan remained lost in thought as she continued traveling towards the Far High Hills.

When she arrived, she was greeted by Tres'Sar. Soon she found herself settled in another set of living quarters, equally as well-appointed as those at Awenasa. She sat on the stuffed sleeping mat and put her head in her hands.

This was not working out. Perhaps she should forget about all the nonsense of finding a mate. But she was there now, so she would go through the motions. She hated to disappoint whoever Tres'Sar had lined up; it was just that her heart was not in it any longer.

At the evening meal, Pan did her best to make conversation. As it had been at the Deep Valley, the Leader, his mate, and some of their family were at the table, along with the males for her consideration. She found herself merely passing the time and waiting for the solace of the quarters in which she was staying. At the morning meal, she announced she would be returning to Kthama. She could see the disappointment on everyone's faces.

Because she had promised, on her return home, Pan stopped again at the Deep Valley, but she hoped to avoid Rohm'Mok if at all possible. The sentries let Hatos'Mok know she had returned, and he and his mate met her at the entrance to Awenasa.

"You are not staying?" asked Deparia.

"No," Pan replied. "I feel a need to get back. I am missing Liru more than I anticipated."

Just as she finished, a voice from behind startled her.

"How is she?"

Pan turned around and stared into the face of Oragur, the father who had rejected his own offling.

"She is fine. She is clever. She is a happy soul, into everything now."

Behind Oragur stood Krin, and Pan pushed away the desire to hug her. "How are you doing? We miss you at Kthama." Pan could see that Krin had tears in her eyes.

"I have taken a new mate," Oragur blurted out. "She is willing to raise Liru."

Pan stared at Oragur. "What are you saying?"

"I want my daughter. We will give you a few days to get her ready before we come for her."

Pan twirled and looked at Hatos'Mok and his mate. Deparia's eyes were soft, and she shook her head as she mouthed, "I am sorry."

"How do I know you will not change your mind again?" Pan asked.

"Guardian, I know this must be very hard for you," said Deparia, stepping toward Pan as if to touch her.

Pan stepped back, avoiding her. She glared at Oragur and tried to calm down. "I will have her ready," she said finally.

Once again, she was grateful for the privacy of the Mother Stream. She made her way to one of the little alcoves and sat down to let herself cry.

It was not fair; Oragur had given Liru up. He had not wanted her. She was Pan's. *Oh, Great Spirit, how is this happening?* The whole trip had been a mistake and Pan wished she had never come. If she had not been there, she would not be thinking about Rohm'Mok, and she would still have Liru—at least for a while longer.

Pan stayed there until she had calmed down, then slowly made her way back to Kthama. She gingerly re-entered the lower level and sneaked to her quarters as quietly as possible, thankful that she had managed it undiscovered. She was not ready to talk to anyone.

CHAPTER 9

After having lived at Kthama, the Sassen's progress in adapting to life at Kayerm had moved slowly. There were some positives. Tyria, a young Mothoc female, had nearly completed her Healer training with the Healer, Pagara. And many of the young offling, who had not known life at Kthama that long, were adapting quickly.

However, the older females still reminisced about the conveniences at Kthama, the biggest being the Mother Stream running through the lower level. Daily trips to retrieve fresh water from the Great River below Kayerm's entrance were time-consuming and had quickly become a burden. The males had to establish new hunting areas, and there was no rich vortex of energy pulsating below Kayerm to help guide them. They had to pick up the weaker fields and rely on visual cues to learn their way around, although, in time, they succeeded. But the most troublesome was the division between Straf'Tor's people and the rebels, which was not showing any signs of narrowing.

Wosot came to give his daily report to Straf'Tor. "Ridg'Sor continues to meet frequently with his group. I am convinced he believes you do not know about these gatherings. Some of our people have reported his followers mingling among them, making statements about how difficult life is at Kayerm and creating more dissatisfaction with life here. Clearly, he is trying to create trouble."

The Leader threw down the stick he was toying with. "I have been more than patient; it is time for this to come to a head. Call an assembly."

That afternoon, Straf'Tor stood before his people. To his right stood his beloved mate, Ushca, and next to her was his son by Toniss, joined by his mate, Kyana, who was holding their youngest offling. The crowd stood murmuring, wondering what it was about.

"As I was waiting to begin, I looked around and saw many of these same faces I have looked upon for so long now. Years ago, we came together to Kayerm to build a new life. With the exception of Ridg'Sor and his followers, it was the choice of each of you to follow me. And it has been your choice every day since to continue living at Kayerm. Yet, despite the passage of time, I am aware that many of you have still not made peace with it. You are consumed by looking back at the life you left at

Kthama instead of focusing on making the best life here."

He walked forward, closer to the crowd. "I know life is harder here, but it is not unbearable. The land is still rich with blessings. However, as long as you are looking back, those of you who continue to mourn Kthama, you are not discovering the many ways in which to move forward and make your lives here more comfortable."

"So I am asking all of you, and especially those who have offling, to stop speaking of Kthama. Stop romanticizing life there. Do not nurse in your offling the dissatisfaction you feel here. This is their life now, and you rob them of their happiness by passing on your bitterness. To what end, I do not know, as we are not leaving Kayerm. This is our home now; there is no place else to go."

He stopped and looked directly at Ridg'Sor, his eyes never leaving the rebel's. "I am also aware there is a faction that has never accepted the arrival of those of us who came from Kthama. Even after all this time, dissent rumbles in the background. And that faction serves only to inflame your dissatisfaction here."

"That is not true!" Ridg'Sor shouted from the back, fist raised.

"And now we see the source of your discontent," said Straf'Tor, gesturing in his direction. "Ridg'Sor, what have I said that is untrue? Let us have it out here and now."

"It is not true that we have nowhere to go. Why should we suffer here when there is a perfectly good place, probably not even being used, where the females used to live. It is only because of the stubbornness of you and your brother that we were exiled here."

"That is true in part, as you were indeed exiled from Kthama when you joined Norcab's band and tried to usurp Moc'Tor's power. Moc'Tor killed Norcab, but he spared you and your followers. As punishment, you were all banished from Kthama, and you are fortunate we allowed you to stay here at Kayerm. But the rest of us who came from Kthama, we left willingly."

"You should have fought to stay at Kthama," shouted Ridg'Sor. "But instead of standing up to him, you kneeled to your brother's authority. And even though you have not seen him in an age, he still subjugates us. Why do we scrape and suffer here when there is a perfect solution—one that has the Mother Stream running through her lower levels just as at Kthama—the adjacent cave system where the females lived, the one that people speak of as Kthama Minor!"

Faces turned to each other, and Straf'Tor saw some nodding heads.

"Kthama Minor is not open to us." Straf'Tor's voice was strong. "We have moved on. It is up to us to create our lives here. There is no going back."

"Maybe not for you. But why should we all suffer

because you and Moc'Tor disagreed? There is no reason not to return. What are they to do? They may outnumber us, but my guess is that we are far greater in strength. I have heard stories about how frail they are. And I imagine that, by now, their latest offling are even more pathetic. When they see our superior power, they will give way."

Ridg'Sor had done his job well. Slowly, year after year, at every opportunity, he and his followers had strewn discord among Straf'Tor's people. With a word here, a statement there, they had kept alive the longing for the easier life at Kthama. Whenever possible, they pointed out the hardships at Kayerm. They drew attention to the toil required to live there. They called up memories of Kthama's huge expanses, the vast numbers of rooms for spacious living quarters, and always the rich blessing of the Mother Stream. They had turned the idea of Kthama into a legend, the solution to all problems.

At that moment, Straf'Tor realized his greatest enemy was not Ridg'Sor. He had not been fighting a flesh and blood adversary. That he could have defeated. No; all this time he had been fighting an idea. The idea that life at Kthama was perfect and that life at Kayerm would never be satisfying. He had misjudged the battle. Ridg'Sor fed the discontent, that was his part, but the real enemy was the idealization of life at Kthama.

As long as they yearn to return to life at Kthama, they will never make peace with living here.

"Listen to me. There is no going back. You cannot turn back time. You do yourselves and your offling a disservice by continuing to compare life here to what we knew at Kthama. You rob them of a future of happiness here, of the real chance of embracing their lives here. From now on, there will be no further mention of Kthama. The name must never be spoken again. Nor will we speak of the Akassa. The past is gone. You cannot go back. And any talk of trying to take Kthama Minor must stop here, now, as well."

"Now go back, and once and for all, commit to your lives here. Stop listening to the voices of dissent; Ridg'Sor does not have your best interests in mind. Our people have been through enough, and he would drag you into a war with the Akassa, falsely believing that will open the way to happiness. The Akassa are not our enemies; they are our brothers, sisters, cousins. We share the same blood, the same history. Etera needs both of us to survive. It is cowardly to blame the Akassa for our troubles.

"You have heard me. Vow today to put Kthama from your thoughts. The time for looking back has passed. Now, be on your way," and Straf'Tor stood tall as he waited for the crowd to disperse as ordered.

Some of the group left immediately. He could have said ahead of time which they would be. But more stayed than had left, which told Straf'Tor that Ridg'Sor's influence was stronger than he had realized.

He looked at Ushca close by and saw her

furrowed brow. He could sense concern coming from his son, Nox'Tor.

"Not now; later. We can all talk later." Straf'Tor put his hand on his mate's back, and he and Nox'Tor escorted her down the hill and through the crowd toward the entrance, forcing them to part to make way for him. As he walked past the rebels, Ridg'Sor said to him, "You have already lost. You just will not admit it."

Straf'Tor stopped and turned to Ridg'Sor. "I spared your life against the advice of many. Despite every chance I have given you, you have chosen to create trouble. But why? That is what I want to know," he said.

Ridg'Sor glared at the Leader and stepped closer. Straf'Tor motioned to his family to keep going without him.

"You and your brother have destroyed the Moth-oc," said Ridg'Sor. "Your *leadership* has led to our ruin. There is little left of the greatness we had. Mothoc blood may still course in the Sassen's veins, but they are a pale comparison to what we truly are. You had the power to take Kthama from your brother and those pathetic creatures he calls his people. And instead, you led your followers here to scrape out an existence in this *krell-hole*—while those *Soltark* crosslings live in luxury at Kthama."

Straf'Tor pushed Ridg'Sor backward and snarled, "You were barely grown when you joined Norcab's group. A spindly male with no mind of your own. A senseless follower of that traitor you thought was a Leader. You have squandered your life on bitterness and resentment. I tell you, this path will take you to your own destruction. You have a mate now. And for reasons unknown to me, she seems to care for you. Some day you will have offling of your own. I do not want to kill you; Etera needs every Mothoc who walks her. This is your last chance. I will banish you and your followers if you do not stop this now."

"My followers and I found and claimed Kayerm after your brother exiled us," Ridg'Sor shouted. "Then you came and took over. I will not rest until you and your brother have paid for your crimes. If I had the power, I would wipe every last Sassen and Akassa off the face of Etera."

Straf'Tor grabbed Ridg'Sor and jerked him around until he had him in a headlock, one arm twisted painfully behind his back. The smaller male was no match for Straf'Tor. With his free hand, he clawed feverishly at Straf'Tor's arm, to no avail.

"Now you listen to me," Straf'Tor snarled into Ridg'Sor's ear. "I am one thought away from snapping your neck and ending your foolishness here and now. But I believe Etera needs every drop of Mothoc blood she has. For that reason, and that reason alone, I am sparing your life. You have until the new moon to gather those who will go with you and leave together. I am being generous because you and your rebels have taken mates and I do not wish hardship on them. I hope they abandon you and stay at Kayerm. How you ever won Tyria is beyond me—you do not deserve the greatest blessing there is, the true love of a loyal mate."

Straf'Tor released Ridg'Sor, who fell to his knees, choking. "If you threaten anyone again, including the Akassa and the Sassen, I will kill you. That is a promise."

He stormed off, leaving Ridg'Sor on all fours in the dirt, trying to recover.

Straf'Tor passed by several of those who remained in the area; they had heard everything, but he did not care. He caught up with Ushca and the rest of his family, who had stopped to watch the altercation, and led them back to Kayerm.

Back in their living area, Straf'Tor comforted a shaking Ushca. Then he put an arm around his son Nox'Tor and drew both into the huddle. He tousled his son's head, a fatherly gesture from centuries ago when Nox'Tor was much younger.

"Shhh. Harden yourselves. It will be over soon. Make no mistake, if Ridg'Sor threatens anyone again, I will follow through on my threat. And just as Moc'Tor did when he dispatched Norcab, I will make it as public as possible. If fear and death are the only things that can convince his rebels to stop this war, then fear and death are what they will get."

E'ranale was surprised to find her daughter back at Kthama. "Pan, what are you doing back so soon? When did you get home? Why did you not let your father and me know you had returned?"

Pan had finished selecting some morning food-stuffs. She was walking toward her customary seating area in the Great Chamber. "I am sorry, Mother. I was not up to talking to anyone. I needed to be alone for a while."

E'ranale followed her daughter and sat next to her. "Tell me what happened. Obviously, something went wrong for you to have returned so soon. We were not expecting you for days."

"Oragur told me he wants Liru back. He and his new mate are coming in a day or so to collect her," Pan said softly, her eyes averted.

"Oh, no. I am so sorry. I know how much you love her. No wonder you are upset." E'ranale bit her tongue; she would not remind her daughter that it had always been a risk. This was not the time for a motherly lecture. So she hugged Pan instead.

"Yes. It is breaking my heart to think of giving her up. And how do I know he or his new mate will not change their minds again?" After a few moments, Pan said, "There is more. I met someone." Her face was a picture of misery.

E'ranale sat patiently, eyebrows raised.

"At the Deep Valley."

"Is that not a good thing? Why are you distraught?" asked her mother.

"He was not supposed to be one of the eligible. He is the son of the Leader, Hatos'Mok. His parents assigned him to be my escort out of consideration for my position. I know I am not wrong; he was pursuing me, even though I made it known I would not leave Kthama to be paired."

"And he is heir to his father's leadership?"

"Yes. I spoke with his mother, and she said he would not be able to leave the Deep Valley. That is when I decided to leave early. I went on up to the Far High Hills but could not get Rohm'Mok out of my mind. I had promised to return to the Deep Valley on my way back. I did not want to, but I had said I would. Luckily, I did not see Rohm'Mok again, but that is when Oragur approached me and said he was coming to get Liru."

"Oh, my sweet daughter. I am so sorry. Two heartbreaks so close together. I understand why you wanted to be left alone," E'ranale said.

"I am going to spend as much time with Liru as I can until they come to get her. I know she is too young to remember me. But at least I will remember her.

E'ranale felt her own heart breaking to see her beloved daughter in so much pain.

The next day, the sentries received word that Oragur was on his way. Pan sat holding Liru. "I love you so much. I did not know I could love someone this deeply. I know you will not remember me, and that hurts even more. I thought you would be mine forever. I have already pictured teaching you to fish, to weave baskets, to make tools. I saw us going on walks around Kthama, enjoying the spring flowers. Teaching you the calls and the names of the birds. Now, none of that will ever happen. And I will worry about you and wonder if you are happy and if I shall ever see you again. I wish I could make you understand that I will think of you and miss you every day of my life." Pan let her tears fall, unable to hold back. Liru looked at her with wide eyes as if trying to understand.

Before long, there was a clack at the door. Pan wiped the tears from her eyes, set Liru on her hip, and went to greet whoever was there. "Oh, hello, Mother. Have they arrived?"

"Yes. They are waiting for you in the Great Entrance."

Pan picked up a basket with the things she had made for Liru, soft hide toys, cuddly wraps, and the fur coverlet from her nest. She walked with her mother to meet Oragur.

Moc'Tor was waiting just before the Great Entrance.

"Pan," he said and put his arm around her. "I am so sorry."

"I know, Father. I am trying to be strong, but it is not working."

Moc'Tor and E'ranale escorted their daughter the rest of the way. As they entered the Great Entrance, Pan gasped.

"What is it? Is it Oragur's new mate?" asked her mother.

"He brought others with him," she replied, her body stiffening.

E'ranale frowned, thinking that was to be expected.

"It is him," Pan whispered.

"Who?" asked her father, now concerned.

"*Him*. Rohm'Mok, Hatos'Mok's son," she answered.

"Oh. The one I told you about," E'ranale whispered to Moc'Tor.

"Ahhhh," Moc'Tor let out a sigh.

Why did he have to come? This is hard enough as it is, thought Pan.

"Come on, dear, best to get it over with. Breathe deep," said E'ranale, and she placed a hand on Pan's back to guide her forward.

Pan avoided looking at Rohm'Mok, knowing she was not composed.

"Greetings, we welcome you back Oragur, Krin, even if only for a visit." Moc'Tor turned to the female he did not recognize. "You must be Oragur's new mate?"

"Yes. I am Neilith. You are Moc'Tor, Guardian,

and Leader of the High Rocks. You are a legend, Adik'Tar," she said and bowed slightly.

"Legends can be good or bad. I hope history will remember me kindly," he replied. Then he turned to the striking male standing next to her.

"I am Rohm'Mok, son of Hatos'Mok of the Deep Valley. Thank you for your hospitality. This is not my first visit to Kthama; I have attended several of the Leaders' Council meetings," he answered.

Silence.

E'ranale broke the awkward pause. "Liru is ready. My daughter gathered her belongings so you can take them with her. Just small items she made for Liru," she said softly.

Pan carefully handed little Liru to Neilith, and the offling looked back at her, astonished. Though her heart was breaking, Pan did her best to control her emotions.

"Thank you," said Oragur, "but if you do not mind, we would like to stay a few days. My mate has never seen Kthama, and Krin would like to spend time with her old friends. Is that acceptable to you?"

"Of course," said Moc'Tor. He signaled for Dochrohan. "Please have suitable quarters prepared for our guests. We will need one for Oragur, his mate, and his daughter Krin. Another for Rohm'Mok, heir to Hatos'Mok's leadership at the Deep Valley. They will all be staying several days."

He continued, "Oragur, you know the layout here. I will skip the formalities of a tour. I am sure you can show your mate around."

"I would appreciate a tour," said Rohm'Mok. "I have only been to the Leaders' council meeting room, the quarters arranged for me then, and the eating area. Perhaps your daughter Pan could be my escort?" he asked.

Pan looked at her mother, silently pleading for help. Before E'ranale could intervene, though, her father replied, "Of course. Let us get you settled and then you can both discuss the tour."

Pan glared at Moc'Tor and looked to her mother, who shook her head slightly.

"While you are all waiting for your quarters to be prepared, come with us to eat," suggested E'ranale.

As she watched Neilith walking away with Liru, Pan held back because she could not stop her tears from falling. She knew she would spend many, many days grieving over the loss of the little offling she loved so much.

Moc'Tor and E'ranale led the guests to the Great Chamber. Pan seemed to be doing her best to keep as far away from Rohm'Mok as possible, but he waited for her.

"I am glad to see you again," Rohm'Mok said as they walked.

Pan looked everywhere except at him. "I had no idea you were coming."

"I thought it would be a great chance to spend some time with you. They wanted an escort, so I was glad to volunteer."

The two lapsed into awkward silence.

Having overheard, Moc'Tor sighed and moved ahead to speak to Oragur. "This is an indelicate question. But since your departure, we are without a Healer. Is there any chance you and your family would return to Kthama?" he asked.

"I have made a life for myself at Deep Valley. I will never return," Oragur answered curtly.

"But Krin has friends here, and Pan has become very attached to Liru. Perhaps during your stay here, you could reconsider," Moc'Tor added.

"Perhaps. But it is best you do not get your hopes up, Moc'Tor," Oragur answered. "Or your daughter's."

Moc'Tor gritted his teeth and said no more. *Oragur has always been brusque and stubborn.* But Moc'Tor realized that, in the Healer's situation, perhaps he would react in the same way.

He looked back at Rohm'Mok, still walking silently next to Pan. He would apologize later for agreeing that she should escort the visitor, but he could have done no less. It would have been a terrible insult to refuse the request because, even though his daughter was a Guardian, Rohm'Mok was the next in line to lead the Deep Valley and also deserved consideration.

Maybe it could work out. Rohm'Mok had obviously volunteered to come, and he was clearly interested in Pan. *Perhaps Rohm'Mok's parents are in for a big surprise after assuming their son would never leave Deep Valley. Unfortunately, that might create a rift between Hatos'Mok and me.* But Moc'Tor had seen before how the Great Spirit worked these things out, and he would not let politics stand in the way of his daughter's happiness. *If Rohm'Mok loves her as I love E'ranale, he will also let nothing stand in his way.*

In the Great Chamber, Moc'Tor guided them to his table. Having been told guests were coming, several of the females brought a selection of food items to them, spreading everything out on the rock slab.

Rohm'Mok took a place directly opposite Pan, and she squirmed in obvious discomfort.

Moc'Tor shook his head. *He is not even trying to hide his interest in her.* Was it some type of game? Pan had suffered enough, and Moc'Tor would have to take Rohm'Mok aside and ask him to make his intentions clear. He would not stand by and let some young buck hurt her further.

When they had finished eating, Moc'Tor stood and addressed Rohm'Mok. "May I have a word with you?"

"Of course, Adik'Tar," he said, standing up to follow the Guardian.

Moc'Tor led the young male down a tunnel to the closest empty meeting room. "Please. Come inside."

"To what do I owe this honor, Moc'Tor? I have been to some of the Leaders' Council meetings but have never had the opportunity to speak with you directly."

"As you have attended meetings," replied Moc'Tor, "then you know by now that I quickly get to the point. My daughter is clearly enamored with you. She has asked to be paired, yet it was stated very clearly that she would not leave Kthama. You seem to be pursuing her company, yet I know you are heir to the leadership at the Deep Valley. I will not stand by and watch you break my daughter's heart by leading her on when you have no intention of joining her at Kthama."

Rohm'Mok replied, "I understand your position as her parent, as Leader of the High Rocks, and as the Guardian. I am glad she has such a protective father who cares so much for her welfare. I am not usually as blunt as you are, but I will follow your lead.

"Adik'Tar, when your daughter stood before the Leaders' Council and said she wanted to be paired, my heart jumped. It was the first time I had met her, and I immediately knew that she was the one for me. I could not get her out of my mind. If you have experienced anything like this, you will understand. The moment I saw Pan, it was as if our souls were joined somehow, and from that moment on, she has consumed my thoughts."

He continued, "When Pan said she was coming to the Deep Valley, I made sure to know when she would arrive. I approached my father and suggested that out of respect for her station as Guardian, it would be appropriate for me to be her escort. To my delight, he agreed."

Moc'Tor, "Alright. But what about *your* station?"

Rohm'Mok paced a few steps and turned back to face Moc'Tor.

"It is true, I am heir to the leadership of the Deep Valley. But I am prepared to vacate the position if your daughter will have me," he declared.

Moc'Tor let out a long breath. "I see. That changes the picture, but what about your parents? I assume they have no idea of your position on this?" Moc'Tor asked.

"Yes, you are correct; they do not know. I have struggled with it because my father has expectations of me. But it comes down to which I could more easily give up—leadership of the Deep Valley or your daughter. Once I put it in that perspective, no decision has ever been easier."

Then he continued, "Adik'Tar, I am not blind to the position this puts you in as far as your relationship with my father is concerned. But I have a very capable brother. At the Deep Valley, there will still be a Leader from the House of 'Mok. It will just not be me."

Moc'Tor thought for a moment before replying. "I believe you. And I do understand how you feel about my daughter. I had the same experience when I met my First Choice, E'ranale. I knew there would never be one such as her. In every way, I knew I had to have her. And in every way, it was the wisest decision I ever made; she is my beloved, my counselor, the foundation of my world. Although I had other females before her, and later Ny'on and Ushca, I rarely touched them. It was she whose company I sought out at every opportunity."

Moc'Tor then changed his tone. "What of your parents? They expect you to take over as Leader of Deep Valley. What if they refuse to allow you to leave?"

"Let me ask you this, with all due respect," said Rohm'Mok. "What would have kept *you* from being with E'ranale?"

Moc'Tor set his hand on the younger male's shoulder, and looking into his eyes, said, "You have my permission to pursue my daughter. Her mother will agree once I tell her of our conversation."

Rohm'Mok nodded and said, "Thank you, Adik'-Tar. I will not hurt her, I promise. I will spend my life making hers as wonderful as I can."

Moc'Tor nodded in return. "Come then; let us go back to the table. By now, Dochrohan should have your quarters prepared."

By the time they returned to the Great Hall, Dochrohan was indeed waiting for them. "Adik'Tar, the quarters are prepared."

Then the first guard turned to the guests. "If you follow me, I will show you to them so you can get settled."

Rohm'Mok looked at Pan and said, "Whenever you are ready, I would love to start that tour."

Pan frowned at her father. From the look on her face, it was obvious she was burning up with the desire to know what he and Rohm'Mok had spoken about.

"I will give you time to refresh yourself, then I will come to your quarters."

Rohm'Mok nodded, and the others stood to join him. They all followed Dochrohan out of the eating area.

When they were far enough out of earshot, Pan turned to her father.

"What is going on? What did you two speak about? How could you assign me to be his escort? *Spending time with him is the last thing I want!*" she whispered.

Moc'Tor looked around to see who else was in the huge cavern. Most had left, so he explained, "I did not mean to put you in an awkward position, but he asked for you specifically. I felt I had to agree, though I intended first to speak bluntly with him as I am not prepared to stand by and watch your heart being broken. Depending on how he answered my questions, I was prepared to withdraw my agreement for you to be his escort.

"I saw how you looked at Rohm'Mok. And I saw how he looked at you. I asked him plainly what his intentions are. Whether he clearly understands that in no way would you leave Kthama to be paired. I warned him not to toy with you."

Unconsciously, Pan held her breath.

"You can relax, Pan. Rohm'Mok assured me that he is serious about his interest in you. He spoke of his feelings for you as I speak of my feelings for your mother. He is prepared to abandon his station as heir to Deep Valley if it turns out you will have him."

"He said that?"

"As clear as the light of a full moon," Moc'Tor answered. "Rohm'Mok's younger brother would take his place in the line of succession."

E'ranale hugged her daughter and beamed at her mate. Pan buried her face in her mother's soft coat and answered a muffled, "Thank you, Father. Thank you."

Perhaps this will ease the sting of losing Liru. Moc'Tor knew that a mate and an offling were different. But the pair would have their own offling someday, and perhaps that would comfort her. "Now you had better wash your face, take a walk in the sunlight, and then go and meet your beloved."

Pan turned to throw her arms around her father's

neck. "Thank you, thank you," she said, and she looked at her mother with a glowing smile.

Pan almost scampered down the corridor to her quarters. She entered and twirled around; arms flung out. *Thank you, Great Spirit. Thank you for this greatest of blessings.*

Still overly excited, she went to her personal area, poured some fresh water onto a small piece of hide, and washed her face as her father had suggested. Then she walked outside to bask in the sunshine for a few moments before going to find Rohm'Mok.

Rohm'Mok was pacing in his quarters. His hands were sweaty. Expecting Pan to show up at any moment, he found he could not concentrate. *This may really be happening.* He had believed from her actions that she was interested in him, but her father had now confirmed it. He might get to spend the rest of his life with Pan and give her offling of her own to raise. He had never been happier or more nervous than he was right now.

Suddenly there was the familiar clack of the announcement stone. Rohm'Mok smoothed down his hair covering and pushed the door open. He broke into a huge smile as he saw Pan standing before him. To his surprise, he suddenly felt shy.

"Are you ready for your tour?" she asked, obviously trying to keep her composure.

"Yes. Thank you for taking the time to show me around."

"It is my pleasure," she answered before looking away. "What would you like to see first?"

"You decide. I am sure our cave systems are pretty much the same. Do you have a special place that you enjoy going to?"

Pan thought a moment, then said, "Yes, I do. It is not far; come." She turned to lead the way.

"I am sorry how it worked out with Oragur. I know it must be heartbreaking to give up Liru."

"It is," she said softly. "She was like my own. The thought of not seeing her every day is so painful. How I wish Oragur would take up my father's invitation to bring his family back here."

"I know it does not help at the moment, but maybe you will have offling of your own someday. Would you like that?" he asked.

"If it were with the right mate, I would. But it would have to be with someone I respected and knew would be a good father to my offling. And I would like to feel about him as my mother does about my father. What they have is very special." Briefly, she looked up at him.

Rohm'Mok met her gaze. "Then make sure you

hold out for the right mate. Because you deserve nothing less than that kind of happiness."

Pan stood transfixed by his eyes, seemingly unable to move. After what seemed like forever, he looked away.

"How far is it?" he asked.

"Not far. Just outside and up one of the paths."

Pan led him out of Kthama and then up the climb to the meadow above. When they reached it, she stopped to give him time to look around.

"This is a sacred place. I can feel it," he said.

"Yes. It is a place of great peace and great power. My father and I come here to discharge our duties as Guardians. Others are allowed here only under very special circumstances."

Rohm'Mok suddenly understood the special consideration Pan was giving by taking him there. "I never thought about you having duties. Is it like meditation?"

"Not exactly. Perhaps in some ways. It is here that we connect with the creative life force of the Great Spirit. And it is here that we enter the Order of Functions."

"I have heard of the Order of Functions. But I do not pretend to understand it," he said.

"The Order of Functions is the wisdom built into every aspect of Etera. It is the pattern of our realm.

An incomprehensible weaving together, so that every piece affects another all according to the rules and pattern that hold together creation as we know it. An intelligence so vast that no individual mind can even begin to understand it."

"If you do not understand it, how do you work with it?" he asked.

"It is not a question of working with it. It is only a question of surrender."

"Sit with me," and Rohm'Mok reached out his hand to lead her to a grassy knoll he had spotted. He waited for her to take a seat and then selected a spot next to her. "I do not pretend that I could ever understand your responsibilities. But I would like to try. I hope we will have many more conversations like this." He looked around. "This place is very special. And very beautiful," he said. "Like you."

Pan felt her face flush. "Thank you." Then she rose and added, "We should be getting back."

"As you wish," he said and stood up. "Pan, do not be afraid. We will take our time getting to know each other. Whatever it takes for you to feel certain about —us. I know you feel something for me," he added. "But I will not push you."

"I do," she said quietly. "I do feel something for you. I just do not want to be hurt."

"I would never hurt you. I want only to take care of you, protect you, make your life easier. I know that sounds stupid; a Guardian, most of all, does not need protection. But it is still how I feel."

"My father told me about your conversation. Would you really leave the Deep Valley? Your parents would not be happy," she said quietly.

"I know. I will speak with them as soon as I return. There is no point in dragging it out because I will not change my mind. My place is with you, and the sooner they know of my decision, the sooner they can focus on my brother, Bahr'Mok. They will be upset, but in time they will come around. Do not let that be of any concern," he said.

She looked at him again, and he gently brushed the back of his hand against her cheek. She raised her hand and covered his. Then Rohm'Mok brought her hand to his lips and kissed it, never letting his eyes leave hers.

A thrill ran through her center, and Pan closed her eyes. More than anything, she wanted to fall into his arms and surrender herself to him as she surrendered to the Order of Functions. It was moving so fast, but she did not care. *I know there will never be anyone for me but him.*

She opened her eyes and looked up at him just as he leaned forward and pressed his lips to hers. She wanted to stop time, to stay forever in this place at his side.

Though she wanted more, so much more, he pulled back from her. "You said we should get back. I hope to see you at evening meal," he said.

"I will make sure someone comes to fetch you."

They walked to Kthama in silence, each filled with visions, hopes, and dreams of a future together.

During the next few days, Rohm'Mok and Pan spent as much time with each other as possible. They had both relaxed and discovered how much they enjoyed each other's company. Moc'Tor and E'ranale could not have been happier for their daughter.

In between spending time with Rohm'Mok, Pan stole as many visits with Liru as Oragur would allow. She knew it was just keeping the wound open, but if there was some chance the little offling would remember her, it would be worth every bit of hurt.

The day came that Oragur and his family were to return to Deep Valley. Rohm'Mok and Pan said their goodbyes in private.

"I will return as soon as I can," he said, holding both her hands.

"These last few days together have been the happiest I have ever known," she whispered.

"There will be many more, I promise."

He leaned down and kissed her, resisting the drive to pull her more dangerously close. "I do want you so. The sooner we are paired, the sooner our life together can begin."

She nodded silently, and they left the meeting room to find the others.

Oragur and his family were standing in the Great

Entrance, waiting on Rohm'Mok. As he and Pan entered, Oragur tilted his head. "That is interesting," he whispered to his new mate Neilith, who was holding Liru.

"I think so too," she whispered back.

"How did you know?" Oragur asked.

"You do not have to have a Healer's Seventh Sense to see what is going on. I am sure everyone else here has noticed it," she chuckled. "I expect we are in for some drama once we return to the Deep Valley."

"Thank you for your hospitality," Oragur said to Moc'Tor as the Leader and E'ranale joined them.

Pan stepped over and placed a kiss on Liru's forehead. Krin took her friend's hand and gave it a quick squeeze as Pan turned away for a moment to hide her grief. A few more goodbyes were said, and then the visitors were gone.

Pan stood next to her father and mother for a while. "Father, when is the next Council meeting?" she asked.

"You miss him already," said Moc'Tor, smiling at his daughter.

Pan felt the color rise in her cheeks. "Maybe a little," she grinned.

"It is not far off. Not as soon as you would like, though, I am sure. The High Rocks must have a Healer, and I need the Leaders' help locating someone from another community, even if he or she needs to be trained before being brought here. It is a great deal to ask, to change homes, but those who are called to Healing are generally self-sacrificing."

"All the young females do it when they are paired with a male from another community," said E'ranale. "The new generations now accept it as the way things are, so whether the new Healer is male or female, the concept is not new. I know it is still very hard for them, though. Change has never been easy for any of our people."

Pan grew silent as she suddenly realized how much Rohm'Mok was giving up to be with her.

CHAPTER 10

Activities outside Kayerm increased with the cooler weather. Although the Mothoc and Sassen subsisted primarily on a vegetarian diet, hunting added fat and protein and was a welcome change.

Straf'Tor and Nox'Tor were crouched in the tree line watching a herd of deer drink from a tributary of the Great River. Straf'Tor had already made a kill, and now it was his son's turn. Nox'Tor signaled that he was ready, and with lightning speed, he rose and flung his spear, taking down the largest buck. The rest scattered, and the two males ran to the fallen beast to make sure it was not suffering. They thanked the Great Spirit for the stag and wished its soul Good Journey on its return home.

Nox dragged the carcass out of the water and up onto the bank. "Kyana and Mother will be glad to see this."

"It will keep them for a few days. The forest is overrun with deer, and we must encourage the others to hunt; otherwise, many animals will perish terribly in the upcoming cold months," said Straf'-Tor. Then he continued, "We must spend more time together. I do not see you as often as I would like. Although there is still unrest at Kayerm, it does not seem as active, so I should have more time."

"I am not convinced of that, Father," Nox'Tor replied. "I do not think Ridg'Sor has given up his quest to incite trouble. I think he is just being more subtle about it."

"You could be right. I will have to ask Wosot what he is hearing—and we need to finish with these deer and get back; I am anxious to show Ushca my kill."

The two males dressed the deer carcasses, packed the meat into their carrying baskets, and hoisted them over their shoulders. They returned and immediately went to find Ushca and Kyana.

Ushca, Kyana, and Ushca's friend, Beala, looked up from their task as their mates entered.

"The Great Spirit blessed us today," said Straf'Tor as he swung his basket down to the rock floor. It made a heavy thud.

"That is great news," said Beala. "Especially since Ushca— Oh." Her voice trailed off, and she looked guiltily at her friend.

"What? What is going on?" asked Straf'Tor.

The three females exchanged smiles, and Ushca stopped and held up what she had been working on. A tiny wrapping made of the softest hide.

"Really?" Straf'Tor exclaimed. Ushca nodded, and he rushed over, crouched down, and took her in his arms.

"I do not know why it took so long, but, yes, I am finally seeded," she exclaimed.

Straf'Tor hugged her tighter and smiled over at Beala, then up at his son.

"That is great news," said Nox'Tor. "I am happy for you both."

"Our offling will know nothing but life here at Kayerm," added Straf'Tor. "If the others would let go of their memories of the past, we could build a true future here."

"Adik'Tar," said Wosot, "We caught Salus and some others making their way to Kthama."

"Ridg'Sor's band?" Straf'Tor asked.

"Yes, but not all of them. Some of our people were with him. I believe they were on their way to scout it out."

"Where are they now?"

"They were easy enough to follow; they made no attempt to hide their tracks in the snow. We tried to force them to return, but I only had a handful of sentries with me, and they refused."

"Gather as many sentries as you can and arm them," Straf'Tor ordered.

By traveling at full speed, after a while, Straf'Tor and his group caught up to Ridg'Sor and his band of followers.

"Stop!" the Leader called out.

Ridg'Sor looked back and raised his hand for the others to halt.

Straf'Tor was dismayed at the number of males accompanying Ridg'Sor. He had thought the dissent was dying down. *This is not just his original group of rebels. I did not realize so many of my people had turned to his way of thinking.* "You will return to Kayerm immediately. All of you," Straf'Tor ordered. Most avoided his gaze. *Good. They should be ashamed*, he thought.

"You are no longer in charge here. These people do not follow you; they follow me," shouted Ridg'Sor.

"Then they follow a fool. What do you hope to accomplish?"

"What you have failed to do. To take care of our people. Claim what is rightfully ours. We struggle and toil while your brother's people and the abominations he created live in luxury. We are stronger than they are, and we can convince them to give up Kthama Minor or face the consequences."

"There are far more of them than there are of your pitiful collection," Straf'Tor countered.

"That may be true, but by force of strength, ours is the greater position," said Ridg'Sor. "Plus, we have the element of surprise," he added.

"I will take care of that right now. Wosot, you and two others go on ahead and warn the sentries at Kthama of Ridg'Sor's plan. The rest of you, come back with me now or leave Kayerm to wander on your own."

Ridg'Sor snarled as the two males led by Wosot ran on towards Kthama.

The members of Ridg'Sor's group turned to each other, their eyes wide.

"Our fathers searched this area thoroughly," said Straf'Tor. "The only cave system close by is Kayerm. If you think life at Kayerm is hard, try living without it. I thought you would have learned that lesson, Ridg'Sor. You were lucky to have found Kayerm after my brother put an end to that despicable traitor, Norcab, and you were exiled from Kthama. You will not be so lucky this time."

Ridg'Sor turned to the group with him. "He is lying," Ridg'Sor countered. "They did search the area, but I guarantee you they quit looking once they found Kayerm. There could be another system around here; you cannot say there is not."

"The cold months are upon us," said Straf'Tor. "If

you do not come back with me now, you will never be allowed to return. You have no food stores with you. You have no tools except the weapons you are holding. And what of your females? Your offling? Are you prepared to abandon them forever?"

Straf'Tor could see his words were having an effect on the rebels. Heads turned as they consulted with each other. More and more now returned his gaze, and slowly, several of them stepped away from the group and walked toward Straf'Tor.

"Cowards!" yelled Ridg'Sor.

Straf'Tor waited until nearly all had joined his side.

"You blamed your brother for destroying the Mothoc. Well, you are doing the same," Ridg'Sor hissed, his face contorted. "The Great Spirit will make you pay for your ignorance, mark my words."

"Take a look, Ridg'Sor. Your followers have abandoned you. You and Salus stand alone. I give you one last chance. Make your decision. Return to Kayerm and accept my rule, or continue on your way. But if you leave, do not approach Kthama. I promise you I will know if you do, and there will be no third chance." Straf'Tor's voice was steel. He started back in the direction of Kayerm, leaving Ridg'Sor and Salus standing side by side.

"Va!" Ridg'Sor spat on the ground, looked at Salus, and they began to follow Straf'Tor back to Kayerm.

Moc'Tor looked up from his meal as Dochrohan approached.

"Adik'Tar," Dochrohan said. "Three of Straf'Tor's males have approached. They came to warn us that the rebel leader, Ridg'Sor, had assembled a group to try to take Kthama Minor from us. Fortunately, Straf'Tor discovered them."

The Leader stopped picking through his food. "Surely such a small group poses no threat,"

"It was not a small group, Adik'Tar. Apparently, he recruited some of Straf'Tor's people. I do not know that they would have succeeded, but they might have done some damage."

"I owe my brother; this is just what we did not want to have happen. Our peoples must be divided and remain divided. Because of my foolishness in allowing the breeding with the Others to go too far, his people are the best hope for Etera, as they carry the most Mothoc blood."

Moc'Tor thought for a moment. "Are the messengers still here?"

"Yes, Adik'Tar."

"Take me to them," the Leader said and got up. They headed for the Great Entrance where Wosot and his sentries stood.

While the three were waiting, they had scanned the area, all so familiar. "It still feels like home," Wosot had said quietly.

Moc'Tor approached them. "Thank you for coming; I wish you to take a message to my brother. Ask him to come to Kthama. Tell him, "*It is time.*" He will understand."

As they left, Wosot stopped to take one last look around what had been their home for so long.

"Straf'Tor was right," said one of the males as they made their way down the path. "As long as we remember and speak of Kthama, there will be no peace at Kayerm. Just that short time considerably stirred up my longing. It would be better if we did not know it existed."

"Straf'Tor was right to order everyone never to speak of Kthama again," added Wosot. "They are not complying, but I see the wisdom in it."

"What are you planning to do?" asked Dochrohan.

"Finish what we started," Moc'Tor said. "Do we have enough sentries to start posting them around Kthama?"

"Yes, depending on how many you want."

"Only a few. Scout the area; consider the approaches. Then place three or four around the perimeter so that next time we will not be caught off guard."

"It will be a boring job," said Dochrohan.

"Ask for volunteers. I am sure some will be more suited for it than others. Right now, hours of solitude surrounded by the beauty of Etera sounds very pleasant to me." Moc'Tor slapped Dochrohan on the back and sent him on his way.

Dak'Tor, Moc'Tor's son, had come looking for him. "Father, Mother is asking for you."

"What is wrong?"

"She is not feeling well and wishes for your company."

Moc'Tor frowned and followed Dak'Tor quickly down the corridor to the Leader's Quarters.

E'ranale was propped up against the wall on their sleeping mat, hides gathered up around her.

"You are cold?" he asked, moving to sit at her side. He took her hands in his. "Tell me what is wrong?"

"The pain is increasing."

"What pain? The pain you mentioned before?" he asked. "The one you said was indigestion?"

"Yes. It is more constant now. Piercing."

Moc'Tor turned to his son. "Send our fastest messenger to the Deep Valley. At once. Ask Oragur to come to Kthama immediately. Tell him E'ranale is in trouble, and we need his help. Do not look for Dochrohan; he is busy with another task. Find Bakru; he will know who to send."

Dak'Tor took off immediately in search of Dochrohan's right hand.

"Bakru," Dak'Tor called out as he approached. The guard was speaking with a group of males and turned to meet Moc'Tor's son.

"Yes, Dak'Tor?" He bowed the slightest bit, recognizing the future Leader of the High Rocks.

"My mother is not well. Something seems very wrong. My father is terribly worried and asks that you please send the fastest messenger to the Deep Valley and get Oragur the Healer to come immediately."

Bakru motioned to two of his males, and they hurried off. "Let your father know it is attended to. Is there anything else we can do?"

Dak'Tor thought a moment. "No, but I need to tell my sisters."

Dak'Tor had soon gathered his sisters Vel, Inrion, and Pan. "Mother is in pain. On Father's orders, I have sent for the Healer, Oragur, from the Deep Valley."

"Can we see her?" Vel asked.

"I am sure she wants to see you all," he replied.

"Let us not go at once," said Pan to her sisters. "It might alarm her, making her think she is in serious trouble. And let us not stay long; Father will be with her, and she is likely upset. While we are there, she will feel she must put on a brave face. May I go first?"

she asked. "I will not be long; I just desperately need to speak with Father."

As badly as Pan wanted to see her mother, she needed her father's advice first. She clacked the announcement stone outside their door.

"Come," she heard her father's familiar voice. Ordinarily, that sound alone would soothe her, but this time her feeling of alarm would not leave. She poked her head through the door. Her mother was curled up in a ball and seemed to be asleep.

"Father, may I speak with you?"

Moc'Tor eased away from his mate and stepped into the tunnel to meet with his daughter.

"Let us walk away so as not to wake her," said Moc'Tor. "This is the first rest she has gotten in some time."

They had to walk a way to reach a smaller room to talk in.

"What is the matter with her? When did this start?" asked Pan. "She is never sick."

"The first I heard her mention that anything was wrong is when she told me she was seeded. It seems it has only gotten worse with time. Now it is far sharper and lasts longer."

"I am afraid, Father. Is there anything we can do while we are waiting for Oragur to get here?" She put out of her mind the hope that Oragur might bring his mate and Liru, and maybe Rohm'Mok.

"The Order of Functions," they said at the same time, just as Vel approached. Knowing she would sit with E'ranale, Pan and Moc'Tor left for the meadow above Kthama.

Before long, they were there. The cold air was refreshing, and they hardly felt the cold.

"First, the creative stream," Moc'Tor reminded his daughter.

They stilled themselves and entered the Aezai-terian flow.

Pan welcomed the peace and ecstasy of being immersed in the creative stream. She sent her aware-ness, her life force, down into the vortex below Kthama and surrendered to the bliss that never grew old. But all too soon, it was time to return and face the Order of Functions.

They opened their eyes, and Moc'Tor asked, "Are you ready?"

"Yes," she replied. Pan had learned how to surrender to the dissipation of her consciousness across what felt like eternity. It was still unpleasant, but she knew full well what to expect and kept in mind the sacredness of her role as Guardian. And it was only temporary.

As before, they somehow knew when to return, and before very long, Pan had opened her eyes again.

Her father looked at her, "That is all we can do. What will be now will be. I pray it is the Great Spirit's will that she recovers."

Pan's eyes widened. "Is it that serious? Are you saying she might—*die*?"

"I do not know, daughter; I feel it is a possibility. I cannot imagine life without your mother, so we must pray that we will not lose her."

Pan shook her head. *How could the Great Spirit take Mother? It cannot happen. It cannot.* "I know that each time we engage the Order of Functions only imprints the divine pattern more strongly on our realm. If it is the Great Spirit's will that Mother passes from us, then I refuse ever to engage it again," she said furiously.

"You are scared and angry, Pan, so I will treat your words as just that. You are a Guardian. This is your duty. It is not for us to say what the future holds."

"How can you say that? You love Mother!"

"*Never doubt that I love her more than life itself.* Like you, I cannot imagine going on without her," her father replied. "Do not take what I am saying as acceptance of her dying. I am only telling you that *if she did*, you could not abandon your responsibilities as Guardian. The weight of all life on Etera, not just your mother's, rests on the Guardian's role," he said softly. Then he put his arms around her and drew her toward him.

Pan wrapped her arms around her father's neck, and for a while, sobbed into his silver-white coat.

"Let us put this from our minds," he said as he kissed the top of her head. "Oragur will be here soon. He is very experienced; let us see what he says. And perhaps your Mother is awake now," he said.

"I told my siblings not to visit her together, but rather to coordinate their visits so as not to wear her out or alarm her." Pan sniffed.

"Wise advice. You will make a great Guardian when the mantle is passed to you."

"I am not ready. Do not speak of it."

"I am not talking about me dying. I am talking about you taking your place as a Guardian while I mentor you. Much as I took over from my father while he was still alive. Nothing more."

"Have I not been fulfilling my role?"

"In part, but I have been bearing the brunt of it."

"That is why you seem tired. I have never seen you tired before," Pan added.

"Difficult times require more of us, and it cycles. Some eras are worse, and some are easier. I will be glad when it cycles back to an easier time," he smiled. "And there is more I must teach you; you have yet to learn how to guide others to enter the Ror'Eckrah, the One Mind. But for now, let us go."

Dak'Tor intercepted them as they came into the

Great Entrance. "Bakru's runner has returned, and Oragur is on his way."

Pan ignored the urge to ask if he was coming alone.

Over the next few days, E'ranale's pain did not abate but continued to worsen. Finally, Moc'Tor was told Oragur was nearly at Kthama.

Moc'Tor, Dak'Tor, and Pan waited for him to appear. Pan's eyes widened when she recognized Rohm'Mok, and with no regard for propriety, she flung herself into his arms.

Rohm'Mok caught her up. "I missed you so, but I am sorry to be here under these circumstances."

"I am so glad you came; I am so frightened," Pan said.

Moc'Tor greeted Oragur. "Thank you for coming."

"Let us go to her; there is no point in delaying," the Healer replied.

Moc'Tor asked Pan, Dak'Tor, and Rohm'Mok to give them some time and suggested that they find Vel and Inrion.

Shortly, Oragur and Moc'Tor were with E'ranale in the Leader's Quarters. E'ranale opened her eyes. "Oh, Oragur. I am so glad you are here," she exclaimed.

"Tell me about your pain," he said.

E'ranale pointed to the right side of her abdomen. "It has only gotten worse."

"When did it start?"

"A few weeks after I realized I was seeded. I thought it was just indigestion," she answered.

He gently felt where she said it was hurting, and she let out a loud cry.

"I am sorry. I do not mean to hurt you."

Oragur ran his hand over his face and looked up at Moc'Tor before looking away again.

A bolt of fear ran through Moc'Tor's center. "What is it?" he asked, clenching his fists. When Oragur said nothing, Moc'Tor forcefully dragged him out into the corridor and down a way to be out of earshot. "*Tell me.*"

Oragur lowered his voice. "The offling is not where it is supposed to be, in the cradle. It is growing, but in the wrong place."

"What does that mean?" Moc'Tor said, steeling himself for the answer. "What can you do to help her?"

"There is nothing I can do, Moc'Tor."

"What are you saying? What will happen as the offling continues to grow? Can she deliver it somehow?"

"I have heard of this before. It is rare, but it

happens. I am sorry; eventually, the offling will rupture her insides," he answered. "Then she will die."

Moc'Tor wanted to let out a mournful wail. He could not believe this was happening. They stayed in the hallway for some time. When they returned, E'ranale took one look at them, and her tears began to fall. *I knew it. I am going to die. I am going to die with my offling unborn.* What would happen to Moc'Tor? And her daughters? And Dak'Tor?

Moc'Tor went to E'ranale's side.

"You do not have to tell me the details. I already figured my situation was dire. I am sorry, my mate. I do not wish to leave you." She leaned against him, grimacing at the searing pain as she moved.

"I cannot lose you. This cannot happen. You are my life. Without you, there is nothing left," he whispered to her. "And it is so like you to think of me and the others before yourself."

He gently moved E'ranale back a bit to look her in the eyes and then laid his hand on her cheek. "I do not know how to imagine a life without you."

"Is there nothing we can do?" He turned back to ask Oragur again.

"I can consult with the Healer from the Far High Hills, but I do not wish to give you false hope. It is best you prepare for the inevitable."

"How long?" E'ranale asked.

"I wish I could tell you," Oragur said. "I can give you something for pain, and you can increase the dosage to keep from suffering. But be careful. It is strong; if you take more than the maximum amount I tell you, it will cause you to journey earlier to the Great Spirit."

Moc'Tor and E'ranale looked at each other.

"I will go and see what is here in the stores in the Healer's Quarters. If what I need is not there, I will have to return to Deep Valley to get what she needs."

Pan, Dak'Tor, and Rohm'Mok were returning with Vel and Inrion.

"Give them a few moments before you go in," said Oragur, pausing before he hurried away.

Pan's hand flew to her mouth. She and Dak'Tor looked at each other, and a terrible knowing passed between them.

Not being part of the family, Rohm'Mok opted to wait outside, and after a moment, the others stepped into the doorway. Their parents were sitting together on the sleeping mat, their mother leaning back in their father's embrace.

"May we come in?" Pan asked.

Moc'Tor waved them over, and they all knelt down beside their parents. "Mama," Pan said.

E'ranale reached out and smoothed the hair on the top of her daughter's head. "Shhh."

"Please tell us you are going to be alright?" Pan asked.

"I am sorry, daughter. I do not believe that I am."

Pan sobbed openly and covered her face with her

hands. Dak'Tor stared at his mother, frozen, while Vel and Inrion also started crying.

"No, no. This cannot be. The Great Spirit cannot be so cruel." Pan's voice broke.

"We must accept this, Pan. All of us. It is not what I want. It is not what your father wants. It is not what anyone wants, but it will be what it will be," E'ranale said softly.

"If the Great Spirit takes you, I will never serve him again," Pan cried.

"No, daughter," said Moc'Tor. "Do not say that. I know you are hurt and angry. I am sorry you are learning so early how hard life can be."

Dak'Tor finally found his voice, "I do not understand. What has happened?"

"Tell them, please. Tell me; I want to know," E'ranale said.

Moc'Tor explained reluctantly. "The offling is in the wrong place. It is not in the water cradle. It is growing in an area inside your mother where there is no room for it. In time it will—" Moc'Tor could not continue.

"You are going to die? How can this be? Maybe Oragur is wrong!" Dak'Tor's voice shook.

E'ranale squeezed her mate's hand. He could almost hear her reassuring him that their offling needed time to accept it—that they all did.

"Oragur is looking for medicine to ease your mother's pain," said Moc'Tor. "Let her get some rest now. You can all come back later and visit again.

Why not bring food from the Great Chamber so we can all eat here as a family?"

Before leaving, Pan pulled herself together, leaned over, and gave her mother a kiss.

The moment she was back in the corridor, Pan flew into Rohm'Mok's embrace. As she felt his strong arms around her, she broke down again. "Mother is dying. My mother is going to die," she cried.

Pan pulled his arms more tightly around her, "The offling is in the wrong place. It is going to keep growing until it ruptures her insides, and then they will both die." Spoken into Rohm'Mok's thick coat, her words were muffled and barely understandable.

Rohm'Mok pulled her closer, "I am so sorry. I am so sorry." He held her until her sobbing slowed.

"First Liru, and now my Mother? I cannot bear the pain of this world," she cried.

"I am here," he said softly. "We have each other, although I know that cannot make up for losing your mother."

"Oragur cannot find what he needs, so he is returning to the Deep Valley," said Dak'Tor. "He said he will be back as soon as he can and that you should stay here," he told Rohm'Mok.

"I would not leave now, anyway," Rohm'Mok answered, leaning his head on Pan's as she stood still nestled in his embrace.

Moc'Tor left E'ranale's side only to conduct the bare minimum of duties and to continue Pan's Guardian education.

He taught Pan how to implement the Ror'Eckrah, the One Mind, and when this ancient ritual could and should be used. Although Pan said she could not imagine what it would be useful for, Moc'Tor knew the time would come when it would be needed.

One day, Dochrohan approached Moc'Tor to tell him the sentries had been recruited. There was no trouble getting volunteers, much to his surprise. "The watchers are in place, Adik'Tar."

"Watchers? Is that what you are calling them?" Moc'Tor asked.

"It seems appropriate since that is what they are doing."

"The title is good. It differentiates theirs from the other roles. As for you, I believe your title from now on will be High Protector."

"That sounds important."

"It is. You are the one who assigns the days' tasks to the other males. And now that we have a viable threat, you are also in charge of these new watchers. I believe the title will give others a sense of security."

Dochrohan bowed his acceptance. "Adik'Tar," he

said more quietly. "We have heard of E'ranale's condition. You can understand that news like this travels quickly. All our people, including the males, are very saddened for both of you. And your family."

"I do not remember in our history losing anyone in this way," said Moc'Tor, "When she said she had pain, I thought it was just discomfort from the first weeks of being seeded. Now—" Moc'Tor had dropped his guard, and he composed himself again. "Thank you for your concern. Please tell the others we appreciate it. If any are inclined to pray, I would appreciate that too."

As they were talking, one of the sentries came into the Great Entrance. "Straf'Tor is approaching."

In all his grief, Moc'Tor had completely forgotten sending for his brother.

Within a few moments, Straf'Tor appeared. Moc'Tor walked to meet him and reached out to put his hand on his brother's shoulder. He was pleased that Straf'Tor did not pull away.

"I will admit, I have missed you, brother, son of Sorak'Tor," Moc'Tor said.

Straf'Tor took a breath and then exhaled deeply. "Despite our philosophical differences, I have missed you too. I wish we were being reunited under better conditions."

"Do you want to talk now or later?" asked Moc'Tor.

"Now is as good a time as any. Let us use one of the meeting rooms."

Straf'Tor sat, but Moc'Tor remained standing.

"How are matters here at Kthama?" asked Straf'Tor.

"E'ranale is sick. It is serious," Moc'Tor answered.

"How sick?"

Moc'Tor told him about Oragur's diagnosis. "She is going to die, Straf," he said.

Despite their differences, Straf'Tor's heart went out to his brother. "There are no words to comfort you, I know," said Straf'Tor. "I can only imagine if I were to lose Ushca. I doubt I would want to continue living. When you decreed that mating could only be between one male and one female, I thought you mad. Now, having shared these years with Ushca, I see that a good pairing is one of the greatest blessings. One female is enough if she is the right one."

Moc'Tor paused before asking, "How is Ushca?"

Straf'Tor hesitated a moment before answering, "She is seeded."

Moc'Tor nodded. "A great blessing; I am happy for you. The circle of life goes on. The life-breath of the creative spirit enters and leaves this realm, taking our loved ones home and bringing new loved ones to Etera."

Silence hung in the air.

"I appreciate your coming," said Moc'Tor. "I know this is not a good time to be away, with Ushca seeded and unrest at Kayerm."

"You will remember that the rebel, Ridg'Sor, and his followers moved into Kayerm and were there when we arrived," said Straf'Tor. "I thought that in time he would accept my leadership and make the best of it. Instead, he has sewn discord and riled others up to believe they have a right to Kthama Minor and should return to take it. I intercepted them on the way here and turned them back to Kayerm, threatening them with banishment if they continued on to Kthama."

"Did they acquiesce?"

"Yes. Ridg'Sor reluctantly returned once the group abandoned him."

"As I remember, he had only a small following," said Moc'Tor.

"*Had* is the operative word. Many have joined him; his years of poisoning their minds against Kthama have produced fruit."

"When we went down this path centuries ago," said Moc'Tor, "we agreed that the division of our people was Etera's greatest hope. I did not realize you had such struggles at Kayerm."

"Ridg'Sor's bitterness is great. He is angry with both of us—you for throwing him out of Kthama and me for taking over Kayerm, which he staked out before we arrived. He is only controlled by threats. Fear and threats are all he understands," said Straf'Tor.

"So the time is approaching to end the Wrak-Wavara. Is that what you are saying?"

"Yes. I believe that without our final intervention, Ridg'Sor will eventually rile up his followers again. Whether they could take Kthama Minor from you, I do not know. But neither of us needs that battle," said Straf'Tor.

"Very well; I will call the Leaders together, and I will send for you when it is time."

Straf'Tor stood to leave. Before he walked off, he placed his hands on his brother's shoulders.

"I am truly sorry, Moc'Tor," he said. "I cannot fathom the suffering of your entire family. But especially you. I know you love E'ranale as I love Ushca."

"Thank you, brother," Moc'Tor replied.

Together, they walked back to the Great Entrance where Straf'Tor left to return to Kayerm.

Moc'Tor sent messengers to the other communities to call the Leaders together.

In the meantime, Oragur had returned from the Deep Valley.

"Take this, but look at it first." He passed E'ranale a handful of herbs. "Chew it well and swallow it. It will ease your pain, and I am leaving the rest here in a basket by your bedside. Take only the amount I showed you, twice a day. You can increase it by a quarter if you need to, but do not exceed that amount. As I explained to you before, while this will help with the pain, too much will cause you to return to the Great Spirit."

E'ranale took the pile of leaves from his hand, stuck them in her mouth, and chewed slowly. She wrinkled her nose.

"I know it does not taste the best, but you will be glad of it in a few moments. There is more than enough here to last—" Oragur stopped talking.

E'ranale nodded her head slowly; she understood.

The Healer stood and turned to Moc'Tor, Dak'-Tor, and Pan, who were all watching. "I will stay for a few days to ensure it is working and to make certain that E'ranale understands how to adjust the dose. Other than easing her pain, there is nothing more I can do," Oragur said. "Moc'Tor," he continued, "step down the hallway with me a moment."

The two males stepped outside.

"Do you understand that given in a large amount, it will do more than ease her pain?"

"Spit it out, Oragur, it is not like you to be so sensitive," said Moc'Tor.

"My new mate is having a good effect on me. Moc'Tor, the time will come when E'ranale's pain will be unbearable. At that point, it is time to let her return to the Great Spirit. Give her a large amount of the medicine so she will fall asleep and suffer no longer."

"You are telling me to kill my mate."

"I am telling you to help her return home. The

desire to keep her with you as long as possible, that I understand. But at some point, it becomes entirely selfish. It is no life for her, living in excruciating pain. And if you wait too long and the offling ruptures inside her, she will suffer unbearably before she finally dies, and *nothing* will relieve *that* pain. That is what is awaiting her.

"And in case it has crossed your mind, there is no saving the offling. Even if it could be removed, it will be too young to survive outside of her. And cutting it out of her—"

"Stop!" Moc'Tor held his hand up. "Stop; I understand. There is more than enough here, you said?"

"Yes. There was a generous supply at the Deep Valley. Moc'Tor, I know my leaving put you at a great disadvantage. If you identify a Healer, send him or her to the Deep Valley, and I will provide extensive training. I also did not realize I had left your Healer's stores in such low supply. The medicine is harvested from the A'Pozz plant, the orange flowers with the profuse, furled petals that bloom in the late spring and through the summer heat. It is something you should always have on hand. Fortunately, there was a large supply at the Deep Valley. Otherwise, there would be no choice for E'ranale but to die a terrible death."

It was the longest Moc'Tor had ever heard Oragur speak. "Thank you. For everything," he said.

Back inside the Leader's Quarters, Pan and Dak'Tor sat one on either side of their mother, each holding one of her hands and keeping her company while they waited for the medicine to take effect. After a while, Pan could feel the tension leave her mother's body, and before long, E'ranale was sleeping peacefully.

Over the next few days, the messengers returned with word that the other community Leaders were on their way to Kthama. Dochrohan prepared the meeting room, making sure everything was in order.

"What is the purpose of this meeting?" asked Dak'Tor.

"When Straf'Tor and his following left Kthama, he and I both feared that a day would come when, to keep our People apart, we would have to put measures in place that were stronger than our directive alone. My brother and I knew that life at Kayerm would not be as easy as life here," continued Moc'-Tor. "And in my error of judgment, I let the breeding with the Others go too far. We are fortunate that Straf's followers did not continue cross-seeding their females as we did, so the strongest Mothoc blood flows in their veins."

"And now, because of the rebel Ridg'Sor and the ideas he has planted in the minds of others, they are a threat to us because ideas have a way of spreading," commented Dak'Tor.

"Yes. So it is time to seal the end of Wrak-Wavara. It is time for this dark stain to pass from memory. Somehow, Kthama and what happened here must be removed from our history. And we must take so strong a measure that no one will dare break the division between our people."

"So that is why the Leaders are coming."

"Yes. You must be prepared to pick up where I leave off; you are heir to my leadership."

Dak'Tor frowned. "You know I do not want to be Leader and that it should fall to Pan," he answered. "She is stronger, and the people have faith in her and recognize her as one to follow."

"Pan has her own responsibilities as Guardian. I have said it before; you are the one born to lead our people."

Dak'Tor shook his head. "Regardless, that is so far in the future."

"No. It is not far in the future," Moc'Tor continued. "The time is coming soon when you will have to step up and lead our people. You must focus on gaining their trust and taking your place. You need to step up, Dak'Tor. Their eyes must be on the future, on you, not on me. I will have to disappear into history along with the rest of this story."

Dak'Tor frowned. "I do not understand. Are you leaving?"

"Remember when you were young, and I would

tell you to stop focusing on your weaknesses. That a warrior who nurses his weaknesses will never build his strengths?"

Dak'Tor nodded.

"You have often nursed your weaknesses instead of building your strengths. We have had many conversations about it. From now on, you must think of yourself as the Leader of the High Rocks and act accordingly. In your actions, in your stance, in your words. Accept the mantle of leadership and do not disappoint me," Moc'Tor said sternly. "Soon, you must walk Etera without either your Mother or me."

'I do not understand! Where are you going?"

"I cannot answer that, son. I can only say that before long, you and your sisters will be the next hope for Kthama. Do not speak of this to them. I will shortly tell them myself," Moc'Tor added.

Dak'Tor walked away quickly, trying to control his feelings, clenching his teeth and his fists. He desperately struggled to push down all the pain and fear that filled his soul. He was not strong enough. *I cannot do this; my Father is wrong. It is one thing to take over the leadership if he is here to guide me, but how can he expect me to take over without him? What would I do?* Was he to lose his father and mother at the same time?

After Dak'Tor had left, Moc'Tor sought out his two oldest daughters. He asked them to sit on the grassy bank and sat between them where he could put an arm around each. "Inrion, Vel," he said. "Your mother is dying. I know you know this, and I am very sorry to be so blunt. There are hard times ahead for you both. You must carry on now, with your brother and Pan. To tell you what is coming would not make it any easier. Just know that no matter what happens, I have faith that you can handle it. Help each other through this; I am counting on you all to be here for each other."

Inrion and Vel didn't understand what he was saying but realized he was trying to comfort them. As Dak'Tor had done, they pestered their father for answers, but he would give them none. He was convinced that knowing what was coming would provide no benefit and do nothing to soften the blow, and there was a risk they might even try to interfere. They must walk the hard path in front of them and reach into themselves to find their strength within.

Though he knew his visit would be short and that he would be called back to Kthama very soon, Straf'Tor was relieved to return to Kayerm. Wosot was the first he saw. "How is Ushca?"

"She is well. The females are all stirred up and chattering nonstop."

Straf'Tor smiled, the first time he had in a while. "What about Ridg'Sor?"

"Pouting. But contained. But I fear it will not last forever."

Straf'Tor nodded.

"As for the rest who went with him, they only returned because of your threats. In their hearts, I believe they still want to take Kthama."

"I am sure you are right. But, in the event that it should come to this, my brother and I made a plan to end it once and for all," Straf'Tor replied.

CHAPTER 11

Word had spread through Kayerm that Ushca was not far from delivering Straf'Tor's offling.

"So. Another 'Tor is about to enter Etera," sneered Ridg'Sor.

"Why do you hate the House of 'Tor so much? Is it because Moc'Tor killed Norcab?" asked Laborn. "But that had nothing to do with Straf'Tor."

"My parents met when my father traveled to the Little River to trade tools and swap ideas with the toolmakers there. He was so smitten with my mother that he promised if she came back to Kthama with him, she would be his only mate. So she followed him back to Kthama. Everything was fine until she met Sorak'Tor, the father of Moc'Tor and Straf'Tor. She was already seeded by my father, and by then, Sorak'Tor had enough females and did not give her a second look. My father said it was never the same between them after that. He helped raise me, but the closeness between them never returned," Ridg'Sor continued. "So the 'Tors have been ruining my family's life for some time.

"Straf'Tor does not deserve happiness. None of the 'Tors do. But perhaps this is an opportunity to strike him a fatal blow. If he were unable to lead, then I think I have a chance of taking back leadership of Kayerm."

"What are you planning?" asked Salus.

The others listened with rapt attention as Ridg'Sor explained his plan.

When he was done, Ser'Hun said, "I will have no part in this. You are going too far. What you are proposing goes against everything the Mothoc stand for. Reconsider. I know you want to lead Kayerm, but I did not believe you were a monster."

Ridg'Sor jumped up and grabbed Ser'Hun by the throat. "Fine. I always knew you were a coward. But if you breathe a word of this, trust me, it will be the last breath you ever take."

Ridg'Sor released the male and pushed him backward.

Ser'Hun rubbed his throat and glared up at Ridg'Sor. He stumbled slightly as he regained his feet. "From now on, leave me out of these meetings." He looked at the others. "And if you were smart, you would also back out." Then he turned and walked briskly away.

Ridg'Sor spat in his direction. "*Rok!* We did not

need that *PetaQ* anyway. He was always weak. And now that he has offling of his own, his loyalty to the cause is gone."

Ushca's seeding seemed to have unified the community. Well-wishers frequently dropped off gifts for the offling—whether small wrappings, dried chews for teething, stacking rocks, and other items. She stacked them neatly in the corner of their quarters, taking them out to admire with Beala and other visiting females.

"We are so happy for you," said Beala. "We know Straf'Tor had offling from other females, but you are his one true beloved. We feared you would never be seeded."

"We have been paired for a very long time, and it was not for lack of trying," she grinned. "Though some have an easier time of getting seeded, overall, since the contagion, it seems we are not the most prolific of species."

"Whether the offling is male or female, Straf'Tor will be ecstatic," said Beala.

Straf'Tor walked into their quarters and smiled at seeing Ushca chatting with her friends. The other females tactfully left them alone, and he was glad to see how happy Ushca was as she picked up one item after another, admired it, and set it back down.

"Your stack of presents has grown, as has your belly," he remarked, sitting down and encircling her with his arms.

"I am so glad you are home. I think it will not be long."

"Look at this," she said and produced a long piece of hide with straps at each end.

"What the *krell* is that," Straf'Tor asked as she held it up in front of him.

Ushca wrapped it around her and demonstrated how it would free her hands while holding the tiny offling safely.

"That is ingenious. Did you invent that?"

"No, Largoth did."

Straf'Tor nodded. Largoth had the most Akassa blood in her of any there.

"Has there been trouble while I was gone? Is anything bothering you?"

"No, it has been fine. A bit of backache, but my biggest problem has been dealing with these gifts. See the pretty gourd that Tyria sent—it's to help with my back."

"Ah," he nodded, then continued, "My meeting with my brother was good, although it was disturbing being back at Kthama. The longing to return is strong, even for me. Despite all our time here, in many ways, it still felt like home. I must soon return for a Leader's meeting, after which, I believe our troubles with Ridg'Sor will end."

Ushca raised her eyebrows, wanting to ask what they had planned but feeling that if Straf'Tor had wanted her to know, he would have told her.

"When you do go, I hope you will not be gone long," was all she said. "In the meantime, I am going to take some of that drink Tyria sent to ease my back."

"I will leave you to yourself, then. I will return later," he said and kissed her sweetly before he left.

Far later that evening than he had planned, Straf'Tor returned with some food, only to find Ushca sleeping soundly. He was happy to see her resting so comfortably, and he eased in next to her, carefully wrapping his arm around her swollen belly.

Within seconds he flew into a sitting position.

"Ushca. Ushca," he said.

"Ushca, wake up!" He shook his mate with no response.

"No, no, no, no," he wailed, the piercing sound echoing through the tunnels. "Nooooooo!" His cry echoed through every level of Kayerm.

Within moments others came running in, breaking all protocol about entering another's quarters unannounced and uninvited.

Beala was first to reach Ushca; she crouched down and tried to help Straf'Tor rouse her.

She raised Ushca's eyelids and peered into her eyes. She placed her hand against Ushca's neck, then laid an ear to her friend's chest.

"I cannot hear her heartbeat, Adik'Tar," she said, her voice cracking.

Straf'Tor flew to his feet. "Quickly, go find Pagara and Tyria!" Then he went on a rampage, knocking over everything in sight. He kicked the pile of offling gifts, sending them scattering everywhere, and pounded his head with his fists. "This cannot be. She was fine when I left her earlier."

Beala had turned to leave when the Healer Pagara and her apprentice, Tyria, came rushing into the room. Tyria moved to one side to give the Healer the space she needed. Pagara pushed through the concerned group of people and, taking one look at Ushca's form on the bed, flew to her side.

After checking the still form, she looked up at Straf'Tor. "I am so sorry, Adik'Tar. She is gone." She then gently placed her hand on Ushca's swollen belly. "Safe journey, to you both," she said quietly.

"I do not see how this could have happened. She showed no signs of any problems other than slight backache." Pagara shook her head before standing and facing Straf'Tor. "What changed? Was she doing anything differently? Did she fall?" She looked to the others for answers too.

"I have been away; I do not know. She was fine

when I was here this morning," Straf'Tor mumbled, rubbing his hand over the crown of his head.

"She was so happy and excited. She was enjoying going through everyone's gifts and preparing the nest for her offling," Beala offered quietly from the back.

Straf'Tor's head jerked around. "Her gifts. She was talking about her gifts before I left her. The last thing she said—" Straf'Tor turned to stare at Tyria, his eyes angry slits. "The last thing she said was going to use that drink you sent her."

Tyria stared blankly at him.

Straf'Tor took a menacing stride toward the young apprentice, and she stepped back, her lips trembling, as the giant male towered over her, his face inches from hers.

"Where is the container it was in?" Pagara asked.

Beala searched Ushca's sleeping hide and found the gourd lying almost hidden underneath. She handed it to the Healer.

Pagara smelled it. Then she ran her finger around what remained and carefully tasted it. "Oh no."

"What is it?" Straf'Tor demanded. *"Tell me!"*

"I know this preparation, Adik'Tar. I know it well. I promise you that neither Tyria nor I could have had anything to do with it," she stated.

Straf'Tor grabbed the gourd out of her hand and sampled it as she had. *"What is this?"*

"It is not the mixture itself, but it contains an ingredient from A'Pozz seeds. It is a plant that blooms early and through the summer—a Healer's staple. We use it to ease pain. But taken in quantities that are too large—"

Straf'Tor threw the gourd against the rock wall, where it shattered. The others cowered away from the flying shards.

"I cannot explain it." Tyria's face was deathly pale. "Straf'Tor, on my life, by the Great Spirit, I promise you I had nothing to do with this. I did not even put any A'Pozz seeds into the mixture. It was to relax Ushca's back, not to take away pain," she stammered.

"*Ridg'Sor*. Did your mate know about this—where to find it, and what it could do?" Straf'Tor demanded.

Tyria gasped. Then she squeezed her eyes closed and nodded. "Yes."

"*How?*" Straf'Tor bellowed.

"When you argued with each other, and you twisted his arm behind his back, you almost dislocated Ridg'Sor's shoulder. His throat was also deeply bruised. He was in a great deal of pain, and Pagara prepared the A'Pozz mixture for him. He knew that if he took too much, he would drift off to sleep and return to the Great Mother."

"The Great Mother?"

"Yes. That is who we answer to, Straf'Tor," answered Pagara. "Females and female Healers call on the Great Mother, the giver of life and love. Though we not often openly—"

"*Bah*," he interrupted. "So Ridg'Sor knew about

this and could easily have slipped it into what you prepared for Ushca."

By now, Tyria was weeping. "Yes. He knew I was making something to give to Ushca. But how could he be capable of this? There is nothing I can say, Adik'Tar, except that if it is any consolation, she did not suffer. I doubt she even knew what was happening."

"*It is no consolation at all!* I will deal with your mate. Prepare yourself, Tyria. I will do what I should have done long ago. Only his passing will not be peaceful, as you say my mate's passing was."

He turned to Beala, Ushca's closest friend, who was in the corner silently crying.

"Stay with her. I know she is gone, but still—" Straf'Tor said.

Beala nodded. "I understand, Adik'Tar," she replied softly.

"Tyria, come with me," he barked.

Straf'Tor stormed out of his living quarters with the young apprentice moving as fast as she could to keep up with him. Near the entrance of Kayerm, he called out for Wosot, who came running.

"Find Ridg'Sor. *Now.*"

"If he fights you, break his legs. Do whatever it takes to get him here, but bring him alive," snarled Straf'Tor.

Before long, Wosot and three of the sentries returned, dragging Ridg'Sor with them. He was barely conscious.

"Once he figured out we were there to take him against his will, he started fighting," explained one of the males supporting the rebel. "We had to hit him over the head to quiet him. Look, he is starting to come around."

"Bind his hands and feet," Straf'Tor roared at the sentries. "Wosot, bring me the jhorallax. Now!"

One of the males whispered to Wosot, "What is this about? I have never seen Straf'Tor so upset."

"I do not know," said Wosot before he left to do as Straf'Tor had ordered, "but whatever it is, I believe Ridg'Sor's time on Etera has run out."

Wosot returned with the jhorallax, a thick multi-tentacled whip embedded with obsidian chips and fragments, designed to cut through a thick coat to the flesh underneath.

Straf'Tor moved into position and raised the brutal weapon. "Step back," he ordered the others.

Straf'Tor repeatedly whipped Ridg'Sor, who had sufficiently come around to feel every excruciating lash. Seldom warranted, the whip's use was a cruel and visceral punishment. When he was done, Straf'Tor had reduced Ridg'Sor to a moaning matted and bloodied hump.

The Leader threw down the jhorallax. "Take him and hold him somewhere and keep him bound; do not worry about his comfort. Make sure there is no way he can escape; post two males outside wherever he is being held. No, make it three. One to stay in the room with him, the others outside.

"No food, no drink. No relief of any kind. He deserves to suffer as much as possible," he added.

Straf'Tor left Kayerm and wandered through the night. His wails of grief echoed through the dark hills and mountains that surrounded Kayerm. Coyotes in the distance heard his cries and echoed his loneliness with cries of their own.

The next morning at first light, Straf'Tor had everyone awakened for an announcement, but by the time they were gathered, most had heard the news of Ushca's death.

The very first rays of the sun lit up the hillside where Straf'Tor was standing, the place from which he always spoke. He ordered Tyria to his side, and her hand flew to her mouth as she watched her bloodied mate dragged up to lie next to Straf'Tor.

The crowd became deathly quiet. Seeing he had their full attention, Straf'Tor began.

"People of Kayerm. For years—centuries—I have asked for your allegiance, your faith in me. Yet instead, some of you have listened to the lies of the rebel, Ridg'Sor, choosing instead to believe that when we split our community, my brother and I did not have in mind your best interests and the best interests of the Sassen and the Akassa. I have done my best to lead you with integrity, but, yet again, some of you chose to follow this *Soltark* in a quest to try to take what is not ours to take—Kthama Minor." Straf'Tor pointed to Ridg'Sor, now held up on display by the guards.

"Did any of you ever stop to question if his mission was one of honor? Did any of you who followed him, who still follow him, consider whether this is someone worthy of your homage? As a result, your stubbornness, your defiance, your willingness to follow him instead of me has cost me that which I hold most dear."

No one spoke, but everyone exchanged glances. Her body wracked with sobs, Tyria had covered her face with her hands.

"My beloved mate, Ushca, who was also carrying my offling—our offling—is dead at his hand."

The crowd was silent.

"Listen to me. Ushca has returned to the Great Spirit and has taken our offling with her. But it was not her time. She was fine earlier when I checked on her. Yet when I returned last evening, she was gone." Straf'Tor turned and glared at the young female. "Tyria, tell them who murdered my mate."

Tyria tried to compose herself and lowered her hands. She took a few hitching breaths and turned to look at her mate, Ridg'Sor, suspended between the three sentries. He was slipping in and out of consciousness after the whipping Straf'Tor had delivered the day before.

She turned back to face the crowd. "My mate, Ridg'Sor, poisoned Ushca."

No one moved as she explained how her mixture had been tampered with and how Ushca had died. Then Tyria lowered her eyes, unable to continue.

"Pagara says Tyria had no part in this, and I believe her," Straf'Tor announced. "And despite the fact that Tyria is paired to Ridg'Sor, I do not hold her accountable for my mate's death—and neither should you," he commanded the crowd.

"On the other hand—" Straf'Tor walked over to Ridg'Sor and roughly grabbed his hair to jerk his head back. "On the other hand," he repeated, staring into Ridg'Sor's glazed eyes. "*You* will pay the ultimate price for what you did. But I want you to suffer a while longer before I end your life," he said. He roughly released Ridg'Sor's head, which dropped forward. Then Straf'Tor turned back to the crowd.

"Execution will be tomorrow morning. Everyone is required to attend. Leave your offling with their older siblings or make other arrangements. I expect everybody else to be here without fail. You are dismissed."

Straf'Tor turned to those still propping up a bleary Ridg'Sor.

Tyria averted her eyes as they dragged her mate

away.

"Straf'Tor," Tyria asked softly, glancing up at him. "Must I be present for that? He is my mate, after all."

The Leader thought a moment before answering.

"I will excuse you. But only because that is what Ushca would want. Despite your pairing with that piece of 'Rok, Ushca always believed in the goodness of your heart and your dedication to your calling. If you wish to be present for his Good Journey, I will let you know when it is to take place."

Tyria nodded. "Thank you for that, Adik'Tar." As she walked away, huge sobs once again shook her slight frame.

Now that his anger had been appeased for the moment, the reality of what had happened washed over Straf'Tor. He walked away, hurrying to get as far away from Kayerm as he could.

When he was far enough to be assured of privacy, he dropped to his knees and wailed. Then he threw his body to the ground and grabbed tufts of the winter grass in his hands.

"Why? Why? Why?" he demanded, cursing the Great Spirit as he ripped clumps of grass from the soil. "Why would you allow this to happen? She was everything to me. Is everything to me. This is my payment for sparing Ridg'Sor's life, which I did out of allegiance to you? So there would not be one less Mothoc walking Etera? If I had killed him long ago, my beloved would still be with me."

"I cannot live with this," he shouted. "I will not live with this. I am done serving you. I have one less duty to discharge, and then I wash my hands of you and your great plan." He stood up and grasped the closest tree, tearing its roots from the ground and hurling it as far as he could. Then the next and the next, until his body was finally exhausted. He dropped back to the ground and let out the rest of his heartbreak, knowing that his grief would never end as long as he lived.

The sun traveled across the sky overhead, and still, Straf'Tor lay there. If he was hot or cold, he did not feel it. Numbness had replaced his grief, but his resolve had hardened, and he knew what he had to do.

Back in the Leader's living area, Tyria was helping Pagara and Beala prepare Ushca's body for her Good Journey. They worked together silently and reverently. Tyria tried to oust Ridg'Sor from her mind and her heart.

He was a monster, after all. The goodness she saw in him must have been an act, an illusion. But how had he fooled her? Perhaps her Healer's seventh sense became clouded when strong emotions were in play. It was the only explanation for her failure to see his true nature. To murder a female? And a mother at that, about to bear offling. What greater cruelty could there be? *I fear he has destroyed Straf'Tor as well as himself. And if that is so, what will become of our people?*

The next morning, Straf'Tor moved immediately to Ridg'Sor's execution. Wosot gathered everyone and had Ridg'Sor brought to the front, bound hand and foot. Though in a lot of pain, the rebel no longer had to be supported and was now fully alert. According to his word, Straf'Tor had sent a message to Tyria, telling her to stay away. She busied herself looking after some of the offling who had been gathered together in one of the larger rooms.

Straf'Tor stood rigid, one fist clenched at his side, the other behind his back.

The crowd shifted nervously.

Only the cawing of crows in the treetops broke the silence. Straf'Tor looked up and counted them. Seven. The number of perfection, of divine order.

Too bad I do not believe in you any longer, Ravu'Bahl, or the one who sent you," he willed his words to the sky above. *"If I did, your appearance would be reassurance from the Great Spirit that no matter how tragic, events are unfolding as they should. And they are not. They cannot possibly be."*

It was time.

Straf'Tor turned to face those gathered before him.

"You are here to witness the penalty Ridg'Sor has brought on himself. You know that though he has caused many of you to turn against me, I have repeatedly spared his life. And for what. For it to come to this? So that he could murder my mate and our unborn offling? That is what my mercy towards him has cost me. *Everything*."

Ridg'Sor looked defiantly at Straf'Tor.

"And just what do you think I have done now, *Adik'Tar*." His words were slurred.

"I know what you have done. You murdered my mate, Ushca,"

"And just how did I do that? I have not even been near her," he mumbled.

Straf'Tor turned to the crowd.

"Do you hear that? More lies. That is all he has ever given you. Even to the last moments of his last breath, he lies. This is the *hero* you have been blindly following.

"But no more." And Straf'Tor brought his other hand from behind his back. In it, he grasped a razor-sharp blade with a wooden handle.

"Drit the Fixer made this for me eons ago, but it is so dangerous that I never found a use for it and had it stored with the other weapons. Now, today, it fulfills its purpose." Straf'Tor brandished the blade, which caught and reflected the sun's rays. It was remarkable workmanship, a testament to Drit's skills.

"Ridg'Sor, for murdering my beloved and my unborn offling, your punishment is death. May your soul spend an eternity in *krell*. Be grateful; this is quicker than you deserve," and with that, Straf'Tor grabbed Ridg'Sor by the hair and yanked his head back.

"I told you, you would pay for your crimes," Ridg'Sor managed to gasp out.

"And now so will you," growled Straf'Tor

He looked into Ridg'Sor's eyes while pressing the blade into the rebel's neck and drawing it across the skin. He heard Ridg'Sor gasp and felt him struggle as his life's blood came pouring out.

Straf'Tor whispered the last words Ridg'Sor would ever hear on Etera, "*I will see you in krell.*"

He released the rebel leader's body and let it slump to the ground. A crimson river of blood flowed down the hillside, and the onlookers' eyes were irresistibly drawn to the spread of deep red.

Ridg'Sor's body jerked and twitched as the last of his life force drained from it.

After a few moments, Straf'Tor spoke. "Wosot. Take this piece of trash and throw it into the Great River."

The crowd gasped.

"Adik'Tar," said Wosot. "What of his mate, Tyria?"

Straf'Tor closed his eyes. "You are right. I promised her she could attend his ritual. Very well. He does not deserve a proper Good Journey, but for her sake, I will allow it," he relented.

"Take it out of my sight for now," and he turned back to the crowd. "Now. For those of you who followed Ridg'Sor, there is no place for you here. Take your mates and your offling and leave Kayerm forever. If any of you return, you will be killed on sight, females and offling both. The days of my mercy for your disobedience and rebellion are over. I will give you until tomorrow morning to pack up your belongings and get out."

Everyone assembled stood frozen. Fear, awe, grief distorted their faces. Never before had a Leader threatened females and offling. Straf'Tor turned to them and met each gaze one by one. Those who were willing to meet his eyes looked away quickly.

Knowing the crowd would not disperse any time soon of its own volition, he allowed them to remain. *Let them share their shock between themselves. Let them go over it and over it and over it until it is burned in their memories forever. If fear and death are all that will control them, then fear and death are what I will give them.*

Straf'Tor walked off, returning to Kayerm, the place he had done his best to make his home. But without Ushca, it now meant nothing to him.

Ushca's body had been prepared for burial. Flowers adorned her head, and garlands of wildflowers encircled her ankles and wrists. Her arms were protectively folded across her belly. The ritual had been set for later that morning, following Ridg'Sor's execution. Once again, a crowd had assembled, and once again, deathly silence filled the air.

Straf'Tor approached his mate's still body. Her spirit had gone, but it was all he had left of her, so he leaned in and pressed his lips to hers. He brushed the hair back from her forehead. He took her one hand in his, and with the other, he softly caressed her face and then her swollen belly. Onlookers turned away as tears fell down their cheeks. Paired mates reflexively grasped each other's hands.

He lowered his head and whispered in her ear, "You were my world. You are my world. There is now no place on Etera for me. There is nothing to hold me here any longer, beloved. Wait; I will come to you. I will find you, wherever you are, and we shall never again be parted." With that, Straf'Tor rested his head on her shoulder. He stood there for what seemed like forever.

Finally, composed, he raised his head and stepped back. He signaled to Pagara, whose place it was as Healer to continue the ritual. After she began, he slowly walked away and let them finish without him.

Straf'Tor had no need to attend Ridg'Sor's ritual. Instead, he sought out his son, Nox'Tor.

"Walk with me," he said, and Nox'Tor followed his father.

"The age of darkness is almost behind us. What

is about to happen will pave the way for easier times. In leading Kayerm, you will not have the struggle I have had," said Straf'Tor.

"Why do you say this? What is about to happen?" asked Nox'Tor.

"I cannot tell you. But you will recognize it when it takes place. Ridg'Sor's followers will be gone tomorrow and will give you no more trouble. Focus on improving life at Kayerm as I have tried to do these centuries; after this, you will have everyone's cooperation. Reinforce the Sacred Laws that we agreed on with the Akassa before we left Kayerm. Do you remember them?"

"Yes," answered Nox'Tor.

"Good."

"Are you handing leadership of Kayerm to me?"

"Yes."

Nox'Tor frowned.

Straf'Tor reached out and drew his son to him and placed an arm around his shoulder. "I have not told you often enough how proud I am of you. What a fine Leader you will be. I am honored to have someone like you to pass the care of our people onto. Seek out only those you trust, whom you find to also be of good character. Listen to their council, but in the end, always do what you decide is best for our people."

"How will I know what that is?" he asked.

"You will know. And what you do not know, you will learn, I promise," answered his father and released him.

"But—" said Nox'Tor.

"No more questions. From now on, only look forward, my son. Now be on your way, into the future of your making."

Straf'Tor watched his son walk off. *I should have told him what will happen. But it is not often our way to coddle the next Leaders too much; we allow them to grow strong in the fires of testing. It is his path to weather this on his own.*

The next morning, Straf'Tor, Wosot, and Teirac, who was Wosot's right hand, watched as about fifty of Ridg'Sor's followers and their families packed and prepared to leave. Only after the rebels had gone did Straf'Tor discover that Ser'Hun had been left behind because he walked out on the group when he heard Ridg'Sor's plan to poison Ushca. He was allowed to stay, though as punishment for not telling anyone, Straf'Tor ordered him severely whipped, leaving him partially crippled.

Straf'Tor looked at the crowd of females with their offling and hardened his heart against them, refusing to feel pity as they shuffled off into the unknown.

"Do not be concerned. Our sentries will follow

until it is certain they will not double back," explained Teirac.

"I doubt they will," said Straf'Tor. "I made it clear there was nothing here for them but death. I am counting on you both, Wosot and Teirac, to make sure that Tyria is not mistreated. Neither of you is paired. Perhaps one of you should consider courting her."

Just then, movement caught his eye, and he turned to see Tyria walking toward them.

"Please, Adik'Tar. A word." Her voice shook, and her glance darted to each of them in turn before fixing on Straf'Tor.

"What is it, Tyria?" asked the Leader.

"I am sorry for interrupting, but please, please contact your brother and ask if I may go to Kthama?" Her eyes were wide and pleading.

"Go to Kthama?"

"Please, Adik'Tar. It is not safe here; I need to leave."

"Wosot and Teirac will look after you." And Straf'Tor motioned to the males standing beside him.

"I do not doubt that. But they cannot be everywhere. And—" her voice trailed off.

"*What has happened, Tyria?*"

"I was hoping I was wrong, but there is no longer any doubt. I am seeded. Soon it will be obvious that I carry Ridg'Sor's offling. It is not so much for me, but my offling should not be made to grow up in a community that will always eye him or her with suspicion. Our people have long memories, and those memories will not be kind."

Straf'Tor closed his eyes and sighed.

"Pack what you need and be back here as soon as you can. I will take you to Kthama myself."

After Tyria had left, Straf'Tor turned to Wosot and Teirac. "From now on, Nox'Tor will lead Kayerm," he said. "He is untested and inexperienced, and he will need your counsel. I expect you to show him the same loyalty you have shown me."

Wosot and Teirac looked at each other. Somehow, they knew what was coming, and this was a time for acceptance, not questions.

There was only one more thing for Straf'Tor to do, and for that, he had to return to the place where this long journey had begun. When Tyria returned with her satchel, there were no words to be said. Straf'Tor hoisted her bag over his shoulder and turned his face toward Kthama.

After making preparations in their own communities, the Leaders had arrived back at Kthama. Everyone was there but Straf'Tor, but Moc'Tor's watchers had alerted him that his brother was on the way and that he was bringing a female with him, but she was not Ushca.

A cold chill passed over Moc'Tor. *Something*

terrible has happened at Kayerm. Straf'Tor is in great distress.

Moc'Tor asked Pan to walk with him and led her to the meadow where they executed their duties as Guardians.

"Are we here to join with the Aezaitera?" Pan asked sharply.

"Yes. And the Order of Functions," Moc'Tor answered.

"No, I refuse. Mother is dying; why should I serve the Great Spirit? Or Etera?" she cried out.

"It is not a choice, Pan; you are a Guardian. In time you will be the only Guardian. Accept your mantle. Surrender to it as you have surrendered before to the Aezaitera and the Order of Functions."

"I will not," she shouted.

Moc'Tor stormed over to his daughter, grabbed her by the shoulders, and shook her, his face inches from hers.

"Stop. You *must* do it. This is that to which you were born. Your Mother would be ashamed to see you act like this. She has always done her duty, never shirked it. Through the terrible years when Kthama was falling apart. Through the arguments with my brother and the other Leaders. Through the hardest days when we had to watch our cousins, sisters, brothers, and children leave our home. She stood by my side when I killed the rebel Norcab before you were born. All of it was as hard for her as your duty is for you." he shouted back.

"Even this? Even to this?" she cried.

"Yes, even to this. And now it is even more important that we enter the Order of Functions," he said.

"But we just did! And what came of it but that my mother is dying," Pan sobbed. "And I told you that if there was a chance she could die, then I would never engage the Order of Functions again."

Moc'Tor released his daughter and let out a long, heavy breath.

"I cannot force you to meet your obligation, but I will remind you that your life does not belong to you alone. You are a Guardian. You know that one day you will be the only Guardian. It falls to you to serve the Great Spirit in ways that only you can," he said. "Now, more than ever, you need to engage with both the Aezaitera and the Order of Functions. But I cannot force you. You must come to accept the mantle in your own time. You may go," he added before lying down and closing his eyes.

Pan stood over her father as she saw his body go limp, knowing he had entered the Aezaiterian flow and would shortly engage the Order of Functions. How vulnerable he looked; she had never fully realized the need for the guards while they did this. Finally, she could stand it no longer. *I cannot leave this burden on his shoulders alone.*

She, too, lay down and surrendered to what was her duty.

Within moments she was swallowed up in the blissful ecstasy of the creative life force. She surrendered more fully than ever, steeling herself against the nearly unbearable desire never to leave. But this time, they stayed the longest they ever had. And their melding with the Order of Functions was the longest it had ever been. Over time, Pan had learned to bear it, but she was greatly relieved when it was over. She opened her eyes to see her father watching her from his customary place a short distance away.

"Thank you," he said.

"Why was it so important, Father, that we did this again so soon?" she asked.

Moc'Tor sighed and sat up.

"I have explained it to your brother and your sisters, and now it is time for you to know what lies ahead."

Pan sat up too and held her breath.

"You must prepare yourself to walk Etera without me. You and Dak'Tor will lead the People now."

"No," she frowned. "This cannot be true. Where are *you* going?"

"The division between the Akassa and Sassen must be sealed. The Leaders and I are preparing to take care of that. I do not expect you to understand, but you will in time. I will tell you no more, as it will not soften the blow. Be strong, Pan; the people need you. Etera needs you." He put an arm around her and held her close.

They re-entered the Aezaiterian flow, and later, together, they walked silently back to Kthama.

CHAPTER 12

By the time Moc'Tor and Pan returned, Straf'Tor had arrived. Upon seeing his brother, Moc'Tor dismissed everyone else from the area and walked briskly over to him.

"Something terrible has happened. What is it?" Moc'Tor asked, placing his hand on his brother's shoulder and glancing at Tyria at his brother's side.

"Ushca is gone," he said. Moc'Tor frowned.

"She is gone," he repeated. "She was murdered by Ridg'Sor." Straf'Tor's face was expressionless.

Moc'Tor shook his head. *This cannot be happening. I am losing E'ranale, and he has lost Ushca.* At a loss for words, he turned to Tyria.

"Why have you come to Kthama?"

"Adik'Tar," she said, eyes lowered, "I have come to ask for asylum."

Moc'Tor looked to Straf'Tor for an explanation.

"Tyria was the mate of the rebellion leader, Ridg'-

Sor, and carries his offling," Straf'Tor explained. "It was her potion, poisoned by Ridg'Sor, that killed Ushca. Under the circumstances—" His voice trailed off.

Moc'Tor signaled to a male nearby. "Take her to one of my daughters and ask them to have quarters prepared for her. Make sure she has all she needs."

"You will be safe here, I promise," he told her.

Tyria thanked both Leaders before following the escort.

Moc'Tor turned to his brother. "Why are you here?"

"To finish what we started," said Straf'Tor, "To complete our mission, so I can find peace."

"Brother. There are no words. We are both facing tragedy. You have lost Ushca, and E'ranale is not far behind."

"Both our beloveds taken. And their offling with them," said Straf'Tor.

"I cannot bear it. And I know now what we must do. I know what we both must do. Hear me out." And Moc'Tor explained what he knew must take place.

"Are you certain?" Straf'Tor asked.

"I have never been more certain in my life. I have never before felt so in line with the Order of Functions," Moc'Tor answered.

"We will need some time to prepare."

"Agreed. Let us meet with the others and put the final steps in place."

Moc'Tor stood before the Leaders' Council and scanned the group. He could not help it; his thoughts returned to a time an age ago when he had stood facing a sea of dark-haired Mothoc bodies, explaining to them that their culture had to drastically change if they were to survive. "Despite our efforts to ensure the separation of our people from the Sassen, the memories of Kthama still haunt the Sassen's memory. Recently, a faction tried to re-take Kthama Minor. Their plans were thwarted by my brother, but in time, others may build their courage and try again."

He continued, "Centuries ago when I stood before those of you who started this journey with me, my brother and I knew there might come a time when only a spiritual solution would seal the division between Straf'Tor's people and ours. This time has come."

Moc'Tor paused a moment for what he was saying to sink in. "Go to your quarters. Rest. In the morning, I will tell you what must be done. If any of you do not wish to be involved, then tell me after I have explained what we must do. But I beseech you to stay; it is imperative that we all agree and act together for the sake of our people and Straf'Tor's and for the sake of Etera herself. It will take all of us to put an end to the Age of Darkness, the Wrak-Wavara"

Moc'Tor dismissed the assembly but intercepted Hatos'Mok. "A moment, please."

The two Leaders spoke for a while. When they had finished, Moc'Tor went to ensure that Tyria was settling in. His oldest daughter, Vel, had taken care of her.

"Tyria is here under our protection; be sure she is welcomed into the community." He looked deeply into his daughter's eyes as he spoke. "I am holding you responsible for her care and well-being. She was apprenticed to the Healer at Kayerm, and others may see that as a betrayal. Vel, she is seeded."

"Yes, Father. I will take her under my wing, and I promise no harm will come to her in any way. It is good she is here because Kthama needs a Healer," Vel added.

"Good. Thank you. Oragur offered to provide training once we found a Healer. Introduce her to him when you can and she can go to him at the Deep Valley after things have calmed down."

Moc'Tor kissed his daughter and headed toward his own quarters to spend with his mate whatever time she had left. *A Healer coming to Kthama.* That was the missing piece. It was all falling into place.

The next morning, having finished laying out what he was asking them to do, Moc'Tor stood waiting before the Leaders. Silence filled the chamber.

Hatos'Mok spoke up first. "I agree. This is the only solution, though it is drastic. But it is necessary if we are to secure the future of the Akassa. We agreed long ago that the Sassen blood must not be any further diluted. This is the only way."

"Fear is all the Sassen understand," Straf'Tor said. "So fear is what we will give them."

The other Leaders nodded their assent.

"You have heard what is planned," said Moc'Tor. "Once this is over, return to your communities, but, except with other Leaders, speak nothing of what happens here. The story of Wrak-Wavara, the Age of Darkness, must pass into history."

Reverence filled the air. Each soul there knew that the role they played would make the difference to whether Etera herself survived. Slowly, they dispersed, all except for Oragur.

"Moc'Tor, there is something you must do. A message you must leave, though I cannot say I understand it. It was given to me in a dream."

Moc'Tor listened, and though not understanding the significance, he agreed.

When the room was empty, the Guardian thought once again of his beloved Kthama. Then he closed his eyes and prayed to the Great Spirit who had brought him down this painful journey. *Look after our son, Dak'Tor. Look after our daughter, Pan, and*

*her sisters. And please, give me the strength to do what
lies before me.*

Everything was prepared just as Moc'Tor had
ordered, although it took longer than he had hoped.
Dochrohan was careful only to use those materials
that Moc'Tor had specified. In between the preparations, the Guardian spent as much time with E'ranale
as he could. The medicine Oragur had brought was
working, though the dosage had to be increased and
she now took it throughout the day. And though
there was no hope for her recovery, at least she was
not suffering, and he knew that in time she would
have peace.

Moc'Tor sat next to E'ranale with his hands
covering hers. She dozed on and off. In between,
when she was conscious, they talked about the
future.

"We knew this day would come, my love," said
E'ranale. "After all, you are a Guardian. We both
knew you would at some point go on without me.
But I know we thought we would have decades yet to
spend together—even centuries."

"When my father returned to the Great Spirit, I
remember consoling myself that if my faith was true,

I would see him again. Now more than ever, I need to believe that," he said.

"You, more than anyone, understand the mysteries of creation. In all the wonders you have seen and told me of, it seems impossible that we do not continue as ourselves after this vessel has failed," she said.

"I am worried about Pan and Dak'Tor," he said, raising her hand to his lips.

"This will be hard for them. But they will have each other, and you," she whispered.

"Stay awake a bit longer if you can. I must tell you our plans. You remember long ago when we vowed to one day put an end to this age? That time has come. Straf'Tor's followers have been influenced by the rebel Ridg'Sor. A band of them were on their way here to try to take back Kthama Minor. They were turned around. My brother executed Ridg'Sor and threw out the rest of his group. All talk of Kthama is banned at Kayerm, and for now, there is apparent peace. But memories have a life of their own." He paused as she started to nod off again.

He waited for her to awaken. Finally, her eyes fluttered open. "I am sorry. I drifted off. I remember you saying that at Kayerm, talk of Kthama has been banned?"

"Yes. Let me try to condense the story. It is time to finish this; Straf'Tor and the other Leaders are here. When we are done, there will be no more thought of contact between the Sassen and the Akassa."

"Never?" she asked.

"For long enough. In time they may outgrow their ignorance. If wisdom dawns, then they will find their way through to the next age. All we can do is set it in motion. The rest will be up to them."

"As for Pan and Dak'Tor, they will have to lead without me," he added.

"Dak'Tor, and Pan, they will be alone now," she said sadly.

"They will not be alone; they will have each other, their sisters, the other Mothoc, and the Akassa. Yes, it will be hard, but I have faith in them," he tried to console her.

E'ranale groaned and grew silent before speaking again.

"Will you be with me in the Great Spirit?" she asked.

"In time, yes," he said. "Sleep now. I will come and get you when it is time."

Moc'Tor sat next to her awhile, watching her sleep. *I did not tell her Ushca has been murdered. She will find out soon enough when Ushca greets her in the afterlife.*

At the appointed time, in the secret depths of Kthama Minor, the selected Leaders came together to take the final step on the journey of leading their people through the Wrak-Wavara.

Kthama Minor was deathly quiet. All activity had been stopped days before. An air of reverence permeated every thought, every feeling, every intention.

Moc'Tor had placed E'ranale gently to the side on soft bedding prepared ahead of time. Next to her was a woven basket. He covered her to make sure she was warm and comfortable, and then he signaled that it was time to begin.

The members of the inner circle took their places. They chanted the ancient sacred words, words which created the vibrations designed to invoke the state of Ror'Eckrah, the One Mind, used to unify their souls and collectively call forth the creative power of the Great Spirit.

In the quiet sanctity of the night, into the mind of every Akassa and Sassen on Etera—a Connection opened. More powerful than had ever been experienced by any of them.

Each one found him or herself pulled into a darkness bleaker than could be imagined. In total silence, a light slowly dawned, just bright enough to reveal a circle of dark-haired, faceless bodies. Though they were legion, they spoke in one voice.

To each Sassen, they said, "*We are Mothoc. We are keepers of Etera; our blood and the Aezaitera are one. What had to be done was done. But no more. Never again, the Wrak-Wavara. This is Rah-hora. Sassen, make no contact with Akassa lest you yourselves are destroyed. Leave the Others to them. We leave you to the future of your own making. When the Wrak-Ayya falls, the Age of Shadows, the true test will begin. We will be watching.*"

For each of the Akassa, the People, they had a different message— "*We are Mothoc. We are keepers of the Others. What had to be done was done. But no more. Never again the Wrak-Wavara. The Others who are our wards are now your Brothers. Learn their language. Make amends. Regain their trust. Leader to next Leader —Kthama Healer to next Kthama Healer—only these may speak of this past. This is Rah-hora. We leave you to the future of your own making. When the Wrak-Ayya falls, the Age of Shadows, the true test will begin. We will be watching.*"

And then, just as those in the inner circle had opened the Connection, so they closed it.

Moc'Tor looked over at E'ranale, and she smiled weakly at her mate before meeting the gazes of the others. They nodded at her and then turned to each other. The time for goodbyes was at hand. Soon they would disperse, each to take the last steps needed to end The Age of Darkness.

Before they parted, Moc'Tor uttered the last words ever to be spoken in Kthama Minor.

"Kah-Sol 'Rin." It is done.

Silently, gently, Moc'Tor picked up E'ranale and the basket at her side. He headed down one of the corridors, stopping to make sure Straf'Tor was following.

They entered a small chamber, which had been prepared ahead of time. It was circular, with high walls. To the right, as they entered, was a giant boulder lying on its side. A pile of wetted clay was in the corner.

Moc'Tor gently placed E'ranale on a stone seat with a solid back and armrests carved into it, one of three situated around the perimeter. He took a large portion of the basket's contents and handed it to her. She looked at him with such love and tears of gratitude in her eyes before weakly placing her hand against the side of his face. Then she chewed and swallowed the large portion of A'Pozz that he had given her. He stayed by her side until her head nodded down. He was not sure, though, if she was sleeping or whether the leaves had already taken effect.

Then he and Straf'Tor moved the boulder into place and sealed it from within with the wet clay. When they were done, they brushed their hands off and looked around. Over the door was the painting Oragur had insisted must be there. High up on the wall was the message that would wait through eternity, never to be seen by anyone if Moc'Tor was wrong about what would come to pass.

Straf'Tor took his place on another of the chairs and signaled to Moc'Tor that he was ready. Moc'Tor took another portion of the basket's contents and handed it to Straf'Tor.

He returned to E'ranale, whose breathing had

slowed. Gradually, it became slower, shallower. He was unashamed when tears rolled down his face as his beloved took her last and final breath on Etera. Moc'Tor placed a kiss on her head as it slumped forward.

Straf'Tor put the A'Pozz in his mouth and settled back against the stone chair on which he was seated.

In the quiet sanctity of the chamber, Moc'Tor waited for his brother to pass. It was eerily peaceful, and he closed his eyes for a moment.

Suddenly, Moc'Tor was standing in a meadow over-flowing with flowers. A beautiful field of unspeakable beauty. The colors were more vibrant than he could have imagined, and the air was fresh and invigorating. A vitality coursed through him that, even as a Guardian, he had never known. Wherever he was, it was a hundred times more beautiful than Etera, and he wanted to stay there forever. Every aspect seemed to be alive, and in the background was a loving Presence. It was as if the life force he knew as the Aezaitera had taken physical form. In that moment, Moc'Tor knew that every soul, every creature, every aspect of their realm was bound together by a love surpassing any understanding.

As he looked around, he saw a figure approaching. It was Ushca. He started running to meet her, but she was already at his side.

"Ushca. It really is you!" He laughed with joy. "Where are we? Is this what I think it is?"

"It is one step along our return to the Great Spirit, yes," she smiled.

E'ranale, he thought, and then she was also at his side. He threw his arms around her and held her tighter than ever. He soothed her hair, gently touched her face, looked her up and down. "My love, you are really here. We are together again. The Great Spirit, it is all true! Life does not end when our forms perish."

Then he stopped. "But I had not yet taken the A'Pozz."

"This is all true, my love," E'ranale said. "But your time to join me in this place forever is not yet at hand. You were brought here for your own peace of mind, so you would know that we will see each other again, and so your faith in the Great Spirit would be restored for what it is you have before you to do—" and her voice trailed off.

In his heart, Moc'Tor knew she was right. He knew that it was not his time to join her. He had known that all along. His part in this was not yet completed.

"My father—" he said.

"He is here. We are all together," said Ushca.

Although it was broad daylight, crystal clear, yet gentle to his eyes, a light brighter than could be imagined began to appear on his right. E'ranale and Ushca turned and followed his gaze.

A figure formed whom he did not recognize. It resembled an Akassa, though he was more heavily coated with what looked like the silver-white body covering of a Guardian. The hairs seemed to move as if each were alive in its own right. He had long flowing silver-white hair on his head, and his eyes were the steel grey of the Guardians. The energy and unimaginable peace and love emanating from him had the same irresistible quality as the life current, and Moc'Tor found himself drawn to the figure as a moth to a flame.

"Welcome, Moc'Tor. I know you are wondering who I am. I am An'Kru, but my name is unimportant. In time you and I will come to know each other well. But for now, because you are filled with self-doubts and self-recriminations, I brought you here to see your beloved and your brother's beloved. You need to hear that you have been a good and faithful servant, that you have led your people with honor and integrity. Do not fear the future. No matter the appearances, no matter what happens, remember my words—everything is unfolding as it should."

As the figure was speaking, Moc'Tor realized he was not hearing words as much as feeling them— that their messages were simply appearing in his mind.

"So am I truly not dead?" Moc'Tor managed to say. "What is this place?"

"No, you are not dead. Your body still lives back in the Chamber of the Ancients as the tomb will become known. This is the place we come to when we leave our bodies in death. But this is only one step along the journey to reunion with the Great Spirit. We call this the Corridor. Does this experience here not feel more real than the one you just left?" the figure asked.

"It feels more real than anything I have ever experienced, yes."

"That is because this is more real than your life-force as it lives on Etera. The world of Etera is only a projection of this world, a pale echo of the reality which is our true home."

"In a moment," the figure continued, "you will return to your body in Etera. You know what you must do. Your daughter Pan has a hard path ahead of her, as do the Sassen and the Akassa. Without your help, the strain of all she must bear will be too much for even her, even as a Guardian. Without your help, your sacrifice, she will not be able to fulfill her role."

Moc'Tor nodded. He had known for some time that he would not be joining his beloved in any after-life for a long time yet.

"Remember my words," said the figure. "Remember this moment. They will give you comfort through the lonely centuries to come."

And then, as easily as he had appeared in this place, Moc'Tor became aware of the stone chairs in the dark chamber and the bodies of his mate and his brother Straf'Tor positioned next to him.

What was now a tomb was still and silent. He sat

there for a long time, in the dark, filled with awe and astonishment at what he had just experienced.

No matter what—

Moc'Tor looked over at Straf'Tor. He was still alive, but his breathing had slowed, as E'ranale's had done. In the next moment, Moc'Tor watched his brother take his last breath.

He is with Ushca now. He has the answers to the greatest mystery of all time. And my E'ranale is waiting for me; in time, we will be joined. But now, I have a duty to do. The last part of my role—my debt, perhaps. Whoever that figure was, I look forward to meeting him again.

Moc'Tor positioned himself on the stone seat and released the tension from his body. He had no need to look upon the bodies of his beloved or his brother. He knew that what was left of them were only empty husks. He knew now they had continued on and that, in time, he would join them.

In time.

Moc'Tor closed his eyes. He sent his consciousness down into Etera. In the next moment, he was immersed in the ecstasy of the creative life force, the Aezaiteria. He drank up every moment, and then, knowing it was what he had to do, sent his consciousness further into the vortex and joined with the Order of Functions, where he would wait— trapped for eternity, if the promises made in the Corridor proved untrue.

As planned, those who had participated in the Ror'Eckrah had left Kthama Minor together. At the entrance, they moved the inner stone in place, upon which had been carved the mark of Wrak-Ayya, the Age of Shadows. Next, they placed the huge outer boulder, upon which had been carved the symbol of Wrak-Wavara.

The shame of the Age of Darkness was sealed in the Chamber of the Ancients, in Kthama Minor, until the time came, if ever, for the rest of history to come to pass.

Finally, they cloaked Kthama and Kthama Minor from the Sassen. When the Sassen awoke, they would no longer remember the location of either.

Straf'Tor's words rang in their minds, "Fear is the only thing the Sassen understand. So fear is what we will give them."

With the last act finished, the Mothoc Leaders released the Akassa and the Sassen from the Connection. When each awoke, they would enter a new tomorrow and every day thereafter would move them separately forward to the futures of their making. As for the Chamber of the Ancients, in which rested the bodies of Moc'Tor, E'ranale, and Straf'Tor, its secrets would wait silently until the descent of the Age of Shadows.

PLEASE READ

If you are just joining the series—welcome! I hope you have found it enjoyable. If you are returning reader from Series One (S1), I am thrilled that you have followed me into Series Two (S2)!

The books planned in this series, Series Two (S2), so far are:

Book One: The Age of Darkness
Book Two: The Chamber of the Ancients
Book Three: The Secret of the Leader's Staff
Book Four: The End of the Age*
Book Five: From the Dust of Etera*

*Titles of unpublished books are subject to change!!

I am speculating there may be more books than these five, depending on interest.

Lastly, positive reviews from readers are the wells of encouragement from which authors drink. If you enjoyed this book, please leave a positive review or at least a positive rating. Of course, five stars are the best.

But, if you found fault with it, please email me directly and tell me your viewpoint. I do want to know.

You can find the link to leave a product review on the book link on Amazon, where you purchased the book.

If you have not read S1, please consider it. S1,

Wrak-Ayya: The Age of Shadows, covers the journey of the People thousands and thousands of years following what takes place in this series. You can find it by searching on my name on Amazon.

Positive reviews on Goodreads are also greatly appreciated.

I wish you well and I hope you continue with me on this journey of *What If?*

Blessings - Leigh

ACKNOWLEDGMENTS

I must acknowledge the love and dedication expressed by the readers of Series One. It is your encouragement and appreciation that has kept me going. Though I had planned on releasing S2 Book One earlier, life had other plans. But you never gave up on me and your patience has been remarkable.

So, in between publishing the books, I will continue to try to entertain you with the sappy, humorous, memes and cartoons I publish on our FB reader group page, The Etera Chronicles.

Made in the USA
Las Vegas, NV
20 February 2024